# SO
# LYRICAL

# TRISH COOK

nal

books

NAL JAM
Published by New American Library, a division of
Penguin Group (USA) Inc., 375 Hudson Street,
New York, New York 10014, USA
Penguin Group (Canada), 10 Alcorn Avenue, Toronto,
Ontario M4V 3B2, Canada (a division of Pearson Penguin Canada Inc.)
Penguin Books Ltd., 80 Strand, London WC2R 0RL, England
Penguin Ireland, 25 St. Stephen's Green, Dublin 2,
Ireland (a division of Penguin Books Ltd.)
Penguin Group (Australia), 250 Camberwell Road, Camberwell, Victoria 3124,
Australia (a division of Pearson Australia Group Pty. Ltd.)
Penguin Books India Pvt. Ltd., 11 Community Centre, Panchsheel Park,
New Delhi - 110 017, India
Penguin Group (NZ), cnr Airborne and Rosedale Roads, Albany,
Auckland 1310, New Zealand (a division of Pearson New Zealand Ltd.)
Penguin Books (South Africa) (Pty.) Ltd., 24 Sturdee Avenue,
Rosebank, Johannesburg 2196, South Africa

Penguin Books Ltd., Registered Offices: 80 Strand, London WC2R 0RL, England

First published by NAL JAM, an imprint of New American Library,
a division of Penguin Group (USA) Inc.

First Printing, May 2005
10 9 8 7 6 5 4 3 2 1

Song lyrics courtesy of Chris Forte and Heather Horton

NAL JAM and logo are trademarks of Penguin Group (USA) Inc.

LIBRARY OF CONGRESS CATALOGING-IN-PUBLICATION DATA:

Cook, Trish, 1965–
  So lyrical / Trish Cook.
    p. cm.
  Summary: The life of Winnetka, Illinois, high schooler Trace revolves around her young, music-loving mother, an unknown father, a voluptuous best friend who may be going off the deep end, and the rich, gorgeous lead singer in a band.
    ISBN 0-451-21508-7 (trade pbk.)
    [1. Mothers and daughters—Fiction.   2. Musicians—Fiction.   3. High schools—Fiction.
4. Schools—Fiction.   5. Running—Fiction.   6. Fathers—Fiction.   7. Illinois—Fiction.]   I. Title.
    PZ7.C773So 2005
    [Fic]—dc22        2004025298

Set in Granjon
Designed by Ginger Legato

Printed in the United States of America

To Steve, the best husband imaginable,
and Courtney and Kelsey, the two coolest kids ever

# ACKNOWLEDGMENTS

Many thanks to:
- My agent, Marlene Stringer, for taking a chance on me
- My editor, Anne Bohner, for making me feel instantly at home
- Team Cook plus Mom and Tom for always having my back
- Suzanne DeMarco for being my muse, savant reader, and biggest fan
- Sue Wilson for always making me laugh and also because she told me she'd be pissed if she didn't have her own line
- Michele Garger, Alison Shotwell, Joanna DePorter, and Julie Mangan for the brave advance reading and liking where I was headed even when I was lost
- Meredith Roholt for being the best cross-generational pal anyone could ask for
- Heather Horton for offering up her awesome songs and even more awesome friendship—go to www.hhroxx.com to find out where you can catch her live
- Chris Forte for sharing his lyrics, opinions, and kick-ass guitar knowledge with me—be sure to check him out at www.chrisforte.com
- Liz Phair (www.lizphair.com) for letting me take her name in vain when I was looking for an agent, giving me a glimpse of what it's like to be a rock star, and giving me the private lesson on *Friend of Mine*

- Green Day, Good Charlotte, and MxPx for making great music I can play along with on my Daisy Rock Venus (www.greenday.com, www.goodcharlotte.com, www.mxpx.com, and www.daisyrock.com)

# CHAPTER 1

"Trace!"

I stuck my head out of my locker and scanned the between-class mosh pit. A blur of faces surfed by, none of which seemed to belong to anyone in desperate need of me. Taking a deep breath, I went back to my excavation. I finally found what I was looking for underneath a week-old lunch bag.

"Gotcha," I muttered, unearthing my trig book. Pens, crumpled papers, and unwashed gym clothes all came flying out after it. I tossed the scrambled mess back inside, slamming the door and throwing myself against it for good measure. I could totally understand the escape attempt. It reeked like tuna and old sweat in there.

"Trace!"

There was that voice again, only louder and more pissed off this time. I scoped the halls until I finally spotted the screamer—otherwise known as my best friend, Sabrina Maldonati. Her body-hugging skirt and sky-high heels made navigating the polished marble floors of Northshore Regional High School a tough proposition. Think beached mermaid and you'll get the picture.

If I could only fast-forward her, I thought, glancing at my watch and hoping I wasn't going to be late for class. Brina made her grand entrance a moment later clutching a piece of paper to her more-than-ample chest.

"Stop bitching and start reading," she said. "Because this is the most unbelievable thing ever."

I faked a big yawn. "Can't Harvard just take no for an answer?" The more over-the-top she gets, the more I like to yank her chain.

"Not funny."

"Your mom wrote a note so you don't have to face the fat calipers in gym today?"

Brina shook her head so hard I thought brains would come flying out her ears in wrinkly pieces. "Wrong again. And anyway, you know how I feel about the *f* word."

"What, fu—?"

"Uh, uh, uh. You quit swearing, remember?" Brina said, interrupting me just in the nick of time. "And the word I was referring to is 'fat.' Last night, my mom offered to get me liposuction for my eighteenth birthday."

"You're so full of—"

"Trace, you're gonna have to try a lot harder if you're serious about cleaning up your language."

"I was about to say 'malarkey.'"

"One of us is lying," said Brina. "Here's a hint. It's not me."

She was right. I wouldn't be caught dead saying anything remotely like, "You're so full of malarkey." That meant the lipo story must be true. Brina's mom, being the anorexic lunatic that she is, probably decided fat-sucking cash was the most thoughtful, generous gift in the history of mankind.

The reality is this: Brina has an eye-popping, curvaceous bod. But instead of realizing that boobs and a butt are normal—even desirable—parts of a woman's figure, all Mrs. Maldonati can see is rolls, rolls, and more rolls. In her wildest dreams, Brina suddenly turns into whichever Olsen twin is the dangerously skinny one. "Don't hold your breath" and "not in this lifetime" are two choice phrases that come to mind, but Mrs. Maldonati refuses to give up hope just yet.

"So if it isn't from Harvard and it's not a reprieve from the claw, what *is* the most unbelievable thing ever?" I asked.

"An anonymous note. Signed by 'slp.' I don't know whether to be flattered or call the cops."

So maybe this really *was* something worth getting excited about. "Hand it over," I told her.

Brina passed the note my way and breathed down my neck. I could almost hear her lips moving behind me as I read.

> Brina,
> I like to watch you from afar
> Always know just where you are
> But not where this might lead
> Maybe you could walk with me
> slp

A lone bead of sweat trickled down my back. Was I jealous? Hell, yeah. Here was some pretty awesome poetry, sweet without being sickening, warm without losing its cool. And once again, I was relegated to the lumpy, frumpy sidekick role—Quasimodo next to Brina's Esmeralda.

"Honestly? It's amazing," I admitted.

"That's what I thought," she said, folding the paper carefully and zipping it into a little compartment in the front of her notebook. I hated how she could be so neat. I also hated that her boobs were so big, and that mine were so nonexistent.

"So what are you going to do about it?" I asked her.

"Do? Nothing." We took a couple more steps before she said, "Why? What would you do?"

"I'd go walk with him."

Brina rolled her eyes.

"I'm serious," I told her.

"Oh, please. Why would I want to stroll around with some loser who's too scared to ask me out?" Brina said, doing a quick one-eighty and dismissing slp as yesterday's news. "Let's just forget about it."

I cleared my throat as a new thought came to me. This would be a kick if it actually turned out to be true. "Maybe slp is a she," I suggested. Brina may have had all the guys in school drooling after her, but up until now she hadn't done a thing for the chicks. "Your Sss-sss-secret Le-le-lesbian Puh-puh-pal." I emphasized the letters so she'd catch my drift.

Brina didn't even stop to consider my theory. "Sorry, Trace. It's just not my thing. If my pal's a gal, we're gonna have to stay friends."

I took one last crack at it. "Have you ever considered it might just be Some Lovesick Puppy?"

"Shut up, Trace, and walk. We've gotta get to trig."

Brina and I slipped into our seats as the final bell was ringing. I kept rereading the note in my mind, trying to figure out who slp might really be. And why he—like every other guy I knew—found Brina so intriguing, and me so not.

Stanley Larsen Pratt?

Spencer Louis Perog?

Shawn Leonard Pearsall?

All great guesses. If any of these names belonged to anyone we knew, that is. And they didn't.

Minutes passed before I, being the incredibly brilliant person I am, solved the slp mystery. There he was—Sam Parish, a cute enough guy if you could overlook his constant sniffling—slumped down in his seat with his feet stuffed under Brina's chair.

I got all excited and passed her a note.

*Brina:*
*Don't look now, but I think slp's behind you. If his middle name is Lester or Langley or Lancelot or Lars, it's him. Identity crisis over.*
*Trace*
*P.S. Maybe it's not an allergy or drug problem like we thought. He could just be trying to inhale your pheromones, or whatever they're called.*

She read it and scribbled back.

*Trace:*
*Good detective work. Let's see if he passes the test.*
*slp's girlfriend*

While the rest of the class was trying to calculate the Pythagorean cosine tangent of the something or other, Brina casually leaned back and whispered, "What's your middle name, hon?"

Sam pointed to his chest—honestly, he looked a little scared—and mouthed, "Me?" Then he just sat there staring at Brina with his mouth hanging open.

She finally patted his arm and whispered, "That's OK. You can tell me later." Brina turned her attention back to the nasty problem at hand, and Sam scrunched down even farther in his seat. He looked like he wanted the floor to swallow him up because he'd just ruined his one big chance with Brina. Or who knows? Maybe he was just trying to hide a huge boner.

Scratch, scratch. Fold, fold. Brina chucked the note back to me.

*Trace:*
*Don't think it's him. Far too shy to have the balls to send me an anony-*
*mous love note. He might write one, but I think that's about as far as it*
*would go.*
*B*

Maybe, maybe not, I thought. He could also be embarrassed at being outed so quickly by gifted me. Scribble, scribble, toss, toss.

*B:*
*Let's keep him on the list for now. I'll put it right next to the one about*
*my dad on my locker door.*
*T*

The other list was necessary because, unless his name really was Mike Graphone like it says on my birth certificate, I don't know a thing about my father. And as cool as my mother is in other respects—especially compared to my friends' parents—she's unbelievably uptight and closemouthed about everything related to Daddy dearest. The only suspects I've been able to pinpoint so far are total shots in the dark: the guys I see hugging my mom in pictures hung around the rock-and-roll shrine otherwise known as my house.

Scritchy-scratchy. Flitter-flutter. Plip-plop. Mr. Flagstaff's eyes darted around the room until they came to rest on the note Brina had thrown my way. It was just lying there on my desk looking guilty.

"Care to try your hand at the board, Tracey?" he asked.

"Sure thing, Mr. Flagstaff," I said in as cheerful a voice as I could muster. Maybe a little enthusiasm would make him forget I hadn't been paying attention for the past half an hour. Since day one, if I'm being totally honest.

But nothing could have saved me. I had no clue how to even start the problem, much less solve it. I stumbled and bumbled with the chalk, creating a powdery mess that made no sense. Not nearly soon enough, the Staffman put me out of my misery.

"Perhaps some extra homework problems will help you catch up to the rest of the class, Miss Tillingham. Your notes tonight will have a lot less to do with your social life and a lot more to do with trigonometry now, won't they?"

I gave him my best conciliatory look and saw a night of terminal boredom and frustration in my future. Once again, Brina had been my partner in crime and I was the only one captured.

Why wasn't I the least bit surprised? Because it happened all the time. Farty old Mr. Flagstaff probably had a crush on her, just like every other man on earth. Having the world's most desirable girl as my best friend was really beginning to suck the big wazoo, no matter how much I liked her.

I went directly to my room after school and changed into my workout clothes. I thought maybe a long, hard run might help me focus on the fact that I was not, contrary to what my mind would have me believing today, the world's biggest loser. Me, my Brooks sneakers, and my beloved green iPod mini were all halfway out the door before my mom stopped me dead in my tracks.

"Hey, Bebe," I said, grabbing a Balance bar and shoving it down my throat. Though my mom's real name is Belinda, I've called her Bebe since I could string a few sounds together. She says that at the time, "Mommy" was just too weird—after all, she was still a teenager herself—and the whole shebang proved to be too big of a mouthful for one-year-old me.

"So Brina got a secret love note today, huh?" Bebe asked.

I swallowed fast. "How'd you find that out?"

"She called and when I asked how her day was, she said, 'Great! I got a secret love note today.'"

"Subtle."

"So what did it say, anyway?"

"Something about watching her from afar and not knowing where things will lead," I said. "Oh, and that maybe Brina should walk *with* him."

Bebe ran her fingers through her hair, looking a little puzzled.

"What?"

"Nothing," she said. "It just sounds familiar and I can't figure out why."

"Right. Well, wouldn't you know it, even the sensitive, poetic types are falling for Brina now."

"Pisses you off, huh?" Bebe put her arm around me and squeezed my shoulder.

"Yup," I said. "I guess I should be happy for her?" I didn't mean to, but it came out as a question.

"Nahhhh. It would piss me off, too." It's almost eerie how Bebe always understands exactly how I'm feeling. The fact that we've never been through that "I hate you" phase most mothers and daughters hit at some point during high school makes me extremely lucky—I know. But when your mom *(a)* is younger than everyone else's parents by at least ten years, *(b)* was a groupie back in the eighties (regardless of whether the overwhelming majority of bands she worshipped were kinda, sorta lame even then and definitely ancient history now), and *(c)* has morphed herself into a successful author of Harlequin-ish romances starring fictional musicians, it's easy to see how we'd relate better than most.

Bebe mercifully dropped the subject of me being caught hunching alongside Brina yet again. "You going for a long one today?"

I gulped down some prerun water. "Eight miles. Why, you need me?"

"My agent always thinks going to a show will inspire my next book, so he bribed me with these," Bebe said, waving a couple of familiar-looking rectangles at me. "Got tenth-row tix to see the luscious Hall and Oates tonight."

"Who's luscious?" I asked her. "Hall or Oates?" I can never keep them straight.

"I don't play favorites," Bebe said, licking her lips, just in case I didn't realize she thinks they are fine, so divine. Believe me, I got it well before the spit dried.

"Can't go, Bebe," I said, thankful for my math punishment now. I mean, yikes. No one's heard from those guys in twenty years. "Flagstaff caught me passing notes in trig class and I ended up with extra homework. Brina got off the hook, of course."

"Don't sweat it. Your teacher was probably blinded by her boobs." Bebe put down the tickets and picked up the phone. "I'll just call Trixie to come with me," she said, hitting the speed dial. Trixie is Bebe's one and only Winnetka friend.

Bebe ended up here—in the world's most conservative suburb— once it became apparent that she had picked up more than just waitressing experience at the shore during her eighteenth summer. Once she started showing, Bebe got shipped off to Great-aunt Betty's house in Winnetka under the guise that it would do her some good to get out of New Jersey for a while. The truth is, it made for a lot less explaining. Never mind the fact that Bebe's parents—my grandma and grandpa Tillingham—are so cute yet so clueless, they're probably still wondering why Bebe hasn't been nominated for sainthood, what with her having had an immaculate conception and all.

To this day, Bebe says living in Winnetka is her sacrifice to me; she wanted me to have as normal an upbringing as possible, given the circumstances. And I can't imagine a better place for a kid to grow up, or a more unsuitable one for Bebe. I mean, she just doesn't blend. Instead of wearing tennis whites and listening to NPR in a luxury SUV, Bebe has holey-kneed jeans and cruises around in a beat-up Beetle cranking Quiet Riot or some other band that horrifies both me and the Winnetka ladies, though for different reasons. I'm embarrassed; they're disturbed by the noise.

"Sure, Trace would love to watch the kids until John gets home from his meeting," Bebe was saying into the phone a minute later, winking at me. And I was pretty grateful for the job—even if she didn't have the courtesy to ask me first—because I might as well make some money while slaving over my math punishment.

\*   \*   \*

The slp note, trig torture, and my nonexistent dad kept rolling around in my mind when I first started my run. But after a mile or two I went into the brain-dead zone, happily listening to my latest and greatest playlist and singing along whenever the spirit moved me.

My mind made it back to the land of the living when I noticed an extremely cute guy jogging alongside of me. OK, he wasn't just jogging; he was laughing. At me. I stopped singing and started scowling. What a reality slap—there was no soundproof bubble surrounding me when I had headphones on like I'd always imagined.

I shot the guy my best pissed-off Jersey Girl look—honed during our annual two-week summer vacation at Long Beach Island with my sweet 'n' ditzy grandparents—and kept running. He didn't seem the least bit intimidated and stayed in stride with me.

"You like Jimmy Eat World a lot, huh?"

I ignored him, even though I was impressed. They're not the world's most well-known band—not yet, at least.

"Know how I guessed?" he asked, belting out their song "The Sweetness" in way too good of a voice. Even all the whoa-oh-ohhh-ohhh-ohs sounded right. And to think, his ears were the recipients of my most recent off-key, a cappella solo. Even worse, after hearing him sing the right ones, I was pretty sure there was a place waiting for me in the Misheard-Lyrics Hall of Fame.

"See?" he said, grinning at me.

"Sorry I offended your virgin ears, Mr. Rock Star." All the good comebacks would no doubt torture me tonight while I was tossing and turning in bed, trying to sleep.

"Not offended," he said, flashing a killer smile. "Not a virgin, either."

Hard as I tried to stay mad, I ended up laughing instead. He took it as encouragement.

"I'm Zander O'Brien," he said, sticking out his hand.

I stared at his long, tapered fingers, not sure what to do with them. After all, we were still moving at a nine-minute-mile pace. I just couldn't imagine the mechanics of the whole thing working out.

Zander gave up on the doomed handshake thing, using that arm to pump again. "How long you running for?" he asked, panting.

By now, the adrenaline shooting through me had picked my pace up to sprint. "Almost done. I'm on my last mile."

Zander seemed like he was about ready to pass out. "Want to hit . . . Starbucks . . . so we can talk . . . without me . . . gasping . . . for . . . breath?"

"Sounds great, but I gotta get home. I have to babysit tonight so my mom can go to the Hall and Oates show."

Zander stopped short. "You do?"

I stopped, too. "Yup."

"I don't think my mother has ever even been to a concert. And the only tunes she listens to are by guys who died a million years ago. You know, like Elvis and the Beatles."

"Not all of the Beatles are dead," I had to point out. "There are Elvis sightings all the time. And Hall and Oates haven't had a hit since the eighties."

"Whatever," Zander said. "At least you don't have to leave the house whenever your mom puts her music on."

If he only knew. "I wouldn't go that far," I told him. "But I will admit, my mom is pretty unique. And we're both really into music."

That's a gigantic understatement. My mom spends her days writing, and cranking out tunes that everyone else—with the exception of those retro shows—forgot decades ago. A dilapidated jukebox in the corner of our basement plays Bebe's prehistoric 45s. The portable turntable left over from her childhood spins the stacks and stacks of albums she spent her entire allowance on growing up. And her boom box, circa 1989, plays the songs contained on the seventeen thousand little cassettes that keep threatening to take over the attic someday.

Thankfully, a brand-new, state-of-the-art home entertainment system in the living room takes care of our continuously growing mountain of CDs. Because I want to save my music from any premature aging, I've separated the CDs into two piles: hers and mine. And it's easy to tell whose is whose. Bebe owns the ones only Oldies 101.5 would play; my bands rock MTV2.

To further prove her musical fanaticism—and make us the biggest freaks in all of Lilly Pulitzer–wearing Winnetka—almost every wall of our house is plastered with photos of Bebe and her now-aging idols.

Autographed ticket stubs, T-shirts, and a bass round out the mix. The absolute kicker is in the family room: a drum set turned coffee table signed by all of Dexy's Midnight Runners. Whoever they were.

Whenever my friends come over for the first time, it's always a big freak-out until they realize they have no idea whom or what they're really looking at. It's always, "Is that Slash from Guns N' Roses with your mom in this picture?"

And I say, "Nope, it's Billy Squier."

Then they say, "Who?"

And I tell them, "Never mind."

Next they study the autographed bass. "Whoa. Nikki Sixx signed this?"

And I say, "Actually, Keith Scott did."

Then they say, "Who?"

He played with Bryan Adams, but they don't need to know that. Instead, I tell them, "If you don't know now, you never will."

Finally, they spot the drum set/coffee table. "Don't even ask," I say before they get totally confused.

Though I normally dreaded this whole routine, I thought I might actually enjoy running through it for Zander. I prayed to the ancient third-string rock gods he would come over for a visit soon.

Meanwhile, he was right next to me in the present tense, trying to make small talk. "You know what? We have a lot in common."

"We do?"

"Yeah. For one thing, we're both into running."

You could have fooled me, I thought. I just watched you and it wasn't pretty. "You're a natural," I said. Obviously, my brain was working just fine—it was only my mouth that refused to let all the good lines out.

"And music. We both love music." Zander gave me a slightly crooked smile that reminded me of Ashton Kutcher's. I was getting sucked in despite the fact I'd sworn off guys just last month. "I'm in a band. Want to hear us play sometime? Maybe you could sing backup or something."

"Ha-ha." I dug my fingernails into my arm really hard, just to make sure I wasn't dreaming. Red half-moons appeared, proof positive I was awake.

"If you're afraid of being alone with me and the guys, you could bring a friend along," he said. "C'mon, I don't bite. Not unless you want me to."

"I might be able to arrange that," I said, hoping I sounded sexier than I must have looked, with the sweat dripping down my face and all.

"Maybe later," he said, flirting like crazy. "After you've showered. So, do you go to Northshore Regional?"

"Yup. You?"

Zander looked slightly embarrassed. "Nope. Country Day."

"Ahhhhh. One of them." Them unbelievably rich people, I meant. Yikes. This guy was so out of my league, I might as well quit now while I was ahead. "Well, gotta run, Zander. Nice meeting you."

He reached out and put his hand on my shoulder to stop me. "You haven't even told me your name yet."

Finally, something I could answer without feeling the need to be clever and witty. "Trace. Short for Tracey."

"So, Trace," Zander said, twirling my name around in his mouth. "You want to come see my band play at the rec center on Friday night or what?"

It was time to admit it: Wild horses couldn't keep me away. "Sounds good, Zander." My tongue must have swollen to gigantic proportions over the past few minutes, because it came out sounding like "Zounz-goozandah."

If he noticed, he didn't mention it. "Hey, in case you don't make it, what's your last name?"

"Tillingham," I said, my tongue returning to its normal size instantaneously.

I started the short run home, making it a full block before I gave in to my screaming mind and turned around for one last look at Zander. By then he was peanut-sized. Figures he'd pick now to turn into a gazelle, I thought.

"Good run?" the back of Bebe's head asked me as I banged through the front door. My mom's face was buried in the computer screen, as usual.

"Great one. I just met the hottest guy from Country Day."

Bebe twirled around in her chair and stopped working on whatever her latest novel was going to turn out to be. "Someone who can cure the T. J. blues?" T. J. was my last boyfriend—the one who dumped me for that slut Claire Russell the day after declaring his undying love for me.

"Could be. It's too early to tell."

"Gonna see him again?"

"Yup. He invited me to watch his band play Friday night."

"Hey, maybe I'll come along!"

I crinkled up my nose at the thought of it. "I don't think so. Not only would that mortify me, but they don't play oldies. Not your style at all, Bebe."

"I'm too cool to be mortifying," she said, clearly delusional. "And Duran Duran is playing the House of Blues, anyway. They can probably still blow the doors off your new boyfriend's band."

"Probably," I said, though I sincerely doubted it was true. I grabbed a water bottle from the fridge and took a chug, wondering if Bebe even realized what a music time warp she was in.

# CHAPTER
## 2

Brina and I were just sitting down for lunch the next day when she whipped out another piece of paper from that little zippery-compartment thing of hers and handed it to me. "I almost forgot to tell you. Slp struck again."

"Really? When? Where?"

"No, I'm lying. This morning. Stuck in the grates of the broken locker next to mine," she replied, shooting off her answers rapid-fire.

Just like the first one, I thought, unfolding the note. I scanned it while Brina tapped her fingers on the table.

*Brina,*
*I like your scent when you walk by*
*Always try to catch your eye*
*But I'm afraid of what you might see*
*Maybe you should take a closer look at me*
*slp*

Brina fake-shivered and showed me the hairs on her arm that were supposedly standing on end. "Is that creepy or what?" she asked. It was so like Brina to question the motives of a guy who was being nice to her. Assholes, she was used to.

"Yeah. Sweet and sexy always scare the hell out of me, too," I said.

"Oh, come on, Trace," she snorted. "What the hell is he talking about, smelling me in the halls? He's going all *Silence of the Lambs,* for chrissake!"

I rolled my eyes. The drama of it all. Anonymous love notes aren't enough for Brina. Oh, no. She has to turn it into a potential murder case.

"If you're really worried, why not talk to Mr. Perry about it during your conference today?"

"I totally forgot about that!" She slapped her forehead so hard I was sure her ears would still be ringing by eighth period. "Who cares about slp? What am I gonna say about college? I have no idea where I want to go next year."

"Tell Mr. Perry you need help, then." The fact that Brina hadn't even begun her college search yet was incredible to me. My applications were practically signed, sealed, and delivered already.

"Never. Never in a million years," she said, repeating it to emphasize the strength of her misguided conviction. "He's way too cute to disappoint. I'll just have to wing it."

Mr. Perry, Northshore's youngest guidance counselor, was the clear front-runner for Hottie Teacher of the Year according to all the girls'-room walls. Rumor even had it that he'd hooked up with the Amazonian captain of the girls' volleyball team last year.

Glancing down the hall, I noticed something that made me feel sick yet oddly satisfied at the same time: Sanford Paulsen, fishing a huge booger out of his nose.

"Brina? Here he comes. Case closed." I could feel the hunch coming out of my back now that slp had been exposed as a nose-picking, flood-pants-wearing geek.

She stamped her foot. "That's not him."

"It is, too. And I'll prove it." I waved Sanford over.

"What can I do for you ladies today?" he asked, trying to indiscreetly wipe his finger on the leg of his pants. The booger stayed stuck. He rubbed harder. Still no luck.

"We're doing a survey about middle names," I said. "What's yours?"

"It's Wendell, but—"

"See?" Brina flashed me a triumphant look. "Told you so."

"Told her so, what?" Sanford asked.

Brina opened and closed her mouth, but nothing came out. I jumped in to help her. "You may not believe this, but you're our third Wendell

today. I bet Brina we'd never get another one, and she said we would."
I turned to Brina. "You win. I'll pay you later."

Sanford looked worried now. "I'm sorry, Brina, but I think it should be a do-over."

Do-over? Jeez, this guy had obviously never made it out of elementary school, maturitywise. How else could you explain his goofy word choices and inability to keep his fingers out of his nose?

"Why?" Brina asked, apparently interested enough in what Sanford had to say to ignore his completely juvenile behavior.

"Because I usually use my confirmation name instead."

"Which is?"

"Luke."

Brina choked on her Diet Coke. When she couldn't stop coughing, Sanford grabbed her from behind. Brina barely escaped getting Heimliched—but not before Sanford had a chance to casually toss off a "So, you wanna hang out with me Friday night?"

Brina smiled sweetly and croaked, "Sorry, I'm busy." She brushed at her sweater a few thousand times to make sure Sanford hadn't left any presents on it and took off down the hall.

Not about to blow his big chance like Sam Parish had, Sanford yelled after her, "What about Saturday, then?" Brina pretended not to hear and just kept going.

I went to retrieve my English-lit notebook from my disaster of a locker, miraculously finding it right away. With a few unexpected minutes to kill before class started, I dug around some more in search of a Sharpie. What a joke. I had to settle for using a bitten-up, thumb-sized pencil to add Sanford to Brina's list. It now read:

> Secret Lesbian Pal
> Some Lovesick Puppy
> Sam ??? Parish (sniffs a lot—note says he likes her scent)
> Sanford Wendell (Luke) Paulsen

Mine was the same as always. Not-so-famous-anymore eighties dude number one, two, three, and four, plus Bruce Springsteen thrown in for good measure. I've really got to find a way to eliminate some of these guys, I thought, making little *x*s around the perimeter of my locker.

That night, I must've tried on everything in my closet before I settled on my usual uniform: superlow Bartack jeans, a cute T-shirt, and funky Steve Madden wedge-heeled boots. I left the pile of rejects slumped sadly on the floor and took the stairs two at a time.

"Bye, Bebe, I'm outta here."

She looked up from her usual spot at the computer and waved. "See ya, love. I'm going out later, too. Duran Duran, remember?"

Don't remind me, I thought. I jumped in the Bug and headed for Brina's, screeching into her driveway on two wheels a couple of minutes later. Then I walked through the door unannounced, just like I always do.

"Brina!" I yelled. "You ready to rock?"

I peeked around the corner and saw Mrs. Maldonati in the laundry room ironing—her favorite thing to do, with the possible exception of not eating. "Oh, hi, Mrs. Maldonati."

She eyed me up and down. "You're looking well, Tracey."

"Thank you." I knew what she meant. Skinny.

Mrs. M. yelled up the stairs, "You really should start running with Tracey. It's done wonders for her."

That last comment stung a little. I wasn't spectacularly fat before I decided to start training for the Rock 'n' Roll Marathon or anything. Just a little squishy around the edges.

"Maybe I'll just start throwing up after meals instead," Brina yelled back. "I hear it works quicker!"

"That's not funny," Mrs. M. said, but I could tell she thought it might actually be a viable weight loss plan. "Go on up to Brina's room, Trace. You know it takes her forever to get ready."

I walked upstairs. "Knock, knock."

"C'mon in!" Brina was still yelling over the blow-dryer's incessant whooshing. She put the finishing touches on her hair and twirled around so I could see her outfit: an Empire-waist peasant top with flared sleeves, skintight Blue Cult jeans, and pointy-toe stiletto sling-backs. Every time I tried to look somewhere else, my eyes were magnetically drawn back to her chest. "So what do you think?" Brina asked me.

"That your tits grew," I said, the words flying out of my mouth before I could stop them. She actually looked stunning. Was I crazy to be introducing her to Zander or what?

"Not everyone can be a double A like you," she said, looking hurt.

"I'm sorry," I said, trying to take back my snotty comment. "You honestly look amazing. I must just be a little nervous about seeing the Vipers, is all."

"The Who-pers?" she asked.

"Zander's band."

Brina put her arm around me. "Don't worry. I'll be right there next to you the whole time."

See, that's what I was worried about.

We bought our tickets and walked into the sweaty gym just as the band was taking the stage. Zander counted off a beat—one, two, three, four!—and the Vipers launched into their first song.

The chorus sounded like it went, "She can run, but she can't sing to save her life." But who knew? My most recent lyrical disaster had me questioning my hearing. It might just as well have been, "It's all fun, but you can't fling your wife."

Brina grabbed my hand and started dragging me through the crowd toward the stage. "Let go," I yelled into her ear. "I like it back here."

"C'mon, have some balls. Let's get up close and personal with your new boyfriend's band," she said. "I want to pick the lucky guy who's gonna be mine tonight." Brina was practically drooling at the thought of being a Vipers groupie. Maybe she was really Bebe's daughter, and I was a misplaced Maldonati.

When Zander spotted me, his smile was so huge I couldn't help turning around to see if he was looking at someone else. Nope, it was me, all right. After the last notes of "Can't Sing to Save Her Life," or "You Can't Fling Your Wife," or whatever it was called, he grabbed the microphone out of its stand and said, "That one was for you, Trace!" That confirmed it. He actually liked me.

I felt woozy. After the whole T. J. debacle, I'd decided to voluntarily withdraw my name from the dating pool this year. I was thinking I had more important things to do, like training for a marathon, uncovering Daddy-o's identity, getting into a good school, and now solving Brina's slp mystery. Oh, well. I'd just have to add jumping Zander's bones to the list.

Halfway through the next song—I didn't even try to decipher this one's words—Zander held out his hand to pull me onstage. There are very few things I hate in this world, but being the center of attention is number one on my list. (Men Without Hats and Flock of Seagulls are a close second and third—a problem only if you live with Bebe, like I do.)

When I didn't take Zander up on his offer, Brina did. Smack-dab in the middle of the stage, she gyrated around suggestively enough to make a stripper proud. All she needed was a pole to complete the picture—no, never mind, the bass player had turned into the pole. A roar went up in the crowd, and people started yelling, "Take it off!"

Wanting to get back in the spotlight like any respectable lead singer should, Zander pogoed his way over to them during an instrumental, and Brina became the cream inside a Zander-and-bassist Oreo. She looked like she'd died and gone to heaven. Here we go again, I thought.

I rolled my eyes and headed out of the place, pushing people out of my way as I went. Welcome back, Quasimodo. The hunch on my back would probably be so big by the time I got to the exit, I wouldn't be able to fit through the door.

The phone rang later—much later. I know because I had to stick my nose right up against the alarm clock so my nearly blind-without-contacts eyes could make out the time: two a.m. I checked caller ID to be sure it wasn't an emergency. Just as I suspected, it was Brina.

I let the answering machine take it. Our message clicked on. "Hi! Trace and Belinda here . . . except we're not. Leave us a message!"

"Trace, pick up. C'mon. It was all in fun."

I grabbed the receiver. "It wasn't fun. It was humiliating."

Brina sighed. "Trace, you're making a much bigger deal out of this than it really is."

I breathed into the phone extra loud just to be annoying. Then Brina said in a singsongy voice, "Zander was looking for you all over the place."

"If Zander wanted to find me, he could've called or come over. Didn't happen. End of story."

"Ahhh, but it's not the end of the story," Brina said. "Far from it. All the good parts happened after you left."

I could almost hear her smiling on the other end of the line, and I felt the corners of my mouth heading upward, too. Brina knew I'd want to hear the dirt as long as it didn't involve her and Zander getting naked. And I was fairly confident that hadn't happened, though I still couldn't be one hundred percent sure.

"So spill it, sister."

"OK. First, Zander grilled me about where you went. So I made up some lame-o excuse about bad cramps—"

"You didn't!" I screamed, hoping Bebe wasn't home yet. If she was, she'd probably think I was getting murdered and call 911.

"Believe me, Trace, Zander thinking you have your period is a lot better than knowing you went all bunny boiler because we were dancing together."

"The fact that I don't like you dry-humping my crush in front of two hundred people does *not* make me a bunny boiler."

"Oh, please," she said, writing off my overreaction. "Anyway, after their set was done, Zander slinks home because you're not there. So I start talking to the bassist, Robb. He's totally my type."

"Lots of muscles, studly, not too bright?"

"Yeah. No. Yeah," she laughed, no doubt realizing it wasn't far from the truth. "So we start flirting and stuff—"

"I'm tired, Brina," I interrupted. "Does this story get any more exciting?"

"Would you listen? By now, Robb and I are all alone backstage—"

I interrupted her again. "Let's just skip to the juicy parts. What did you and Robb do once you were all alone?"

"Let's just say I was a very, very bad girl."

Going to bed late and then talking on the phone in the middle of the night was definitely not the motivation I needed to get up at six a.m.

and run the fifteen miles my schedule said I should. So when my alarm rang, I hit the SNOOZE button and snuggled back under the covers.

Unfortunately, my conscience wouldn't let me fall back asleep. First it said, "You made a commitment." Then it moved on to, "You are a lazy sack of . . . oh, yeah, I'm not supposed to swear anymore." And for a finale, it told me, "Remember what was really in the sack? Not the potatoes, but the other stuff? That's what you're gonna feel like if you don't get up NOW!"

Admitting defeat, I pulled on my running gear, chugged a couple of glasses of Gatorade, and hit the pavement. I took my usual route down Sheridan Road, where I can people-watch as I run past the beaches dotting the shore of Lake Michigan.

A couple of miles in, all that liquid hit my bladder. I felt like I might wet my pants if I didn't do something about it soon. And thirteen more miles was not going to be soon enough. I searched high and low for a proper bathroom—one with a door and a toilet that flushed—but it turned out all the public restrooms had been closed for the season as of Labor Day. Even the Porta Pottis were locked.

Desperate, I ran down a long flight of stairs and settled for a secluded patch of sand instead. I glanced around to make sure I was alone, and then let 'er rip. Much better, I thought, pulling up my shorts.

But also much, much worse. On my way back toward the steps, I bumped right smack into Zander. He'd obviously witnessed the whole episode. Besides being extremely embarrassing for the both of us, it gave him yet another round of ammo in the Trace-is-cute-but-such-a-goofball war.

He was laughing at me, of course. "When I fantasized about seeing you with your clothes off, this wasn't exactly what I had in mind."

Witty repartee eluded me once again. "I really had to pee," I explained lamely.

"I could see that."

I threw a handful of sand in his direction and changed the subject. "You guys were really great last night."

"If we were so great, why did you take off?" he asked. Then he got a weird look on his face and said, "Oh, I forgot. Are you feeling better?" I could've sworn Zander was staring at my crotch, probably looking to see if a humongous maxi-pad was bulging out of my shorts.

"Much, thanks," I said.

Zander picked up a flat, smooth stone and expertly tossed it at the water. It skipped four times before disappearing into the lake. "Hey, what's the deal with your friend Brina?" he asked me.

"Who wants to know?"

"Robb. He seemed pretty blown away by her."

So maybe *that* was what Brina meant about being a bad girl last night. Yikes. "I think she likes him, too," I said, not sure that was necessarily true. Brina might have just thought Robb was fun to play with for a night and now the thrill was gone. My cat is like that with new toys, too.

Zander rolled his eyes. "That's nice, considering she was in his pants an hour after meeting him."

"Oh, come on. Brina didn't do anything major with Robb," I said. Well, OK, maybe she did, but who was I to judge?

"That's not what I heard."

I don't know why I felt the need to defend my best friend's getting-more-questionable-by-the-second honor, but I did. "The whole player thing is a big act."

"I don't think so. Robb's totally honest, even if he isn't the sharpest tool in the shed," Zander said. "Not to be mean, but this is a guy who forgot to drop the second *b* when he shortened his name from 'Robby.' "

I laughed. What did I care if Robb and Brina had possibly indulged in some serious nooky last night? Zander hadn't been sucked in by her obvious charms, and that's all that mattered. "What would Rob-buh think if he heard you say that about him?"

"He probably wouldn't get it," Zander said. "What would Brina say if she knew you knew her smutty little secret?"

"She'd probably deny it," I said, realizing a second too late it sounded like I was admitting her guilt. "Because it didn't happen," I added quickly.

"Yeah, right."

Then it hit me. "Hey, wait a minute. How did you know I was

gonna be here this morning? Are you psychic?" Even *I* didn't know I was gonna be here this morning.

"I actually thought you came to see me," he said. "You did know that's my house, didn't you?"

I looked up at what might as well have been Buckingham Palace. "Whoa."

"Want a tour?" he asked me. "I'll be sure to point out all the bathrooms."

"Drop it already. I have to stay hydrated during my long runs. Which reminds me, I've really gotta get going." I threw out a spontaneous invitation for him to join me, never thinking he'd take me up on it, what with his lack of wind during our last unscheduled training session. "Want to come along?"

"How long is a long run?" Zander wanted to know.

"About thirteen more miles," I said. "Fourteen at most."

"Jeez." He hesitated for a second and then said, "OK, but only if you promise to tell me all about yourself. And give me mouth-to-mouth if I drop from overexertion."

If it would get my lips on his, I'd keep our pace at a sprint the entire run. "Not a problem."

Zander must've read my mind, because the next thing I knew he was pulling off my baseball cap and untangling the headphone cords from my hair. Then he planted a long, sweet kiss on my lips. Before it could progress into a major make-out session—which, believe me, I was up for—Zander pulled away and started walking up the stairs toward his house.

"Wow," I said, trying to catch my breath.

He grinned over his shoulder at me. "I'll be right back. Wait here, OK?"

I couldn't have moved if I wanted to, so I sat down and tried to stop smiling. I felt like a goofy, infatuated idiot. To be honest, I pretty much was.

Thirteen miles gave us plenty of time to talk. And at the slow pace we were taking, speaking was even semidoable.

"So what's your family like?" Zander asked me.

I shrugged. How could I explain my crazy circumstances?

"Let me guess," he said. "You're little orphan Tracey?"

"Not even close. Anyway, I already told you about my mom with the bad taste in music. She's an author."

"You didn't tell me she was a writer. Have I ever heard of her?"

I wished I could avoid the subject entirely. I mean, aren't we weird enough already? "Maybe. Her name's Belinda Tillingham."

"I love her!" Zander practically screamed. Oh, crap. Bebe's readership was almost universally female. Had I misread all the signals and Zander was really gay?

"You know her stuff?"

Zander blushed, realizing his mistake. "Uh . . . well . . . I . . ."

Good. He wasn't gay, just a musical romance-reading geek. Even I could successfully flirt with someone like that. "Fess up, baby," I said, touching his arm.

"OK, my old girlfriend Buffy was a huge fan, and she got me hooked." I didn't know which was worse: his liking Bebe's books or having an ex named after a loofah sponge. Zander shrugged it off. "You might as well know the gory truth. At this point, I've read everything she's ever written."

I concentrated on my feet. Bebe and Brina. Brina and Bebe. And now some chick named Buffy. Wasn't there anything else to talk about?

"Did I say something wrong?" he asked.

"No," I said quickly, hoping to get back to some light, flirty conversation.

But it just wasn't in the cards. "So how old were you when your parents got divorced?" Zander asked.

"I wasn't," I said. "And they didn't."

"Oh," he said, looking confused by my cryptic pronouncements.

"My parents broke up before I was born," I explained.

"Don't feel bad. Practically none of my friends' parents are still together," Zander said. "Do you do the every-other-weekend thing, too?"

"Um, no."

"Your dad lives too far away, huh?"

"I couldn't really say," I admitted. "I kind of don't know where he lives."

"What?"

I decided I might as well let the truth fly and deal with whatever the consequences might be. There was no point in lying to someone I hoped would be sticking around for a little bit. "If you can believe this, I've never met him," I said, taking a deep breath before I delivered the final blow. "To be brutally honest, I don't even know who he is."

"That *is* brutal." Zander groped around for a polite response. It's not like he could look it up in Emily Post's *Teen Etiquette* or anything. "I'm sorry," he finally said.

I could practically see sympathy oozing from his every pore. It wasn't exactly the emotion I was hoping for. I wanted Zander to think I was sexy and fun, but even more than that, I wanted him to think I was normal. So far, I'd only proved to be a lyrically challenged, heavy-flowing, outdoor-peeing, illegitimate-but-who-knows-by-whom kind of a girl. Definitely *not* normal.

"So, do you have *any* idea who your dad might be?" Zander asked me after miles of silence.

"I'm keeping a suspect list inside my locker door," I said. "I haven't quite figured out how to go about proving or disproving any of my theories yet, so no one's been added to it or crossed off in a really long time."

"Anyone interesting on it?"

"Actually, it's pretty lame," I said. "With the exception of Springsteen."

Zander's face lit up like a Christmas tree. "As in Bruce?"

"None other." I could barely meet his eyes—I felt so stupid admitting my suspicions. Like some major rock star could actually turn out to be my dad. Even if there was the remotest possibility, which there clearly was.

Zander eyed me up and down. "Hair color, no, but the curls are a yes. Nose is a no—thank God—but maybe I see a little resemblance around the mouth. Who else made the cut?"

"Let's make it a game. I'll name their most famous song. You name the band."

"I take it your mother has a thing for musicians."

"Didn't you just say you've read everything she's ever written?" I asked, shooting Zander a look that practically said "Duh." "I mean, haven't you noticed by now that every book ends with the rock star professing his undying love to the regular girl?"

"Right," Zander said, looking like he wanted to clonk himself in the head for making such an inane comment. "OK. You're on."

" 'Sunglasses at Night,' " I said, feeling triumphant. "You'll never get it."

"That's what you think," Zander said, a sexy smile curling up his lips. "It's Corey Hart. He's one of your suspects?"

"No, but the guy who played keyboards on one of his tours is."

"Interesting," he said, looking very uninterested.

"Moving right along." I was confident I could stump him with the next one. " 'Sister Christian.' " I started singing the tune badly and chock-full of apparently mangled words, since Zander felt compelled to correct me.

"Let me guess," he said after the lyric lesson was over. "Night Ranger's . . . ummmm . . . bassist?"

"You're good," I said. "But I'm under the impression it might be the drummer. How do you know these old songs, anyway?"

"Not to sound dramatic or anything," he said, sounding dramatic and everything. "But music is my life and I know practically every song in the universe."

"Great, then let's keep going," I said, busting out into the next song, "The Kid Is Hot Tonite."

Zander rolled his eyes. "Sooooo easy. That's Loverboy."

"Fine," I said. "Ruin all my fun."

"It's still fun for me," he said, flashing me another winning smile. "Which Loverboy do you think it might be, anyway? The bandanna guy?"

"Didn't they all wear bandannas?"

"Nope," Zander said. "Only the lead singer."

"Oh. I don't know, then," I said. "I'll have to look at the picture more closely when I get home today. Ready for my finale?"

"Already? Lay it on me."

I made the universal "rock on" sign with my fingers and threw my arm in the air. " 'Stroke me, stroke me,' " I sang, trying to make my voice all raspy and sexy. I sounded like a ninety-year-old Nicotine Nancy instead.

Zander was quiet for a minute.

"Sorry, did I scare you?"

"No. I'm stumped," he finally admitted.

"It was Billy Squier. 'The Stroke.' My off-key singing probably threw you."

"It wasn't that," he said. "It's just that I've never heard of him."

"I thought you knew every song in the universe."

"Make that every song minus one."

"Let me fill you in," I said. "This guy is the only one who made decent music out of the whole bunch. With the exception of Bruce, of course. And he's by far the best looking, too."

"Well, that settles it, then. He must be the one."

A slow heat overtook my face as I nearly melted under Zander's sweet compliment. My tongue was too tied up to even thank him.

After a few blocks featuring nothing more than the slapping of our sneaks against the pavement, Zander ventured on. "Have you ever thought about contacting these guys, Trace?"

That got me speaking again. It was a topic of conversation Brina and I had analyzed and picked apart endlessly, always coming back around to the same conclusion. "And say what? You're in a picture with my mom and I figured you're about as good a guess as any, so hey, are you my dad?"

Zander shrugged. "Something like that."

"You know how many weirdos claim stuff like that all the time? I'd get arrested for being a psycho stalker. At the very least, they'd slap a restraining order on me."

"OK, then, did you ever consider sitting down with your mom and asking her to please tell you everything?"

"Been there, done that," I said. "No dice. She says we've made it this far without testosterone interfering with our relationship, and there's no need to add any now."

# CHAPTER
## 3

By the end of our run, I felt incredible, like I had just climbed Mount Everest or discovered a cure for PMS. Zander, on the other hand, was limping and panting and looking generally sweaty. It all added up to one really hot guy, and I mean that in the best possible sense.

He leaned over and put his hands on his knees. "You know, we run around the field a lot for rugby. But why in God's name did you randomly choose fifteen miles to torture me with today?"

"It wasn't random," I told him. "And I can't believe I forgot to tell you. I'm training for the Rock 'n' Roll Marathon in San Diego this spring."

"Inspired by your mom's last book?" Zander's perceptive response blew me away.

"Uh-huh."

"Well, it was totally hot, how they finally got together at the finish line, after all the lies and stuff. That rocked."

"Yup." *Running on Empty* was my favorite Belinda Tillingham book to date because of the amazing happy ending.

"So maybe I'll do it with you."

That sounded pretty dirty. And I was feeling pretty dirty, too, after all that running. "Maybe I'll let you," I said, winking at him.

Zander laughed at me for the millionth time in our less-than-a-week-old relationship. "The marathon, I meant."

My cheeks lit on fire, and I wondered if even peeling them off my face and throwing them into Lake Michigan would douse them out.

"Oh, that." How could he even pretend we might still be friends, or whatever we were, eight months from now? What a joke.

Zander took my hand and led me toward his house. "C'mon, Trace," he said. "Nobody's home but the little brat, and he'll leave us alone as long as Brenda's home."

"Who's Brenda?" I asked.

"His very own personal slave," he said. "I mean au pair."

"Yours, too?" I imagined a stacked Swedish girl giving Zander a nightly sponge bath, and then shook my head to clear the vomitous image.

"Hardly," he said. "First of all, she's only a year older than us. And second of all, she's . . . well . . . she's Brenda. You'll see."

Instead of heading inside the fairy-tale castle, we walked around back. The view took my breath away. Even though I've seen Lake Michigan practically every day of my life, I had never looked at it from this vantage point before: the wraparound porch of a Victorian mansion perched on the bluff. The Caribbean-blue water and equally blue skies seemed to go on forever.

"Like it?" Zander asked, wrapping his arms around my waist from behind me.

"I love it." Thump-thump, thump-thump. My heart was ready to jump out of my chest.

Zander started kissing my neck. It was heavenly . . . until I remembered the fifteen-mile sweat covering my body. Oh, God, I must smell like a pig, I thought. Not to mention taste like day-old seawater.

"Zander?" I didn't want him to stop, but my brain wouldn't stop reminding me about my probable stenchiness.

"Hmmmmmmmm?"

"I'm so sweaty. Doesn't that gross you out?"

"Actually, Trace, I was really getting into it. But if it makes you uncomfortable . . ."

"Who, me? Uncomfortable? No way." I turned around and threw my arms around his neck, trying to lead him back to business. No such luck.

Instead, Zander covered my eyes and led me to the far corner of the porch. I heard a familiar bubbling I couldn't quite place. "Surprise!" he said, dropping his hands from my face.

In front of me was a gigantic hot tub waving its frothy foam at me. "Hi," it said. "The water is great," it told me. And before I could figure out what I should wear—or not—Zander had stripped off his clothes and hopped in.

"Well? Planning on joining me?" he asked.

I hesitated, unsure of how to handle the moment. If I asked for a bathing suit, I'd look like a total stiff. If I stripped naked and jumped in, I'd look like a total slut. And if I kept my sports bra and panties on, I'd look undecided. Not to mention incredibly dweeby.

I chose dweeby and undecided, taking off my running shorts and T-shirt but keeping everything else on. My sports bra had a neon green paisley pattern on it, and I reasoned it could easily pass for a bathing suit top. Not surprisingly, my panties looked more like underwear than bikini bottoms. Still, I was grateful I had chosen the Victoria's Secret black microfiber ones from the drawer this morning instead of the giant white cotton briefs with the period stains. Like Zander really needed to be reminded about my menstrual cycle again.

I eased myself into the superhot water inch by inch. When I finally submerged myself up to my chin, I leaned my head back against the edge of the hot tub and sighed. "This feels great."

"It would feel even better with you next to me," he said. "C'mon, Trace. Take pity on a guy who ran a half marathon just to get close to you."

I scooched over and Zander pulled me onto his lap and started attacking me. In a good way. I tried to act nonchalant, but it wasn't easy. Now I understood what Brina was up against last night, and how hard it was to take things slowly when you were having fun. Believe me, it was really hard.

I thought we could go on like this for—I don't know—say forever, when his little brother and Brenda the au-pair-slash-slave appeared out of nowhere.

"Say hi to Mom and Dad! They're home a day early from the summerhouse!" the little guy announced gleefully.

Brenda, whose pale freckled skin and screaming orange curls made her look like Carrot Top's lost sister, laughed so hard she almost fell out of what must have been her size thirteen Dr. Scholl's. I bolted to the other side of the hot tub and looked to Zander for a clue how to handle this unsettling news. He gave me a "Don't worry—it's cool" kind of gesture, so I stayed put.

"You must be Brenda," I said, trying to make small talk. I sounded like a squeaky-meeky little mouse. Being caught in your underwear by a guy's entire family can do that to a person.

"And you must be Zander's conquest of the week," she replied in a thick German accent. Good one, I thought. And it wasn't even her native tongue. I must be missing my comeback lobe—there was no other explanation for it.

Zander made polite introductions as his parents appeared on the porch. "Mom, Dad, I'd like you to meet my friend Trace," he said. I'm actually surprised anyone could hear him over the pounding of my heart.

"How pleasant to meet you, Tracey." Mrs. O'Brien actually looked like she found me completely repulsive. At least Mr. O'Brien didn't seem horrified by the situation. In fact, he seemed rather intrigued by what was happening under all the foam.

Unsure of the proper etiquette involved in meeting someone's parents when wearing only undergarments—that's not in Emily Post, either—I went for sincere with a bit of suck-up thrown in for good measure. "It's lovely to meet you both. Thank you for allowing me to enjoy your hot tub," I said. "Zander and I just finished a two-hour run, and we thought this would be a good antidote for sore muscles."

His father tore his eyes away from the water long enough to glance at Zander. "Why so long? That's foolishness. Won't help you get into Stanford, either."

"Why not? It felt great," Zander answered.

"I gather that's not the only reason you feel great, son." Mr. O'Brien gave me the once-over and winked. With his silver hair and startling green eyes, Zander's dad was certainly a good-looking enough man— if you like fifty-year-old guys, which I don't. My feeling is, if a dude's already out of college, he's too old for me. I even find it hard to believe that Brina thinks Mr. Perry is attractive. I mean, he has to be at least Bebe's age.

"I need a drink," Mrs. O'Brien muttered, stepping through the sliding glass door into the kitchen.

Not so easy to get rid of was Mr. O'Brien. This was more than a minor problem because I couldn't put my sweaty clothes back on and start running away until Zander's dad got lost.

"Maybe I'll just jump in for a little soak with you two," he said.

Zander and I stared at each other. I was mortified. This, of course, made Zander egg his dad on even more.

"Oh, would you, Dad? That'd be great."

"Sure. I'll just go grab my suit." Mr. O'Brien walked in the house, probably imagining a kinky father-son ménage à trois.

I waited a few seconds to make sure he was really gone and then sprang out of the tub like it was fire. I looked around. There wasn't a towel in sight. Dripping wet, I grabbed my shorts and tried to pull them on. I couldn't get them past the middle of my hips, turning my butt into a four-leaf clover: two cheeks above the waistband and two below it. I threw on my XL T-shirt to cover up the whole mess. It would have to do.

Zander was cracking up. At me. Again. "You're a regular speeding bullet. Usually it takes my parents at least five minutes before my friends go running for their lives."

I tied my laces with shaky hands. "Zander, I really do have to go now." Those horrendous cramps Brina made up for me last night weren't fictional anymore. Diarrhea, my body's typical reaction to fear. "Thanks for the company, though. And please tell your parents I said good-bye." I started running up his driveway toward the street.

"Let's pick up where we left off sometime soon and see where it leads us," he called after me. I stopped running, the groaning in my intestines subsiding for the time being, and scooped back around toward Zander.

"I can tell you right now I'm not going there with you," I said, jogging in place. Not yet, anyway, I thought. Check back with me in a month or so.

Zander shrugged, undeterred. "For now, let's just go for another run. E-mail me our training schedule."

I raised one eyebrow, my specialty. It sort of looks like a question mark when I do it. "Our schedule?"

"Yeah, ours. I'm in this thing with you."

He couldn't be serious. Could he?

I returned home to find Bebe freaking out. Very Mom-like. Very un-Bebe-like.

"Where the hell have you been?"

Bebe never questions me about what I've been doing, especially not in broad daylight, so I decided to tread lightly. "Hello to you, too, Bebe. You OK?" I could see from the veins sticking out all over her forehead she most definitely was not.

"The problem is you went for a run at seven this morning and didn't come back until the afternoon. I thought you were dead." Obviously, Bebe had gotten knocked out and woke up thinking she was Carol Brady.

I squinted, checking carefully for goose eggs on her head. I didn't see any.

"You still haven't answered my question," Bebe said, crossing her arms and tapping her foot impatiently. "I asked you where you were."

"If you must know, I was running," I said. "See? Got my running gear on." I hitched up my shorts to their rightful spot just below my waist, my butt bouncing back to its normal shape.

"An entire marathon wouldn't take that long."

Though it rubbed me the wrong way—I mean, why should I start telling Bebe my every move now when I've never had to before?—I decided to give her the scoop. "I bumped into Zander and he ended up tagging along with me. Then we went back to his house for a while."

"In the future, I'd appreciate it if you'd ask before going over to his place."

"And I'd appreciate it if you'd bring back my mother, you alien," I said. "Since when do I need your permission to hang out with a friend?"

Bebe's face tightened even more. She was going to end up looking like Joan Rivers before the end of this conversation if she kept it up. "Since I decided you may need some more traditional mothering than you've been getting."

I was floored. What could Bebe possibly have against Zander? She hadn't even met him yet. "All this because of a guy? You never acted this way when I was with T. J."

"T. J. wasn't a musician." Ahhhhh. Now we were getting somewhere.

"Have your books gone straight to your head, Bebe? He's not a *musician* musician. He's a good student who plays rugby and just happens to strum a little guitar on the side." I couldn't help adding, "And he lives in a castle with a hot tub overlooking the lake!" I was still kind of overwhelmed by the whole thing myself.

But Bebe wasn't swayed by my list of Zander's many fine attributes. "Trace, doesn't it seem like things are going a little too fast with this guy?"

"Yeah, I usually don't jog with someone until I've known them for at least a year." When I'm pissed off, my first line of defense is sarcasm.

"All I'm saying is, it's better not to date rocker boys. In my experience, they're never just hanging around for the stimulating conversation."

I felt my face flush as I caught her drift. Ewwwwwwww. I did *not* want to go down this path with my mom. I hitched up my running shorts to nerd-land—over the top of my belly button and halfway to my armpits—thinking that may have been what prompted the comment. "We had that little birds-and-bees discussion when I was eight, Bebe. I can take care of myself."

"That's what I thought, too, and look where it got me."

I felt like I'd been punched in the stomach. "It got you me," I said, turning away so she couldn't see the tears welling up in my eyes. "Is that so bad?"

She walked across the kitchen and tucked my sweaty hair behind my ears. "I'm sorry. I didn't mean it that way," she said. "I'm just trying to protect you from going through the same heartache I did."

"I wish you wouldn't protect me, Bebe. I wish you'd tell me all about it." I wiped my eyes and nose on the shoulder of my T-shirt. "I have a right to know about my dad, you know."

She sighed. "You already know everything you need to know. He bails on people he supposedly loves without even a backward glance. Baby, he was born to run. End of story."

I ran upstairs, slammed the door, and peeled off my disgustingly wet clothes. Shivering, I turned on the shower and hopped in once the water felt hot enough. And it wasn't just the soap getting me in a huge lather.

Who was she kidding, I had to ask her before I went to Zander's again?

Just when did she decide, in her ultimate wisdom, that my company was so unstimulating a guy could want only possibly one thing from me?

And what the fuck was she talking about, I already knew everything I needed to know about my father? I didn't know anything at all, except that my mom had just quoted Springsteen lyrics when she was going off on him downstairs. That alone would've been enough to move Bruce up my suspect list a spot or two, but there was nowhere else to go. He already occupied the number one position.

I suddenly realized my "what the f—" brain wave had just made me lose the not-swearing battle, even if it was only in my head. Tough shit, I thought, I'm on a roll.

I was wrapping my hair in a Turbie Twist when the phone rang. I dived for it before Bebe could pick up downstairs. "Hello?"

"Hi, Trace." It was Zander. Not that I wanted him to know I knew that, of course.

"Who's this?" I asked.

"It's Zander. Who did you think it was?"

"Zander," I admitted.

"I've been doing a little research on your dad mystery."

"You have? How?"

"Ever heard of a little thing called the Internet, Trace? It's been around for quite a while now."

"Yeah, I know about it. I also know that every time I type into Ask Jeeves, 'Is my father the guy who plays drums for Night Ranger?' I don't exactly get the answer I'm looking for. I'd be better off asking my Magic 8-ball."

"We can borrow my brother's Ouija board if you like."

"It'd probably give me more information than the Internet has so far."

"Trace, maybe you've been going about it the wrong way," Zander said. "I actually got lots of scoop just by Googling your mom's name."

Now, why hadn't I thought of that before? Probably because I assumed I already knew all there was to know about Bebe. With the exception of who impregnated her, of course.

"So what did you find out?"

"Number one, the Stone Pony in Asbury Park, New Jersey, is where she met the musician she models the leading men in her books after."

"Who's that? Richard Marx?" He seemed to get the most consistent play in our house, and all the guys on the covers of Bebe's books had dark, wavy hair like his.

"Actually, the place is legendary, Trace. It's where Springsteen got his start."

The hairs on the back of my neck stood up like a zillion tiny soldiers in the battle to find my dad. "No way," I whispered.

"Way," said Zander. "And listen to this. Bebe said that she and whoever this guy was got into a lot of trouble together."

"Getting pregnant at eighteen is pretty big trouble. She didn't name names, did she?" I was already deep into a daddy-daughter reunion fantasy: me, running up the gargantuan Rumson, New Jersey, lawn of Bruce and Patti Scialfa, who of course greeted me with open arms. Their four kids clambering at my feet, psyched to have the big sister they'd always dreamed of as part of their family . . .

Zander's voice popped my big ol' bubble.

"Nothing printable, at least. But maybe someone who still hangs around the joint knows who this guy was. Like an owner or a bouncer or a townie, maybe?"

I opened my desk drawer and pulled out a pad of Post-its. Ticket stubs, pens, and an old bag of Cheetos tumbled out with it. Like locker, like drawer, I thought. I caught one of the pens before it hit the floor, and scribbled: *(1) Check out the Stone Pony.* "Got it," I said.

"OK, clue number two. Bebe was quoted as saying Billy Squier had a magic touch," Zander told me. "Maybe she meant his guitar playing. And then again, maybe not."

I laid the pen down on my desk and spun it, watching it make circles before it rolled off to the floor. "He's already on my list."

"Move him up a space or two, then," Zander said, sounding all excited. "Hey, guess what? In a weird karmic kind of thing, Billy's actually playing a benefit show here in a few weeks. I bought us three tickets."

"Three?"

"Yeah. One for you, one for me, and one for Bebe. She's gonna love me, don't ya think?"

"She will absolutely pee her pants."

"You both have that problem, huh?"

"Shut up, Zander," I said, trying to cover up my giggles by coughing. I didn't want him knowing I actually thought the jokes he made at my expense were funny.

"You OK?"

"Yeah. Just swallowed the wrong way. Anything else?"

"Wasn't that enough?"

"Absolutely. One good clue is better than what I had before, which was nothing."

"I just gave you two clues, you poor thing. Are you doing OK in math?"

"Yes," I told him, lying. Actually, trig was still killing me on a daily basis. It was getting so hopeless, Mr. Flagstaff had called Bebe in for an emergency meeting next week. I was shitting a brick about that one. I needed to pass trig to get into college. "Zander?"

"What, Trace?"

"You rock. Thanks so much for your help."

"Anytime. Now send me that running schedule so I know when I'll get to see those gorgeous eyes again."

"You got it," I said, feeling warm all over. "Bye."

The phone rang the second after I put it down. "Hello?"

"Trace?" It was Zander again.

"Who is this?"

"Didn't we already play this game?"

"Oh, yeah. That's right," I said, grinning like a fool.

"I forgot to ask you something," Zander said.

"What's that?"

"Wanna be my date at the Country Day Cotillion?"

"Sure I do," I said. "What is it, anyway?"

"A fancy dance," he said. "I think Robb's gonna ask Brina."

"Cool," I said. "Any special instructions?"

"You'll do fine just as long as you don't get behind a microphone."

"That I can handle."

"And Trace?"

"What?"

"Sorry about my lecherous father. He was very disappointed to find you gone when he got back to the hot tub."

"He's nice," I said. "But I think I'll stick with you."

"You won't regret it."


After we hung up, I heard a soft knock at the door. "Nobody's home," I said.

Bebe popped her head into my room anyway. "Trace."

"Mother."

My sarcasm wasn't lost on her. "Spare me. I know I went off on you back there, and I wanted to apologize. I was just scared you were lying on the side of the road somewhere, bleeding to death."

"Thanks for your concern," I said, contempt oozing out of my every pore.

"I also wanted to say I'm sorry for the mean things I implied about your new boyfriend—"

"Friend with potential," I interrupted.

"OK, friend with potential. Of course he's not just in it for the physical thing. You're an amazing person." Then she added, "And you don't need any father to tell you that."

I jumped right into that opening. "Thanks. But I actually would like my dad to tell me that. So if you're willing—"

"It has nothing to do with my willingness," she said, shaking her head. "And everything to do with his."

She looked so sad and pathetic I went over and hugged her. "Maybe I could change his mind," I whispered, resting my head on her shoulder.

"It's not even remotely possible."

"Why? Is it because he's too famous or something?"

Bebe pulled back from our little lovefest and eyed me curiously. "Why would you say a thing like that?"

Two could play at this Little Miss Innocent game. "Why wouldn't I?"

"Trust me," she said. "You have no idea what you're talking about."

# CHAPTER
## 4

On Monday, I drove to school with Bebe riding shotgun. "Tell me one more time what's going on in trig?" she said.

"I'm trying my best. I just don't get it," I told her, neglecting to mention my lack of real effort until recently, when it had finally dawned on me that I was in serious trouble. "And I'm scared I never will. I need to pass this class to get into college."

"Don't worry," she told me. "I'll handle Mr. Flagstaff if you can handle some serious tutoring."

"From you?" I asked her, not believing she could do any better with it than I could. Math was not Bebe's strong suit, and I had definitely taken after her.

"God, no," she said. "I can barely balance the checkbook. I signed you up for classes at the Northshore Achievement Center Tuesday and Thursday mornings before school."

I panicked. "That's really gonna cut into my sleep time, Bebe."

"Better than screwing up your life," she said as we approached the main entrance to school. I had to admit, she had a point.

We walked up the steps and I tugged on the heavy oak door. It opened with a jolt, and I let Bebe go first.

"Are you sure you remember how to get to Mr. Flagstaff's classroom?"

"Piece of cake," she said, looking around like she didn't have the first idea where to go.

"It's that way," I said, pointing down the hall.

"Yeah, right," she said. "Catch ya later."

"Be cool," I called after her as she walked out of sight. "Don't agree to anything too outrageous." As if twice-a-week tutoring sessions at the local underachievers' center wasn't outrageous enough.

I glanced at my watch. Still half an hour to kill before first period. I walked into the cafeteria and bought a large Pepsi, hoping the caffeine jolt would help me get through some last-minute homework. I opened my trig book and triangles swam in front of my face.

A second later, they disappeared as everything went pitch-black. That's because someone's freezing hands were covering my eyes. "Guess who?" Brina said from behind me.

"Why are you here so early?" I asked, turning around to look at her.

"Another meeting with that dreamy Mr. Perry," she said. "I actually ran into Bebe on the way out. She needed directions."

"She must have gotten lost on her way to meet with Mr. Flagstaff," I said. "And there are a thousand other guys at Northshore, Brina. Pick on someone your own age."

"Got your period again? That's the third time this month," she said, totally cracking herself up. "Oh, well, maybe this will brighten your day. It sure did mine." She handed me a piece of paper folded into a smallish square. I unfolded it and smoothed the note on the table in front of me.

*Brina,*
*I like to imagine us together*
*Always envision our lives entwined*
*But I can't seem to wrap you up in mine*
*Maybe you could get tied up in me*
*slp*

I screamed. The entire cafeteria turned what looked like one giant head my way to see what all the commotion was about.

"What's wrong?" Brina asked, her eyes bigger than UFOs.

I let a totally exaggerated shiver go down my spine and pretended I could barely hold on to the note—my hands were shaking so much. "This one's even scarier than the last!"

"Don't be silly," she said, grabbing it from me and tucking it back into her neat-as-a-frickin'-pin notebook. "It's totally sweet."

I shook my head. I just never knew how Brina was going to react. "I can't believe Sam's still at it."

"How many times do I have to tell you, Trace? Sam is not slp."

"Sanford, then."

Brina gave me a menacing look, like she wanted to slug me or something. "It's not him, either."

"Think what you like. But until you find the real guy, I've got bets on both of them."

"Trace, it says right here he wants to tie me up," Brina said, pointing to the fourth line. "Sanford hasn't even had his first kiss yet, no less moved on to kinkier pastures."

"You never know," I said, though I silently agreed with her assessment. "Don't judge a book by its cover and all that."

"Not buying it, Trace."

"Well, then, Sam seems like he might be sexually adventurous," I said, trying to remember who his last girlfriend was. Unfortunately, all I could see in my mind was Mr. Flagstaff's nose hair breathing down on me as he tried, unsuccessfully as ever, to get me to understand the most basic trigonometric concept.

"Sam was too scared to answer me when I asked his middle name," Brina said, interrupting my math-phobic thoughts. "I can't see him all of a sudden turning into a take-charge kind of a guy in a relationship."

"Still," I told her, "it's not a deal breaker. I'm leaving Sam on the list along with Sanford, that booger-picking fool."

"If you say so, Trace. But it's not either one of them. I guarantee you that."

I didn't get to torture Brina any more during school, so the rest of the day was stupendously boring. When the clock finally hit three, I sprinted home. Ridiculous, 'cause I was running home to go for a run, but I just couldn't help myself.

I tossed my jeans, T-shirt, and boots into the corner of my room and pulled on a sports bra, tank top, thong—just in case Zander and I ended up in the hot tub again—and running shorts. Then I practically skipped the two miles to Zander's house.

He was waiting out front, and wrapped me into a huge hug when I got close enough. I'm only five-three. Zander is six-two. My face smushed right into his chest.

"Hey, I missed you," he said. From anyone else, I would have thought this was pussy-whipped drivel. From Zander, though, it seemed just about right. He was so cool, I didn't get turned off like I usually do when guys actually treat me well.

"You did?" I said, gasping for air. My voice was totally muffled in his shirt.

"Most definitely," he said, hugging me even tighter, if that was possible. Then he pulled back to look at me. "Hey, how fast did you run here? Your pulse is totally racing."

"That's from you, not the running," I admitted. My heart went bananas whenever I got the slightest bit close to him.

"If that's the case, maybe we should go straight to the hot tub," he said.

"Don't tempt me," I said, feeling very tempted. "I need to stick to the training schedule."

"Have it your way, Tracey Buzzkill. I can be patient."

We started our nine miles at a good clip, with at least me thinking about what was to come later. No pun intended. A few blocks down the road, Zander asked me, "So did you do any sleuthing since we last talked?"

"Yep." I'd actually been hard at work, banging my head against a big brick wall. And I had bumps and bruises all over my ego to prove it. Let's just say that eighties rock icons, along with some lesser idols, don't exactly jump at the chance at being interviewed for a "school paper." Maybe part of being a rock star, or ex-star, is knowing how to smell an ulterior motive half a continent away.

"So talk."

"I couldn't find anyone at the Stone Pony who's older than dirt and was around when Bebe hung out there," I said, ticking off my feeble attempts to discover something, *anything,* about my dad. "The place has been totally revamped since the eighties."

"Moving right along."

"Next, for some reason, Steve Van Zandt, Nils Lofgren, Max Weinberg, Clarence Clemons, and Soozie Tyrell seem to have no interest in being featured in the *Northshore Courier*. Neither does Billy Squier, Loverboy dude, Night Ranger stick man, or Corey Hart's keyboard guy, for that matter. The silence in response to my e-mails was completely deafening."

"No shit," Zander said, smiling and winking at me. "Can you believe the nerve of those people?"

"Yes, I can." It was actually pretty funny when I thought about it—some random high school girl having the balls to ask veritable superstars (along with has-been sorta stars) for an interview. As if they were actually going to be like, "Why, certainly. I thought you'd never ask!"

Mercifully, Zander directed the subject away from my pitiful detective work. "Did you tell Bebe about the Billy Squier show yet?"

"Yup. She freaked out and went shopping."

"For a new outfit to impress him with?"

"I guess so. She came home with an armful of bags."

Zander wiped the sweat from his brow with the end of his shirt. When his face reappeared, he said, "I'm glad the concert's on a Thursday, 'cause we have to start practicing."

"For what?"

"For college. I hear Thursday is the biggest night out all week."

"At Stanford or everywhere?" I asked him.

"Everywhere," he said. "So when I'm at Stanford, where will you be?"

"USC, UCLA, Santa Clara, or Fairfield." One of these things is not like the others. Here's a hint: California, California, California . . . Connecticut.

Zander squinted at me, sizing me up. "You're clearly a misplaced USC or UCLA girl. Forget Fairfield—wherever that is. I've never even heard of it."

"I'm only applying to make my grandfather happy. He went there about a million years ago," I explained. My whole life, Grandpa has regaled me with squeaky-clean stories of his days at this little Catholic college. From the looks of the deluge of communications they've been sending me, things haven't changed much. Everyone there still looks a hundred percent scrubbed and clean-cut—no piercings, no tats, no dangerous-looking future rock stars. Not exactly what I envisioned for my wild and crazy college years.

After our fifth mile, running was getting totally monotonous. I tried to whip up some excitement by slapping Zander's butt. "Ooohhhh, that thing is rock hard, baby," I said, shaking my hand like it hurt.

"You better believe it," he said, grinning.

Spotting something that looked like even more fun, I said, "Turn in here." We ran down the steps of one of the public beaches and Zander let me go first at the water fountain. Unlike the public bathrooms, it was still in operation. Figures. Without water, I'd only get dehydrated. Without a public bathroom . . . well, we already knew the humiliating end to that story.

I sucked in as much water as possible and then turned around and sprayed Zander in the face. He looked shocked for a second, then wiped his eyes and moved quickly on to retaliation.

"You shouldn't have done that," he said, racing to the fountain and sending a river that drenched my shirt. Then he tackled me in the sand and pinned my arms above my head. "Say 'Zander is the man.' "

"No way," I said, shaking my head. "Never."

"Say 'Zander rocks,' then."

"Nuh-uh."

His hair was dripping down on me, adding a new layer of wetness. I glanced down at my chest. Headlight city. I looked like Jennifer Aniston in at least one scene of every *Friends* episode. "Say 'I wish Zander would shut up and kiss me already.' "

Now, that sounded good. "OK. I wish Zanmmmphhhh . . ."

This was the kind of action I'd been looking for, but just as things were about to get a little too PG-13, we took a cold shower. Literally. A guy had taken a pail of lake water and thrown it at us.

"Hey, you two. Get a room," he said. "I've got my kids here!"

"Sorry," we mumbled, shaking sand from our hair and clothes and trying to look presentable.

"Kids today. It's always sex this and sex that," the guy was muttering. "I was born twenty damn years too late." Then he walked off down the beach, bending over every few steps to look at sea glass with his children.

Zander took my hands in his and looked me straight in the eye. "Trace, just so you know. If we ever end up taking this any further, it won't be on a beach or in the backseat of a car. It'll be special. Just like you." I tried to memorize what he'd just said, and repeated it over and over in my head so I wouldn't ever forget his words the way I mangle lyrics.

By the night of the concert, I was a major wreck. "Bebe, let's say I'm sick and blow this thing off."

She put her arm around me. "Trace, I wouldn't miss it for the world. I'll be cool. No farting. No burping. No flashing Billy from the front of the stage like I used to."

I rolled my eyes. "Statements like that are what scare me."

"Just chill. Everything will be fine—you'll see," she said. "I even have a surprise for you guys after the concert. It's so awesome, even I don't believe it." I could only imagine what kind of embarrassment awaited us.

Bebe whistled quietly as we pulled into Zander's driveway. "Holy crap, that's a big house. What did you say his parents do?"

"His dad is CEO of some kind of packaging company. And his mom is one of those typical tennis-playing, Lilly-wearing types."

Bebe took a deep breath, opened her door, and got out of the car. I stuck to my seat like I was superglued to it. Bebe made some rude gestures at me to get out. I still stayed put.

"Now who's having a problem being presentable?" she asked, collaring me like a mama cat and dragging me onto Zander's front porch. Bebe rang the bell and Mrs. O'Brien appeared.

"Hello, Tracey," she greeted me. I wondered if that wineglass was permanently attached to her hand. "I thought Zander said your mom was taking the two of you out tonight."

"I *am* Tracey's mother," Bebe said, sticking out her hand. "Belinda Tillingham."

Mrs. O'Brien turned into one of those ridiculous bobble head thingies right in front of my eyes. "You're Tracey's mom?" she said, her head bouncing back and forth between Bebe and me. "Forgive me—it's just that you . . . she . . ."

"Don't think twice about it," Bebe said, waving away the uncomfortable moment. "I get that reaction all the time."

Sadly, it's true. When Bebe and I go out together, people are forever asking if we're sisters. I mean Bebe's young, but get real. Not that young.

Mrs. O'Brien took a big gulp of wine, draining the glass. "Excuse me," she said, heading toward the kitchen. Just as I started wishing a freak tornado would suck us out of the mansion of horrors, Zander came walking down the stairs.

"Mrs. Tillingham, it's a pleasure to meet you," he said in a charming but misguided attempt to endear himself to Bebe.

"You've just succeeded in making me feel about a hundred years old," Bebe said, her mouth forming a thin line that looked like a kid drew it with a supersharpened pencil. "Which I'm not. So 'Bebe' will do just fine."

"Sorry about that, Bebe," Zander said, blushing.

"It's OK," she said, still not smiling. "Just don't do it again."

So far, so bad. And with Bebe's potentially frightening surprise later, I guessed the only way things could go from here was down.

I was wrong. The ride to the city was actually kind of fun. Zander had burned a new mix just for the occasion, putting on it his current favorite bands like Trapt and Puddle of Mudd, some original Vipers tunes, and at least one song each from the groups our suspects played in. Bebe didn't seem the least bit suspicious, though I can't imagine why. She couldn't possibly think Zander would normally listen to her stuff, could she?

Apparently she could. "Nice to hear some retro songs in your mix, Zander," Bebe said. "Trace wouldn't dream of admitting she likes eighties music, even though I know she must."

"Not," I muttered under my breath.

"I listen to it all the time," Zander lied.

"Not," I said again, less quietly this time.

Bebe punched me in the shoulder. "This guy's got good taste, Trace. You should hang on to him." And to think, just a few short weeks ago she was convinced all Zander wanted was a little play from me. It was amazing what a trio of Billy Squier tickets could do.

We spotted a parking space just down the street from the Five Star Fajita Bar and screeched into it before anyone else could. Zander opened my door and helped me out, running around to the driver's-side door to do the same for Bebe. Then he linked his arms through ours and we half walked, half skipped into the restaurant, belting out "Can't Sing to Save Her Life." I got the words right, for once.

A spunky blond waitress came over to take our drink order immediately. "Dos Equis for me," Bebe said.

"Me, too," I added, flipping out my never-fail fake ID before the waitress even had a chance to ask for it.

"Uhhhh . . . Coke for me," Zander conceded, undoubtedly knowing he'd be carded and shot down if he tried to get served. "I don't have an ID," he mumbled when Miss Energizer Bunny was out of earshot.

"We'll just have to do something about that, won't we?" Bebe said, ruffling Zander's hair like he was two years old. I gave her a menacing look. She ignored me.

"You'd help me get one?" Zander asked, brightening.

"Nope, not even close. Come to think of it, I don't even approve of Trace's," Bebe said, shooting him down without a second thought. "But I will order you a great virgin drink."

Bebe motioned to the waitress, who ran right over, her ponytail gleaming under the bar lights. "Can you get a nonalcoholic Sex on the Beach for this underage hottie?"

Zander examined his fingernails and tried to change the subject. "Know what, Bebe? We seem to have a lot in common." Oh, come on. Did he use that same tired line every time he met a girl?

"Well, we certainly like a lot of the same music," Bebe said. God, she was so dense.

"And we're both writers," Zander said, drowning out all the shrieking in my mind. "I'm a reporter for my school paper."

This was news to me. "You are?" I asked, wondering why he'd never mentioned it before.

"Uh-huh," he said, nodding his head. When Bebe turned around a second later to pay the waitress for our round, he shook it and mouthed, "No way."

After Bebe was done settling the tab, Zander got right back into character. "I was wondering if I could interview you for the *Country Day Reporter*. It would be quite a coup for me."

Bebe dug into the guacamole with an extra large chip and took a slug of beer. "Sure, why not? Fire away."

As if by magic, Zander produced a notebook and pen from his pocket. He even looked like the real deal. "How did you get started as a writer?" With a boring, pedestrian interview question like that, Bebe would definitely figure out Zander was a fraud.

Wrong. "I was actually more of a frustrated musician looking for a creative outlet," Bebe said. "I had tried taking up guitar a million times, only to quit a few weeks later when I got disgusted with my bleeding, blistered fingers that couldn't pick out anything vaguely rockin'." She was giving Zander more information than she'd ever offered me, her only child, before. I chalked it up to beginner's luck.

"And then . . . ?" Zander asked, trying to lead her even farther down the path.

"When it became clear I was never going to be a rock star, I decided the next best thing would be to meet some and write about them instead."

"Easier said than done, isn't it?" Zander prodded further.

"Not when you've got a friend with connections and totally unsuspecting parents," she said. "Every time I went to a concert, I made it sound like an educational experience."

"Your parents bought that?" Zander asked. He looked like he couldn't believe anyone would be that gullible. But he didn't know my grandparents. Those two wouldn't have thought in their wildest dreams that anything illicit could possibly go on backstage. This is how out of it my grandparents were—and still are—about anything remotely related to pop culture: Once, Bebe told Grandma and Grandpa she was going to see Molly Hatchet and Lynyrd Skynyrd—both Southern rock bands from back in the day—and they automatically assumed she was referring to the kids who were recently crowned homecoming king and queen. Bebe didn't even try to correct them.

"Bought it? They thought it was great I was exposing myself to the arts."

I leaned over and whispered to Zander, "She exposed herself, all right."

He kicked me under the table. "So who'd you end up meeting?" Zander asked her.

"Only some of the greatest bands ever. Loverboy, Night Ranger, Corey Hart, Billy Squier . . ." Bebe looked flushed as she conjured up her glory days. Maybe it was just the beer. Or maybe it was remembering how she used to swing from the ceiling with all those guys. ". . . Even Bruce and the E Streeters. Now, that was one of the biggest thrills of my life."

Regular thrilling, I wondered, or the orgasmic kind? I jumped into the interview uninvited. "How did you do it?" I asked, wondering if she could give me some pointers on how to get backstage at the next Strokes show.

"Like I said, my friend had connections," she answered, sighing. "That was one crazy summer."

Zander went in for the kill with his next question. "So why did you quit . . . uhhh . . . groupie-ing?"

"I was always just a music lover. Nothing more," Bebe answered, unfazed.

"OK, let me rephrase that last question," Zander said, not so easily deterred. "When did you quit being a music lover?"

"Never have, never will." Jeez, talk about banging your head against a brick wall.

Still, Zander wasn't quite ready to quit yet. "Then why did you stop following your favorite bands?"

"My friend and I had a falling-out. It just didn't seem fun after that," she said, finally giving him an inch. "I guess being very obviously pregnant had something to do with it, too."

"How did that one go over with your gullible parents?" Zander asked.

"They were pretty confused, to say the least, but they supported my decision. And then they shipped me off to Great-aunt Betty's, here in Illinois," Bebe said. "Where I waited for the light of my life to come along."

That sounded promising. Like she was waiting for my dad—the light of her life—to come after her and say he wanted us to be family after all. "And who was that?" I asked Bebe, kicking Zander under the table.

"You, of course, Trace. Who did you think I was gonna say, David Lee Roth? I mean, he's lots of fun, but hardly in the light-of-my-life category." Bebe was still laughing when she got up and excused herself to go to the ladies' room a minute later.

That left me and Zander, who was just sitting there with a shit-eating grin on his face. "Why are you so happy?" I asked him. "We haven't even gotten a decent lead yet."

"I just can't believe your mom knows the guys from Van Halen."

"She doesn't," I said, watching his bubble burst. "I hate to tell you this, but she met David after he went solo."

Bebe got back just as the waitress plunked our burritos down on the table. She held up her beer and made a toast. "Here's to a great night and a great concert!"

Zander and I raised our drinks and we all clinked glasses. His pink, girlie concoction slopped all over the place.

# CHAPTER 5

Even I had to admit, Billy put on a pretty good show. He opened with "The Stroke"—the same song we'd played Name That Tune with when I was making Zander guess about all the Dad suspects. I leaned over and said, "Recognize it now?"

He shook his head. "Nope. This is his most famous song?"

"Yup."

"Then what's he going to play for an encore?"

"Good question." I glanced over at Bebe, who had her head thrown back and was singing every word to every song loud enough that people five rows ahead of us could hear her. I slumped down in my seat and pretended I'd never seen her before in my life.

After a couple more riff-laden rock songs, Billy sat down on a stool in the middle of the stage and picked up an acoustic guitar. Bebe grabbed her purse and started rummaging around in it frantically. She looked like she was about to cry.

"What's wrong?" I asked her.

"I can't find my lighter!"

"Since when do you smoke?"

"Since never," she said. "Oh, here it is. Thank God." She pulled a yellow Bic from her bag, lit it, and started waving her arm back and forth to the music. This would have been completely mortifying if every other thirty- and forty-something woman in the audience hadn't been doing the same thing.

Bebe closed her eyes—amazing, since she hadn't taken them off

Billy since he took the stage—and belted out the words to this song even louder than the ones that came before it. The final dramatic line was something about Billy trying to find his way, and if he did, he would stay with whomever the song was about forever.

"I wish he'd stayed with me," Bebe whispered in my ear during an instrumental. "Too bad. I'm sure it would have been incredible." Then she went back to her flame-waving, ballad-warbling rapture.

OK, I thought hysterically, was she trying to tell me something? Was this her way of saying Billy was really my dad? I kicked Zander, who had fallen asleep. His eyes flew open. "What?" he said, rubbing his ankle.

"Billy Squier," I hyperventilated, pointing at the stage.

"I know. I bought the tickets, remember? Now let me get some rest."

"No," I said. "I think he's the one." Bebe's last comment spilled out of my mouth like it was one very long word: "Iwishhedstayedwithme-toobadimsureitwouldhavebeenincredible."

"How are we going to find out?" Zander asked, wide-awake now.

"I don't know!" I said, totally freaking out.

"Breathe," Zander said, grabbing me by the shoulders. "You can do it. Bebe's already halfway down memory lane. You just have to make her go all the way."

"That's what got her into this mess," I said, patting myself on the back for the quick comeback. Then I realized the mess I was referring to was me. Oh, well. Maybe Zander hadn't picked up on it.

"You're not a mess," he said, kissing my cheek. "You're awesome." OK, so he had picked up on it. But the kiss and the compliment were worth tripping over my tongue for.

"Thanks," I told him.

Billy closed the show with "In the Dark." We were all on our feet and dancing by this point, even Zander. As the last note faded, the entire stage went pitch-black. Even if it was a little overblown, I went wild, screaming and whistling for Billy like he was actually one of my guys, not Bebe's. Bebe started digging around in her purse again, and refused to believe the show was over until the lights came on and middle-aged faces started streaming up the aisles.

"No encore, huh? I guess I won't be needing this after all," Bebe said, tossing the lighter back in her bag. "Follow me, guys."

She led us down the aisle in the opposite direction of everybody else. We fought our way against traffic until we came to a door marked EMPLOYEES ONLY. Bebe knocked on it three times. She paused, then knocked three times more. Nothing happened.

"Spike! Open this door right now, you asshole!" Bebe finally yelled.

A big, tattooed dude peered out the door, nearly doubled over with laughter. "Just like the old days, huh, Bliss?"

Bliss? Did he have Bebe confused with someone else? "Who's Bliss?" I asked her.

"Just a stupid nickname," she said, waving away my question with the flick of her wrist. "Spike used to work security for Survivor. Liked to give me a hard time back then, too."

Bebe turned her attention back to Spike. "Got me again," she said, punching him in his jiggly Santa Claus belly. Spike gathered Bebe in his massive arms and twirled her around the room. Zander and I stood pinned in the corner behind them, not sure what to do.

I cleared my throat. "Aren't you going to introduce us to your friends, Bebe?"

"I just did," she said.

"What about Billy and the band?"

"I . . . I . . . can't." Bebe stared at the floor and shifted her weight from foot to foot.

"Why not?" Zander asked.

"I'm too scared," she finally admitted.

"You don't have to be afraid," Zander said, draping his arm over her shoulder. "I'm sure he'll be happy to see you and Trace again."

"What?" Bebe asked, looking at Zander like he had two heads. "Who will be happy to see us again?"

"You don't have to put up a front with us anymore, Bebe," Zander told her. "It's OK. We know the truth."

"Maybe he'll even want to get back together with you," I added, putting my arm around Bebe's other shoulder and squeezing tight.

"What are you two talking about?" she asked, looking more confused than ever.

"You know. My dad, Billy. And you," I said.

"Now, that's a threesome that will never happen," Bebe answered. "And I don't know what's gotten into you guys, but let's get Spike to make the introductions."

"I thought you and Billy already knew each other," Zander said.

"Yeah, so did I," I said. "And there's a picture hanging in the downstairs bathroom to prove it."

"It may look like Billy and I are old pals in it," Bebe said. "But the truth is, I only met him once and when I did, I was so nervous I could barely squeak out three dopey words: 'I . . . love . . . you.' My friend snapped a picture of us, and that was the end of it. He'll never remember me."

"There's one person you can cross off your list," Zander whispered to me, sticking out his hand to shake Billy's.

That Saturday, I was idly scratching Billy Squier's name off my Post-it list as I waited for Zander to pick me up for the Country Day Cotillion.

"Trace, your chariot awaits," Bebe yelled up the stairs. "Look out front!" I peeked out the window and saw Zander's head sticking out of the moon roof of a stretch Navigator limo. He had a rose clenched between his teeth.

"Don't wait up," I said, kissing Bebe on the cheek and stepping through the front door carefully, trying to stay upright in Bebe's Jimmy Choos.

Zander let out a whistle when he saw me and yelled, "Hey, baby!"

I twirled around, grinning. "Hey, baby, yourself."

Zander's head popped back in the limo and a minute later, his whole body came out the door. He took the rose out of his mouth and handed it to me. "You look gorgeous," he said, helping me into the car.

Inside were three other couples, the female halves of which looked like they'd just waltzed out of *Gone with the Wind*. I hadn't realized there was that much taffeta and tulle in all of Chicago. The whole posse eyed me like they'd just picked me up at the Kato Kaelin house and wanted to know where the main estate was.

"Nice outfit," the girl in the pastel pink said as I slid into the seat next to her. Bebe had talked me into wearing vintage clothes instead of going to a cheesy store at the mall to pick out an even cheesier dress.

And as outdated as her musical tastes are, I have to admit that Bebe's fashion sense is rockin'. The low-slung velvet pants fitted me like a glove, and the black halter made my flat chest almost noticeable.

"*Très* retro," added the chick in baby blue.

"Where did Zander find you?" asked the stunner wearing a simple ivory gown.

I assumed it was a rhetorical question and kept my mouth shut. Zander came to my rescue. "I picked her up on the street. Saved her from a life of too much running, too little playing." He casually leaned into my shoulder and whispered, "Don't worry about the candy cane girls. They're just jealous."

Zander turned to the group and started to introduce me to the rest of the gang, who looked totally uninterested in participating. "Trace, this is—"

"This is my fuckin' favorite song, dude!" Robb interrupted, cranking the radio up so high I could feel the bass thumping throughout my entire body. I never found out anybody's name right then, not that I really cared. It didn't look like I was going to be making any new best friends, anyway.

Next stop, Brina's house. She looked ravishing in a hot little number cut down to her boob cleavage in the front and butt cleavage in the back. It was like that dress J. Lo wore to the Grammys a few years ago, only in black.

The volume on the stereo was still maxed out. "How are you going to sit in that getup?" I yelled in Brina's ear as she settled into the seat between me and Robb.

"Twat? I cunt hear you! I've got an ear infuckshun!" she yelled back. Her idea of total hilarity. Luckily no one heard.

"I said, watch your boobs. They're trying to escape."

"I'll be sure to keep my eye on them," she said, hitching up the straps of her dress. The minute she let go, those giant bazongas started bouncing around underneath the silky fabric. It almost looked like they were laughing at her. Robb, along with every other man in the car, couldn't peel his eyes away from the natural wonders.

"So will everyone else," I said.

"Wow," Robb said, never raising his eyes higher than Brina's chest.

She grabbed Robb's cheeks and forced him to look up. "Down, boy. The night is young," she yelled over the music. Everyone laughed, even the rotten fairy-tale triplets. Then Brina put her mouth right up against my ear and screamed, "Who the hell are these chicks?"

I rubbed my ringing right ear and wondered whether it was possibly I'd suffered permanent hearing loss. "Thank God we don't go to Country Day, huh? I don't think we'd quite fit in," I said.

"Who'd want to?"

Zander dug around the various compartments in the limo, finally coming up with a bottle of champagne. He popped the cork and started passing around glasses of bubbly. The Ivory Princess was the only one who declined.

"The headache kills me," she said, passing it on over to her date.

"It always killed me, too," Zander shot back, winking at her.

Whoa. This was going to be hard to swallow. Zander had obviously had some kind of fling with this chick before he met me. I prayed it wasn't serious, and that it was good and over.

"Surprise, surprise. The princess is a prude," Brina said in my ear.

I laughed and wondered whether Zander still had a thing for her. Why wouldn't he? She was beautiful. And definitely not the type who'd get caught peeing on his property.

The limo stopped short as we pulled up to Lakeview Club. I was pleased to see the pink and blue girls spill champagne down the fronts of their dresses. "Shit!" Pinky screamed, sounding very unprincessy. The two of them took off for the bathroom, making swishing noises as they wiped beads of liquid from the taffeta.

"So who's your old girlfriend?" I teased Zander on the way in, making sure everyone else was out of earshot.

He looked everywhere but at me. "That's the infamous Belinda Tillingham—reading Buffy I was telling you about the other day."

"Oh," I said, kicking some loose gravel with my Jimmy Choos. I wished I hadn't asked.

"It's no big deal," he said. "We broke up months before I met you. The only person sad about it was my mother—" He clapped his hand over his mouth to try and stop the last part from flying out, but of course by that time it was too late.

"She was pretty disappointed, huh?" That goddamn hunch was back, and worse than ever. I did a few discreet neck rolls, hoping to loosen it up.

"It would have looked good on the social register someday, that's all. Buffy's a St. Claire," Zander said, as if that explained everything.

"She's a what?"

"You know, St. Claire? The luxury hotel chain?"

"Gotcha." So my new boyfriend's ex-girlfriend was Paris freaking Hilton, with a father richer than 99.9 percent of the world. How lovely. If my father turned out to be someone other than Bruce Springsteen, I'm sure he was probably drumming on old plastic tubs in the subway for change at this point.

Zander put his arm around me. "You're the one I want, Trace. Only my mother cares about the designer genes, I swear." The poor thing was starting to sweat, and he wiped his forehead with the sleeve of his tux. "Let's just have a good time tonight."

I couldn't help throwing out one last parting shot. "Couldn't you have at least mentioned that she was going to be here tonight?"

"Would it have made you feel any better, knowing beforehand?"

Good point. "I guess not. I probably would have hid in my room all night, pretending I wasn't home."

He shrugged. "Well, there's your answer."

"I still think I need a drink."

"OK," he said, leading me over to the bar. "A Coke for the young lady, please."

"That's not exactly what I meant."

"It'll have to do," Zander told me. "Your fake ID isn't gonna work at this dance. Not with everyone's parents here. They'd have a fit."

"Why so many chaperones? You Country Day kids go wild at school dances often?"

"Trace, don't you even know what a cotillion is?"

"Sure I do. It's a fancy-schmancy name for a dance," I said.

"Wrong. It's an event where girls are presented to society."

"What is this, the fifties?" I asked him. "Why don't boys have to be presentable?"

I felt a tug on my hair and turned around. It was Brina. "Let's hit the ladies' room."

"I don't have to," I said with a forced smile. I had actually been preparing myself to hold it in all night, just in case Buffy wanted to get her well-manicured claws back into Zander.

"Then come keep me company," Brina said, grabbing my hand and dragging me away.

"Chicks," I heard Zander mutter. "Can't even pee by themselves."

"I can't stand another minute of this," Brina said once we were inside the bathroom.

I checked myself out in the mirror. Not so bad. The hump had nearly receded. "Of what? Having a good time?"

"I am not having a good time, if you hadn't noticed. Robb is a disgusting, horny pig."

I provided a little reality check for her. "Excuse me for pointing this out, but didn't you get up close and personal with that oinker last weekend?"

"Only my hand did," she admitted. "And you know what? He's hung like a two-year-old. It was so gross—I felt like I was yanking on his big toe."

This time, I really was in danger of peeing in my pants. The bubbles from the champagne and then the Coke were making me totally giddy, and the "big toe" was quite possibly the funniest thing I'd ever heard.

But Brina didn't even crack a smile. "Trace, I'm gonna blow this Popsicle stand before Robb thinks he's getting an instant toe-pulling replay." She glanced at her watch. "I'll call you later."

"Brina, where are you going? How are you getting home?" I bit my polished fingernails one by one. I was afraid Brina might do something stupid or dangerous. Probably both.

She tossed off my concerns with her patented head-flip thing that sent dark hair cascading down her shoulders. "Never fear. I have a plan. Later, Trace."

With that, she was off. I returned to our mingling spot sans Brina. I couldn't imagine what I was going to say about where she went, so I hoped no one would ask. Of course, the first thing out of Zander's mouth was, "Where's Brina?"

"Ummmmmmmm . . . ," I stalled.

"Did she hook up with someone else?" he asked, scanning the crowd.

"Not quite. Just took off. Decided she didn't like Robb after all." I held my palms upward and shrugged my shoulders in a lame little apology for my fickle friend.

"Yeah, I usually feel that way after getting naked with someone, too." Zander gave me a distracted kiss on the head. "Kidding. Thank God you're normal. Well, almost. Wait here—I'm going to try to fix things up."

I stood sipping my soda, not bothering to clarify that Robb was in fact the only one who had gone au natural during their hook-up, as Zander walked over to where Robb was standing. He must have explained about the disappearing act of Brina and her Great Bazongas, because Robb looked like he was about to blow his top. Zander kept talking and patting Robb's shoulder until he seemed calmer, and then steered the guy across the room toward a group of dateless debutantes. The plan totally worked, because seconds later, Robb was walking around with a harem.

The lights flickered on and off, our cue to move on to the dining room. I followed Zander to our table, where he did the gentlemanly thing and pulled out my chair. Unfortunately, I am not all that accustomed to good old-fashioned manners, so instead of my butt finding the chair, it hit the floor. The Country Day crew howled like I was the grand-prize winner on *America's Funniest Home Videos*.

"What a clod," I heard Buffy say. "I don't know what Zander sees in her."

I wished I could make myself invisible, and then slam one of those snails from the appetizer up her nose. No such luck.

"Don't worry about it," Zander whispered in my ear. "I like everything about you. Even your pratfalls." Then he said loudly enough for everyone else to hear, "That was your best Chris Farley imitation yet, Trace. Buffy's just jealous because she got booed off the stage during Improv class junior year."

I don't think they bought it, but I had to give Zander huge points for trying. "I'll be right back, Trace. I have to hit the head," he whispered to me. I wanted to grab on to his pants leg and beg him not to leave me alone with these people, but I controlled myself.

The minute he was out of sight, I heard Buffy say, "I actually feel kind of sorry for her. She's clearly retarded. What other explanation is there?"

Buffy was obviously talking about me. Not only didn't she keep her voice down; she was looking straight in my eyes. She wants me to hear her, I thought. I got so pissed off I couldn't see straight.

"You're so off base, Daddy's girl," I hissed, not sure how I pulled off the presto chango from fat Chris Farley to a skinny snake so quickly.

"Oh, and who's your daddy, honey? Our mechanic or our pool boy?" Buffy's hand flew to her mouth, like she hadn't meant to say it out loud. It was obvious she had.

"He's . . . he's . . ." What in hell was I gonna say now? He's an astronaut on an eighteen-year space mission? A CIA spy who's stuck in the Middle East, defending the U.S. from potentially deadly virus attacks? Bruce freaking Springsteen? C'mon, think, I urged my brain.

"Oh, I see. He's a big fat nothing," Buffy said ever so sweetly.

"Do you normally refer to world-famous rock stars as nothing?" I asked her, immediately regretting it. Way to go, Trace. Now Buffy could tell everyone at Country Day that Zander's new girlfriend was a mentally disabled, schizophrenic klutz.

"Yeah, right. And I'm the queen of England." Her statement was probably way closer to the mark than mine.

Zander came back from the bathroom and sat down next to me. He chatted on and on, but all I heard was, blah-blah-blah, you are the world's biggest loser, blah-blah-blah. I added a "Hmmmm?" here and an "Oh, really?" there so he'd think I was paying attention.

I ate the rest of my dinner in silence, trying to wrestle the slimy escargot and purple-hued rack of lamb into submission before it escaped my fork and landed in someone's lap. But if I had to humiliate myself again, I at least hoped Buffy would be the recipient of the flying food.

During dessert, when the fathers introduced their daughters to society—the chauvinism of which made me want to barf—I suddenly realized I could never be one of them. Not that I'd ever compromise my feminist ideals that way, but it would have been nice to know my dad would stand up for me if I ever went completely mental and decided to become a debutante. But the fact was, he wouldn't. Couldn't. Because in my life, he didn't exist, except maybe on CDs and stages where I'd never be able to get close enough to find out if it was really him.

Tears threatened to fall from my eyes. Zander must've thought I was getting all gushy about the old-fashioned ceremony, because he put his arm around me and said, "See? I knew you'd like it."

The thing was, he couldn't have been further from the truth.

I arrived home to find Bebe freaking out again, though thankfully not about me this time. "What the hell happened, Trace? Mrs. Maldonati called raving about how she just found Brina passed out."

I shook my head, not surprised in the least bit that this was how Brina's night had turned out. "Bebe, you know what a wacko she can be. She decided she didn't like Rob-buh anymore, so she split."

"Mrs. Maldonati said her feet were all bloody. You don't think she walked home that whole way, do you?"

"I have no idea. She said she had a plan. You know I can't stop her when she gets like that," I said, ducking into my room and getting ready for bed.

Bebe peeked her head in the door. "Sorry. I forgot to ask how your night was."

"I would classify it as heavenly in its horror." Brina and I coined the phrase back in seventh grade when we couldn't decide whether Matt Casey's French-kissing was completely great or entirely disgusting. We finally agreed that his lips were fabulous (soft and plumfy) but his tongue action was gross (it felt like he was screaming into your mouth). And so, playing spin the bottle with him was heavenly in its horror.

"Let's start with the horror." Bebe lay down next to me on the bed and stared at the ceiling, her hands behind her head.

"OK. Horrifying was the fact that Zander's beautiful ex-girlfriend Buffy was there in ivory taffeta, flanked by her friends Muffy in pink and Fluffy in blue."

Bebe flipped over on her stomach to get a better look at me. "No shit?"

"Muffy and Fluffy are aliases, but the dresses and Buffy were all too real," I told Bebe. "She's only your run-of-the-mill debutante with a spectacularly wealthy father. Last name's St. Claire."

Bebe's eyebrows shot up into her hairline. "Of the bazillionaire St. Claire hotel family? Whoa. And heavenly was?"

I held my hand up. "Not so fast, Bebe, the horror's not over yet. Next, Brina tells me her date has a tiny willy and takes off."

"Talk about too much information," she said, crinkling her nose.

"Sorry," I giggled. "And for my grand finale, I landed on my butt when Zander pulled my chair out at the dinner table."

Bebe laughed even harder about the chair thing than I did when Brina first told me about the big toe. "Trace, you remind me so much of myself when I was your age, it's scary."

"I do?" As always, Bebe made me feel like she knew exactly what I was going through.

"Trace, I have fallen on my ass so many times I'm surprised there's not a permanent bruise on my rear end."

"You have?"

"Yup. I actually started writing about strong, sexy women who always get the guy in the end because they are the total antithesis of me."

"You did?"

"Honestly," she said, punching me softly on the arm. "I was never one of those girls who had every guy drooling over me. You know, like the ones with the stripper names."

"Hate to be the one to point it out to you, but 'Bliss' is a stripper name," I said, trying to conceal a smile. "And how can you say the guys weren't after you? You've got tons of pictures of rock stars groping you."

"I was trying too hard with the Bliss thing," she said. "And everyone who ever met those guys probably has pictures like that, too. Didn't you learn your lesson with Billy Squier? You imagined I'd had some sort of wild affair with him when the truth was I was just another starstruck fan who met him once."

"But what about the Night Ranger dude? Or Loverboy? Or Corey Hart?"

"Same, same, and same."

"Wasn't there *anyone* famous you actually became friends with?" I asked. I wanted to say "lovers" but chickened out at the last minute.

"Sure," she said, smiling. "I actually had some really good times hanging out with the E Street Band. They were totally cool."

Score! "Does that mean you and Bruce . . . ?" I ventured, sticking a big toe—a real one, not like Robb's misplaced appendage—into the sea of *Is he my daddy?*

Bebe laughed and waved off my question with a flick of her wrist. "Oh, please, Trace."

"So you're saying you didn't live up to your stripper name with him, then?"

Once again, Bebe sidestepped my question. "Really. You should know by now I'm more nun than stripper."

It was fairly close to reality, at least these days. To my knowledge, Bebe hadn't gone on a date in over a year, and I was positive she hadn't had sex in even longer. At this point, I wouldn't be surprised if she told me her virginity had grown back.

Bebe took my hand and stared at my palm like she could figure out what was going to happen next from the lines on it. "Can I hear about heavenly parts now?"

"Heavenly was slow dancing with Zander."

"I used to love to slow dance with your father. Our song was 'Fourth of July, Asbury Park.' "

"Never heard of it," I said. "Who the heck does that one?"

A secret little smile took over Bebe's face and she looked lost in a dream. "The Boss, of course," she said, sending my heart into near convulsions. How could my father *not* be Bruce when every time I brought the subject of my dad up, the word Springsteen always followed close behind? "There's a line in it that goes, 'Love me tonight and I promise I'll love you forever.' "

"That sounds romantic," I said, hoping Bebe would forget herself in the memories and tell me more.

"Everything was romantic for us," she said. "But I should've seen what was coming next from the final verse. That's the one that goes, 'Love me tonight for I may never see you again.' "

"So how did everything change from forever to never, anyway?" I was so close to finding out who my dad was, I could almost taste it. And his initials, I assumed, were "BS"—hopefully not standing for "Bullshit."

Bebe snapped back to reality. "Never mind."

I knew I was probably pushing things just a little too far, but I had to try. "Bebe, it's crystal you two were totally into each other. What could've possibly come between you?"

"Distance," she said, sighing and looking like a lost little puppy. "We were just going in different directions."

Distance, as in the number of miles between Jersey and the various stadiums across the world my dad was playing at, maybe? "Where were you headed that he wasn't?"

Bebe looked at me with hurt eyes and held my gaze long after I wanted nothing more to do with our little staring contest. "Trace, when will you accept the fact that he decided I wasn't the one?"

"Even if you weren't, Bebe, why wasn't I?" I asked her, those damn tears spilling out yet again.

"It's not as simple as that," she said, wrapping me in her arms and gently rocking us back and forth. "Nothing in life is."

# CHAPTER
## 6

**H**ard as I tried to answer the phone that was ringing so rudely in my ears, I couldn't do it. Drool had sewn my lips to my pillow. My eyes were glued shut. Serves me right for coming in so late, I thought.

The answering machine clicked on and the minute the message ended, Brina starting yelling into it. "Pick up, Trace! You're not gonna believe what happened last night!"

I unstuck my face from the pillow and felt around the nightstand for the phone. "Huh. Mummpphhhh . . ." I could feel myself falling back to sleep as I mumbled what might have been construed as a greeting in a very rude culture. I'm not the most pleasant person in the morning.

"Wake up," she yelled. "You gotta hear this."

"What time is it?" I groaned. Brina knows calling me before noon on a weekend is sacrilege, punishable by the silent treatment for the rest of the day.

"Noon."

I stuck my nose against the clock. Ten a.m. "In what country?"

"Look, will you forget about the time? I think I know who slp is, and it is friggin' shocking." Brina dangled the last part out there, just waiting for me to pounce on it. I took my time. I didn't want her thinking she had a better adventure than I.

"You know what's shocking? I fell flat on my ass in front of the Country Day debutantes and then for an encore, I told my boyfriend's ex-girlfriend my father was a rock star."

"My shocking outshocks your shocking any day," Brina said. "Guess who gave me a ride home from the ball?"

"Billy Squier?"

"Who?" My friends always turn into owls when I mention one of Bebe's bands.

"Never mind," I said, adding, "He's not my father, you know. I'm actually this close to being convinced Bruce Springsteen is, though."

"Trace, listen, I know you're obsessed with finding your dad, but I never thought that's who drove me home," she said. "I actually hooked a ride with Mr. Perry. Wanna know what his first name is?"

"Stupid?" I couldn't believe Mr. Perry would give Brina a ride home after all those rumors flew about him and the volleyball girl last year.

She ignored me. "Steve."

"Like the guy from Journey?"

"Who?" she asked, all owly again.

"The lead singer from one of Bebe's bands," I said, feeling like I was showing someone new around my house. "So what happened?"

"I ran into Steven, I mean Mr. Perry, just before I made you go to the bathroom with me. I told him my tale of woe and he offered me a ride." She sounded all mushy-gushy.

"Brina, get real. He was just being nice."

"If you say so."

"Did you go home with him?" I asked, wanting to see if there were any really juicy parts to this story that didn't involve blood. "Did you kiss?"

"No, but I think he wanted to. We talked and flirted the whole way," she said. "He kept asking me for directions to my house, but I knew I couldn't invite him in or anything. My parents would go insane if they found me making out on the couch with a twenty-something-year-old guy."

"Brina, I really don't think Mr. P. would have accepted your invitation inside," I said. "And he's more like a thirty-something guy."

"Think what you like. I was getting vibes from him." Brina has this theory that she can actually feel vibrations from people who like her. It's a load of crap. Miss Cleo has a better track record predicting things that actually come true. "Anyway, I made him drop me off at Bobby Pantano's party instead. It was too early to go home."

Get to the gore already, I thought. "At what point in this story do you start bleeding?"

"After that asshole wrestler, Stu, turned into Robb all over again and tried to maul me in the bathroom. So I kicked him in the family jewels and walked home."

So very Brina-ish, walking home in November. And still no mention of the blood. "What about the blood?" I asked, fed up.

"It wouldn't have been an issue if I hadn't shotgunned so many beers," she explained. "And the stiletto heels didn't help, either. Had to go barefoot."

Dopey move. "Smart move," I told her.

"Whatever. When I got home, I was so tired. Everything was spinning and I just wanted to go to bed," she explained. "But my feet were a little cut up and you know how my mother is about her white carpets. . . ."

"So you decided your best bet was to sleep outside?" I interrupted.

"Not outside, exactly. More like on our porch." I could just see Brina shivering on the uncomfortable wicker furniture with her feet oozing all over the jute rug. This would drive Mrs. Maldonati only slightly less crazy than Brina's bleeding on the pristine living room velvet/plush.

"Is that where your parents found you?" I asked her.

"Luckily they didn't," she said. "Sully did."

The name sounded familiar, but I couldn't quite place it. "Sully?"

"You know, my little brother's jock friend—the tall guy with dreads and a pierced eyebrow?"

"He's pretty hot," I said. And he was. "In a very funky, sophomore kind of way, of course." I felt the need to add that last part because it's totally taboo at our school for a senior girl to even notice a sophomore guy. Not so the other way around, of course. There was that damn chauvinism again, rearing its ugly head.

"I don't know about hot, but he was certainly a gentleman—probably the last one on earth," she said. "My left boob had fallen out of my dress when I was passed out, and Sully was polite enough to cover me up before he carried me into the house. Then he washed my feet, helped me into my pajamas, and put me to bed."

"You've got to be kidding me."

"Oh, I wish I was, but it gets even more embarrassing. I decided to go sleep in the bathroom so I wouldn't have so far to go to throw up," she explained. "And that's where my mom found me. She thought I tried to commit suicide when she saw me lying there in a pool of blood."

I didn't say anything. I couldn't. I was laughing too hard.

"You haven't heard the best part of all yet," she said.

"Your mom banished you to living in the doghouse?"

"No, nothing that extreme," she said. "But she did make appointments for me to see a nutritionist *and* a psychologist. Thinks being fat is making me crazy."

"You are not fat," I said. "You're perfect just the way you are."

"Try telling my mom that. She still hasn't gotten over being called Chubby Debbie in sixth grade," Brina said. "And anyway, that's still not the best part."

"What is?"

"You're going to be my personal book carrier all week. My mom made me go to the ER this morning, and a very cute resident gave me a tetanus shot and put both my feet in soft casts. I'll be on crutches the whole week."

"Oh, crap," I said. This was so like Brina, it wasn't even funny. If she's got a headache, it's not just a headache—it's a brain tumor. A swollen gland is lymphoma. And now her sore, scraped-up feet had warranted a vaccination and casts. "I betcha this is a total turnoff for slp," I teased her.

"Who, Steven? I don't think so," she said. "I got another love letter from him in the mail today."

"Give it up, Brina," I said, exasperated. "Mr. Perry is not slp."

"You know, now that I think of it, you actually haven't heard the most shocking part of my night yet," she said. "Know what Mr. Perry's middle name is?"

"No." I hoped it was Xavier or Zacharias. Anything but an *L* one.

"It's Lee."

"I'm coming over right now," I said, jumping out of bed way earlier than I ever would have without a crisis.

\* \* \*

When I walked through Brina's door fifteen minutes later, she threw the latest slp poem at me, stuck her hands on her hips, and waited impatiently as I read it.

> *Brina,*
> *I like to save you from the bad guys*
> *Always want to be your knight*
> *But you're still in the dark about who I am*
> *Maybe you should shine your light on me*
> *slp*

"Brina, you said this came in the mail, right?"

"Right."

"It couldn't possibly be from Mr. Perry, then."

"Why? Why couldn't it be?" Brina wanted to know.

"Think about it. He just dropped you off at ten o'clock last night. Even if he scribbled the note right after and threw it in the nearest mailbox, it still wouldn't have gotten here already," I said. "We are talking about the U.S. Postal Service here, not FedEx, right?"

"Let's just see what the postmark says, little Miss Smarty-pants," she said, turning the envelope over for a better look.

I peered over her shoulder and my jaw dropped to the floor. There was no postmark. No stamp, either. Slp must have dropped it through the Maldonatis' mail slot sometime between last night and this morning.

"That still doesn't mean it's from Mr. Perry," I said. Well, OK, it looked pretty fishy, but I wanted to give him the benefit of the doubt.

"How can you even say that?" she asked. "It's so obviously him."

"Can we just assume for the moment that it isn't?" I said, hoping beyond hope it really wasn't. It would be a huge scandal if anything ever happened, not to mention the fact it could cost Mr. Perry his job.

"OK," she said, shrugging her shoulders. "If that's the way you want to play it."

"Brina, what would it take for you to go out with slp?"

"If he wasn't Mr. Perry?" she asked. " 'Cause I would totally go out with him in a heartbeat."

"Right," I said. "Slp is not Mr. Perry." I figured maybe if I repeated it enough, Brina would start to believe me. Even if I wasn't sure I actually believed me. After all, every other guy in school was gaga over Brina. Why would Mr. Perry be any different?

"I guess he'd have to be totally hot, then," she said. "Too tall, too short, too fat, too skinny, too brainy, listens to crappy music like Bebe, or has a horrible singing voice like you? Any one of those and no way."

I sighed. "Well, that just about rules out everybody in the world."

"Yup. Everybody except the hotties." She grinned.

Next stop on this trip, guilt. "So his looks and coolness factor are the only things that matter?" I asked Brina. "Even after he wrote you all these great poems?"

"You just don't get it, do you, Trace? You can't choose who you fall for. It's purely a chemical thing."

I tried to think of sexy guys who didn't fit her mold to show that you don't always have to stick to your type. "What about Justin Timberlake?" I asked.

Brina stuck her finger down her throat and pretended to puke. "Britney's castoff? Too skinny. Too curly. Too girlie, for that matter."

"OK, so he was a bad example. What about Tobey Maguire?"

She shook her head. "Doesn't do a thing for me."

I punted in desperation. "Jason Biggs?"

"You can't possibly think I'd date a guy who put his dick in a pie."

"He was acting, Brina."

"Oh, that's different," she said, nodding. "OK. Sure, I'd give him a chance."

Finally. The opening I was waiting for. "So why not give slp a chance, no matter who he turns out to be?" I asked quietly.

"I absolutely intend to," she said. "Because he's not the pie fucker. He's Mr. Steven Lee Perry."

"No, he's not."

"Yes, he is," Brina said stubbornly. "And by the way, I was just kidding about Jason Biggs. I wouldn't give him a chance, either. Not a single one."

I sighed. Poor slp. I wanted to tell him to forget the poetic notes. That all his romantic ideals were wasted on a girl like Brina. And that unless, by some off chance, he actually was a certain hot guidance counselor, there was simply no hope for him.

At school, Brina regaled everyone with the thrilling tale of how she ended up with not one but two casts on her feet. She embellished her story a bit more every time until all the kids at school believed she was a cross between Wonder Woman, all three of Charlie's Angels, and Lara Croft.

Unfortunately, all she ever said to me was "Trace, can you get my backpack?" and "Trace, pull a chair over for my feet," and "Trace, hold the elevator—I'm gonna be late for class!" Never mind that being at Brina's beck and call made me late for class all the time, with three detentions to prove it.

After a full week of this, I was feeling hunchier than ever, and not just in the metaphorical sense. My neck and shoulders were positively killing me from having to carry around both our backpacks, though Brina never even noticed.

My loyal servitude ended on Saturday when her casts came off. Even Brina must have finally realized the torture she'd put me through all week, because she invited me over for her special homemade gravy and pasta to thank me for all my help.

"Smells heavenly in here," I told Brina as I walked in the kitchen. Her T-shirt was stained with tomato sauce and there were little dots of flour on her nose and cheeks. "By the way, that's a good look for you."

She walked out into the hallway and stared in the mirror. "All the fat Italian models are wearing it this season," she said, coming back into the kitchen laughing.

"For the millionth time, you are not fat."

"Says who?" That nasty remark came from Brad, Brina's little brother. He always reminds me of a golden retriever puppy, tripping over these big hands and feet he hasn't quite grown into yet. "Hey, *chicas,* it's Hip-hop Day at the rink. Wanna go?" he asked us.

Brina shot him an evil look. "Three words. No. Freakin'. Way."

"Oh, you're too cool to even go ice-skating now?"

Brina chucked the wooden spoon she was using to stir the sauce at Brad's head. It missed, leaving a big splat on the wall behind him. Brina rushed over with a sponge, scrubbing away the mess before her mother could freak out. "I wouldn't be caught dead with you and your geeky friends."

Poor Brad. Brina never wanted to talk to him, no less be seen with him. "Forget the wench, Brad. I'll come with you," I told him. I've known Brad practically his whole life, so I feel like his honorary sister. The nice one.

"You can't mean that, Trace," Brina shrieked in mock horror, clutching her chest. "Your social life will be ruined!"

"I don't think Zander's gonna dump me if I hang out with your little brother, Brina," I said, rolling my eyes at her. "And quite frankly I don't care what anyone else thinks."

Brad high-fived me. "Right on, sister." Then he looked at me in all seriousness and said, "Trace, could you do me a huge favor?"

"Sure thing, sweetie."

"I'd appreciate it if you'd go your own way once I start rapping with the chicks."

Brina snorted. "The only chicks you'll ever get that close to are at the pet store, doofus."

"Not when I'm with Sully," he said, giving Brina an evil glare. "He's a regular chick magnet."

Brina opened and closed her mouth a few times before anything actually came out. "Well, you and your flock is something I can't possibly miss," she finally said. "Just let me ask Mom to keep an eye on the spaghetti, and we'll be on our way."

A half an hour later, the three of us were doubled over, trying to put on our puke brown rental skates. A low, gravelly voice interrupted our efforts. "How're you feeling, Brina?"

It was Sully. He was even cuter than I remembered. In fact, he was smoking hot. This made it rather hard to remember he was jailbait.

Brina smiled up at him from her half-laced skate. "Better, thanks."

"That was some crazy shit you pulled the other night." Uh-oh. Sully was going to get his head bitten off in a second—I was sure of it.

"Yeah," Brina admitted without even taking a nibble. "I guess it was."

"Good thing I came to your rescue," Sully said, pulling Brina to her feet. "You healed enough to take a spin around the rink?"

"Ummmmm . . ." Brina glanced around at the A-list crowd that was milling around the lobby. "Maybe later."

"Whatever," he said, putting a hand on Brad's narrow shoulder and steering them both out onto the ice. "Let's go, buddy."

"Are you insane?" I asked Brina once they were out of earshot. "That boy is gorgeous!"

"The key word being 'boy,' " Brina said. " 'Baby boy' is more like it. He's practically still in diapers."

I held the door open for Brina and we skated out to find that Brad wasn't kidding. He and Sully were already surrounded by a group of girls. A couple I identified as underclassmen, but there were also a few juniors and seniors thrown in the mix.

"Guess they aren't scared to be seen with a very hot sophomore," I said to Brina.

"Guess not." She put on her tough-girl face and skated off alone.

Without Brina to hang out with, I found myself gliding next to a little girl in a sparkly purple velour dress and white headband. She was waving wildly at a man in the stands, staring at him with a mixture of awe and adoration. "I love you, Daddy," she called happily as she skated by.

It was such a sweet scene, I got a little teary-eyed. I put one finger alongside each of my temples and squeezed hard—a trick I learned to keep from crying when Jimmy Dolan decided to steal my winter hat every single day in second grade.

I felt a tug on my pink puffy jacket, and the little girl said, "Don't be sad. I'm sure your daddy will come skating with you next time."

"I'm sure you're right," I told her. "Thanks." If I knew for sure who he was, I thought, I'd definitely invite him along—though I couldn't quite see Bruce making an appearance at the local skate-o-rama with me. It would cause a complete riot, not to mention I'd feel pretty silly twirling around the rink with the Boss on my arm.

"Hang on," the little girl said, grabbing my hand and making me the end of a very long chain of people. A second later, I found myself shooting around the rink and clinging on for dear life.

It was way too much fun to hog all to myself, so I grabbed on to

Brina's hand at the next corner. She picked up Brad, who stuck out his hand for Sully to get in on the action. "Hey Ya!" echoed as we whipped around the rink.

When the last chorus faded into silence, the people chain fell apart. I slammed into the wall, Brad flew clear across the rink, and Brina tumbled to the ground. After unsuccessfully trying to do a hockey stop, Sully landed right on top of her. For a second it seemed like time stood still, and they just lay there staring at each other. Then Sully got up and dragged Brina to her feet, and they both skated away in opposite directions like it never happened.

"Did you two just shake it like a Polaroid picture out there?" I asked Brina as we were returning our smelly rental skates.

She put her hands on my shoulders. "Do I have to keep repeating myself? It is not going to happen. I'm about as attracted to Sully as I am to Justin Biggs."

"Do you mean Justin Timberlake or Jason Biggs?"

"Either. Both. It doesn't matter," she said. "There's not a chance in hell I'll ever end up with Sully, so you can stop pushing it right now."

I grinned at her. "Methinks you doth protesteth too much."

Brina punched me in the arm. "And methinks you're an insane loser. So give it up already."

On Wednesday, Brina had a huge smile on her face when I saw her in the hall bright and early. Her teeth were practically blinding me.

"Trace, you-know-who wrote me again!" she said, waving yet another lovey-dovey yet cryptic note in my face.

I fished my sunglasses out of my bottomless pit of a backpack and slid them up the bridge of my nose. "Give that to me," I said, snatching the paper from her hands. Here's what it said:

> *Brina:*
> *I like to feel the warmth of your heart*
> *Always long to touch your soul*
> *But your fire's just too hot, my love*
> *Maybe you could do a slow burn with me*
> *slp*

"Steven's totally heating things up, isn't he?" Brina was gushing. It was all I could do to keep from barfing my bowl of morning cornflakes.

"How many times do I have to tell you? It's not Mr. Perry."

"You can't ruin my buzz, so don't even try," she said.

Brina was clearly not paying attention. "I can guarantee you it's not Mr. Perry, and that whoever it is wouldn't interest you in the least if you knew who he was."

Brina glanced at me sideways, trying to see whether I had any inside scoop or not. "Why would you say that?" she asked, deciding it might be possible.

"First of all, because the guys you like can't read, no less think up clever notes." Mean, but true. "Plus," I said, pointing to the first line, "it says right here, 'I like to feel the warmth of your heart.' That means you've already been up close and personal with slp—that he's probably already touched you, for God's sake—and you obviously weren't impressed."

"I've met Steven Lee Perry. And you know what I forgot to tell you happened when he dropped me off after the cotillion?"

Here we go again, I thought. "No, what?"

"He gave me a hug," she said, looking smug. "That's about as close as you can get to the warmth of my heart."

"Two meetings to pick out colleges, a ride home to keep you from being killed, and a friendly embrace do not add up to his being slp, Brina."

"It doesn't mean he's not, either."

I put my hand on her shoulder. "Listen. Even if slp was Mr. Perry—which he isn't—there's not a thing you can do about it. He's too old for you. He'd get fired. It'd never work."

Brina frowned, refolding her note. Nothing like pissing off your best friend before you've even hit homeroom.

"I'll see you tomorrow," I called after her as she stomped down the hall.

"Not if I see you first," she yelled back over her shoulder.

Though Brina and I had planned a wild night of drinking and debauchery at some junior football player's open house, she left a short, pissed-off-sounding message on my machine nixing it. "Can't go tonight, Trace. I've got cramps. Yeah, that's it. Really bad ones. Sorry."

I knew she was just trying to get back at me for not buying into the Mr.-Perry-is-slp theory—though even I had to admit there was the slightest possibility it could be him—and also for expressing my disapproval of their union if it turned out to be true. I also knew I wasn't really up for going to the party alone or with the cheerleaders Brina and I sometimes hung out with, so I got in my jammies and went in search of my mama.

"Want to watch *Almost Famous* with me again tonight, Bebe?"

Every time we see it, she always says, "I feel like Penny Lane and I could have been best friends." Penny is this hot groupie for bands that actually rock—we're talking more along the lines of Led Zeppelin than Culture Club—so the truth was, the two of them really didn't have all that much in common. In fact, I'd be willing to bet Penny would have thought Bebe was a total dork.

"Thanks, but no, thanks," she said, carefully applying lipstick. "I've got plans." I should have known. She never wears makeup otherwise.

"What's on your agenda?" I asked, wondering if I could get any more pathetic. My own mother was going out for a night of drunken debauchery, while I stayed at home and watched reruns of her life. Well, not really her life, but a cooler version of it.

"Some dinner. A few drinks," she said. "And hopefully a little nooky for a nightcap."

"You just crossed the line," I said, shaking my head to try to get the gross picture I'd conjured up out of it. "Who's the lucky guy? Or should I say, who's the guy who's gonna get lucky?"

"Actually, Trace, he's—" The doorbell interrupted her. "Would you go get that? I'm not quite ready yet."

"Sure." I ran downstairs. "C'mon in," I said as I opened the door. "Bebe's almost—" I stopped short as my tongue went into shock.

"Hi, Tracey." It was none other than Mr. Perry. "Who's Bebe?"

"My mom." My jaw must have been hanging somewhere around my knees by this point.

"I thought her name was Belinda."

"It is," I said, still gawking.

He shrugged, looking a little confused. "I guess Belinda . . . Bebe . . . what am I supposed to call her, anyway?"

"Belinda, I guess."

"I take it she neglected to tell you we were going out tonight."

"Isn't Bebe a little too old for you?" I muttered under my breath.

"Sorry, I didn't catch that," he said, giving me a look that told me he actually had. Uh-oh.

"Nothing," I said.

"If you're referring to Melinda the volleyball captain, let me just stop you right there," he said, apparently having borrowed Superman ears for the date. "It's an urban legend that just won't die. Melinda's my cousin. I drove her to school once in a while, and people got the wrong impression. That's it."

"Yeah, right," I muttered again.

"It's true."

"Well, then, what about that ride home you gave my best friend the other night?"

"Who, Brina?" he said.

"You make a habit of picking up random high school girls at cotillions?" I asked. "Yes, Brina."

"She was going to get herself raped if she followed her original plan, which was hitchhiking home wearing that dress," he said. Oh, yeah, I thought. The J. Lo one. He was right. "I couldn't in good conscience let her do it, so I drove her home. End of story."

"You actually drove her to Bobby Pantano's house," I corrected him. "Remember Brina's week of hobbling around with her feet in two casts? That's really the end of the story."

"You'll have to tell me all the gory details sometime," Mr. Perry said, laughing. "That girl is quite a drama queen, isn't she?" OK, so maybe it wasn't so bad that Bebe was going out with him. At least he laughed at my jokes.

"Hey, wait a minute," I said, still suspicious. "Why were you at the cotillion, anyway? It seems a little sketchy, if you ask me."

"It was my cousin Melinda's big coming-out party," he said. "My whole family was there."

I was about to launch into the rest of Brina's tale of woe when Bebe came down the stairs wearing these awesome Paper Denim & Cloth low-slung flared jeans and a tight black button-down shirt that hugged her curves just the right way. Unlike me, Bebe actually has some, though they're not nearly as big as Brina's.

"Hi, Steve," she said. "I see you sprung our big surprise on Trace." She turned to me. "Remember the day I had to go meet with Mr. Flagstaff about your trig problems?"

"How could I forget?" I said. "I got demoted to the sped class after it."

"Well, I got lost as usual trying to find the right classroom," she said. I wasn't surprised. Bebe couldn't find her way out of a paper bag. "So Steve here volunteered to be my escort. It was all the way over in Building C, so we got to talking. Turns out we have a lot in common."

"Like our taste in music, for one thing," he said, smiling at Bebe. If that was the case, he was absolutely perfect for her and they could spend the rest of their lives listening to the Buggles sing "Video Killed the Radio Star." It was a frightening thought.

"I waited a while to call, to see if I could get Belinda out of my head, but I couldn't. I hope you're not upset, Tracey."

"I think it's great you two found each other," I said, opening the front door for them. Hey, wait, I thought, those are *my* jeans. I should have known Bebe would never have something so trendy in her closet. "Nice pants," I told Bebe on her way out.

"I kinda thought you'd like them," she said, winking at me over her shoulder. "I'll make it up to you later."

"Make what up later?" Mr. Perry wanted to know.

"Wouldn't you like to know?" Bebe said, patting him on the cheek. My God, she was actually flirting and having fun. I hadn't seen her like this in—oh, I don't know—let's say my whole entire life?

"You kids be careful," I called after them as they got in the car. "Don't do anything I wouldn't do."

"That shouldn't be hard," Bebe said, her head disappearing into Mr. Perry's red Mini Cooper. "It doesn't leave much."

"Ha-ha," I said, and went to put the popcorn in the microwave.

# CHAPTER
## 7

When Bebe and I arrived at the Maldonatis' the next morning, the big bird preparations were already in full swing. Though we offered to help in the kitchen, Brina's grandma and aunt shooed and *tsk*ed us out.

"You young girls go have fun. Let the old ladies do the cooking." Aunt Rose's cheeks were flushed from the heat. Probably from all the wine she was guzzling, too.

"Ina!" I heard her say to Brina's grandmother. "The oven temperature is way too high. Turn it down or the turkey will be dry as a bone." Then she added under her breath, "Just like last year."

Grandma Ina got right in Aunt Rose's face. "I learned to cook back in the old country, Rose, so clamp it," she said, trying to tower over Rose. Grandma Ina was wider than she was tall, and she looked like she was carrying half a basketball under the back of her dress. I prayed I wouldn't look like her when I got old. "You'll see. This turkey will be so juicy you'll need two napkins and a bib."

I could barely tear myself away from the old-lady bitch fight, but I guess Bebe wasn't quite as engrossed as I was. "I'm going to go find Debbie to see if there's anything I can do to help her get ready for dinner," she said, and took off in search of Mrs. Maldonati.

"What are you staring at?" Grandma Ina asked me, all annoyed that I was still standing there. "Haven't you ever seen anyone cook before?" The truth was, I had—just not a baby humpback whale.

I stopped gaping and went to find Brina. I found her lying on the floor of the family room, watching TV and looking like hell. Her grandpa and dad were playing poker at the portable card table while her uncle Mario snored on the couch loud enough to shake the rafters. His pants were already unbuttoned, even though the meal wasn't supposed to be ready for hours.

"He chowed down on a whole platter of calamari and then complained about being bloated," Brina said when she noticed me staring. "Says squid gives him gas."

"Well, that explains Uncle Mario," I said. "Now how about you? Are you sick or something?"

"No, I'm totally fine," she said, putting her finger to her lips and shushing me quietly so her dad wouldn't hear.

But Mr. Maldonati seemed to have acquired super hearing powers, too. "Brina came rolling in way after curfew last night," her dad said, his eyes peeking over the top of his cards. "We think she's got the Irish flu today."

"I already told you I was late because Reece's car died and we had to wait for that dope Stu to jump-start it," Brina said.

I couldn't believe she had blown me off for Reece, Northshore's bright and beautiful cheerleading captain. She knew I hated Reece. And why Brina was even talking to Stu again was a whole other can of worms I wasn't ready to open yet. "And I am not hungover, Daddy," Brina said, looking totally hungover.

"A likely story," Mr. Maldonati said, turning his attention back to his cards.

I gave Brina the evil eye. "I spent the night watching TV while you went to the party with Reece?"

"I'm sorry, Trace," Brina said, groaning as she rolled over. "That was pretty sucky of me. I was just pissed at you about the slp thing and—"

"Brina, there's something I have to tell you about that." I was going to explain about Bebe's date with Mr. Perry, but just then an explosive fart levitated Uncle Mario off the couch and dropped him back down again. It blew away any thoughts I had of telling Brina about Bebe's budding romance. Literally.

We nearly died laughing. Her father looked up from the game long enough to ask, "What's so funny?"

"Uncle Mario . . ." Brina stopped to swipe big tears from her face.

"... bad calamari ..." I added, my shoulders shaking from laughing so hard.

"... might need a Depend ..." Brina and I continued to howl.

"... and someone should check to make sure ..."

"... except it won't be me ..."

"... or me ..."

Brina's grandfather dismissed us with a wave and a "Bah!" Her father shoveled pretzels in his mouth and continued to survey his cards.

"What did I miss?" asked Brad, walking into the room and noticing our doubled-over bodies. That set us off again.

"Chicks," said Sully.

"Freaks is more like it," said Brad.

Brina and I sat up and tried to compose ourselves. "You had to be there," I told them, wiping away the tears that were streaming down my face. Fart jokes just don't seem funny in the retelling. Besides, I was trying to protect Brina, who can't even say that word without blushing and getting all uptight. And God knows she'd certainly never admit to doing such a thing.

"What smells—?" Sully started to ask.

"So good? Must be the stuffing," finished Brina, thinking she'd bypassed any more gas talk.

"You meant 'like moldy ass,' didn't you, Sully?" Brad said. "If that's any part of our meal, we might as well hit McDonald's right now. What do you say?"

"Thanks, but I'll brave this one out. It looks like fun in here, even if it is a little rank."

Brina's mother walked in the room with Bebe trailing behind her like a puppy dog. Mrs. Maldonati had already put Bebe to work, stacking her arms with freshly ironed white linen napkins. Once Mrs. M. caught a whiff of Uncle Mario's little present, she started yelling at her husband. "For God's sake, Jerry, open some windows in here. It smells like a stable."

"OK, dear," he said, not moving a muscle.

"Can we play, Dad?" asked Brad, fingering the bills stacked in the middle of the table.

"If you've got the *dinero*, we've got extra seats."

Brad and Sully plunked a couple of bucks into the pot and sat down while Grandpa dealt a new hand.

"C'mon up to my room for a second," Brina said, grabbing on to my hand and pulling me out of the chamber of ass gas. "I want to get your opinion about something. You come, too, Bebe."

"OK," Bebe said, handing the napkins to Brina's mom.

"Don't you want my opinion?" Mrs. Maldonati asked as we headed upstairs.

"Maybe next time," Brina called down to her mom. "Or maybe never," she whispered to me and Bebe.

When we got to her room, Brina pulled out a painted ceramic heart-shaped box from her bureau drawer and took out the five slp letters she'd received to date. She unfolded each one carefully and spread them out on her bed.

"Here, Bebe," she said. "Take a look and tell me what you think."

Bebe picked up the notes and read them one by one. When she put down the final piece of paper, Brina jumped all over her. "So how about it? Slp's a great poet, right?"

"Oh, Brina," she said, shaking her head. "He's something else entirely."

"What do you mean?"

Bebe dropped a bomb. "These aren't slp originals."

"Crap. My poet's a plagiarist," Brina said, flopping herself down on the bed. "You were right, Trace. The guys I like can't put two sentences together on their own."

Bebe bent down and smoothed Brina's hair from her eyes. "I can't figure out exactly who wrote this stuff, or where I've seen it before," she said. "But it's actually unbelievably sweet. Right out of *Cyrano de Bergerac*."

Brina and I looked at each other, then back at Bebe for an explanation. Neither of us had a clue what she was talking about.

Bebe threw her hands up in the air in disgust. "What the hell am I paying taxes for in this snotty-ass town, anyway? Don't they teach fine literature anymore?"

Brina and I shrugged, unsure of how Bebe wanted us to answer. Silence seemed the best plan of attack.

"OK, since you two obviously don't read, does the movie *Roxanne* ring any bells? With Steve Martin? And Daryl Hannah?"

I remembered having watched it on the Oxygen channel with Bebe one boring night. I quickly ran through the plot in my head, finally got her point, and gasped. "The one where the dude is so embarrassed about the size of his nose, he has a friend read his poems to the chick he likes?"

Brina's face fell. "I think I saw that on a *Brady Bunch* rerun once."

But Bebe was still grinning like a fool. "That is the most romantic thing I can think of. You should be incredibly flattered, Brina."

By now, Brina was picking at an invisible pull in her sweater, looking completely down in the dumps. "Flattered some guy with a humongous honker is sending me recycled lines? I don't think so."

"I'm surprised you two didn't pick up on it," Bebe said, apparently not noticing Brina had traveled far into major bummer-land. "I mean, look at the structure here. The first line of the poem always starts with 'I like' plus a verb. The second line starts with 'always,' the third with a 'but,' and the last one with a 'maybe.' "

"I should have known," I moaned. "Forgive me for sucking at English AND trig!" I fell to the floor in a dramatic heap.

Brina ignored me, stepping over my body and sitting down next to Bebe. "So what do you think I should do about it?"

This was right up Bebe's alley—it was totally something that would happen to one of the characters in her books. "That depends. What have you done so far?"

Brina squished her toes into the carpet and avoided eye contact. "Nothing."

"Jeez, what does it take to impress you, girl?" Bebe asked her.

"Chiseled pecs and shit for brains," I said.

"No one asked for your opinion," Brina said, and stopped scrunching her feet into the rug just long enough to kick me.

"I think you should write him back, Brina. Pick an awesome poem, just so he knows you get it," Bebe said, pacing the room. "In fact, let me just run home to grab my favorite poetry book."

"There's no need for that, Bebe," Brina said, a weird little smile on her face that I realized was actually a grimace.

"No problem at all," Bebe told her, totally missing the point that Brina had no intention of sending gushy poetry back to Mr. Schnozola. "I'll be back in a jiffy."

"Take your time," I called after Bebe as she ran out the door.

"Be polite, Brina," I told her once Bebe was gone. "Write down the first thing you see and then toss it out when Bebe's not looking. If you act like you're not going to write back, she'll bug you and bug you until you completely break down. Trust me, fake compliance is the only way out."

"Don't you worry, Trace," she said. "I am the queen of deception when it comes to parents."

"Oh, yeah? I seem to remember you didn't do it so well after the cotillion."

"What, are you crazy? I totally convinced my 'rents I was puking that night because I ate bad shrimp."

"Like they actually believed that."

"They did," she insisted, and flipped open her iBook and logged on. "Still do. Now let's see if we can figure out who slp is fronting."

First, we tried Googling a bunch of different lines from the slp notes to see if we could pin down the actual author. No such luck. Then we moved on to keywords. Nothing relevant there, either.

"It doesn't really matter who wrote those poems, anyway," Brina said, looking even more miserable now than before we started our research, if that was possible. "My knight in shining armor has a deformed face and not an original thought in his head. So who needs him?"

I knew Brina well enough to know the notes had provided her a much needed thrill this semester, despite her loud protests that they meant nothing to her. "So you're totally over Mr. Perry, then," I said, jabbing her in the ribs to let her know I was kidding.

Brina drew in such a deep breath I thought I'd really hurt her. "Wait a minute, Trace," she said a second later, most definitely OK. "Maybe Mr. Perry had a nose job when he was younger, but he still has an inferiority complex about it. That, plus the age difference, might make him turn to anonymous notes and flowery poetry to get my attention."

I sighed, shaking my head. "My, my, you have a big imagination."

We were so involved in our slp discussion that we barely noticed a sweaty Bebe gliding back in the room holding an oversized, ancient-looking hardcover book. "Aha!" she said, finding what she was looking for within seconds. "This was always my favorite."

"Good one, Bebe," I said, rolling my eyes at Brina when I had finished reading it.

"What? What is?" Brina wanted to know.

"Emily Dickinson," Bebe said, shoving the book under Brina's nose. Brina read out loud:

*Wild Nights—Wild Nights!*
*Were I with thee*
*Wild nights should be*
*Our luxury!*

"That's great, Bebe. I'll use it for sure."

Brina caught my eye and winked. I winked back. Everything was going according to plan. Until Brad and Sully burst into the room applauding, that is.

"Bravo!" said Sully, clapping madly. "Author! Author!"

"I think she's dead," Brina muttered, blushing madly.

"Wild nights, wild nights," Brad started screeching in a balls-in-a-vise falsetto. "Come taketh me, between the sheets, between my thighs—"

"Shut up, dweeb," Brina hissed, whipping at him in retaliation the wooden paddle brush she uses to give her hair one hundred strokes every day. But Brad was so used to Brina throwing things by now, he easily ducked out of the way. So the brush whizzed past him and landed in the middle of Sully's face with a loud thunk instead.

"I am so sorry, Sully," Brina said as she rushed to Sully's side and took his face in her hands to get a better look. "Are you OK?"

"Christ, a person could die around here," he said. "If the stench doesn't get you, the wench will." His nose was swelling up like a balloon and turning eggplant purple.

"Can you ever forgive me?" Brina asked him, looking really worried now.

"Don't worry about it," Sully said, smiling and then wincing in pain. "I'm fine. It was an accident."

"Yeah, it's all fun and games until someone breaks a nose," I said, thinking I was pretty funny.

Brina shot me a deadly look and mouthed, "Shut up, shut up, shut up."

Bebe, who had raced downstairs to rustle up some first aid supplies, came back into Brina's room carrying ice wrapped in a paper towel. "Believe it or not, it's safer up here than down there," she said, handing the ice pack to Sully. "Ina and Rose are about to claw each other's eyes out, and Mario is still stinking up the den."

"OK, then, we need to come up with fun things to do while we're stranded in Brina's room. Any ideas?" I asked everyone.

"Hunt for snail trails in Brina's underwear drawer?" Brad suggested.

"Murder my brother before he can touch my panties?" Brina countered, smiling sweetly at him.

Sully came up with the winner. "Draw straws to see who goes downstairs to steal a bottle of wine for us all?"

"Oh, God, this means I'll have to join the adults," Bebe groaned. "I can't be caught drinking with a bunch of minors."

"See ya, wouldn't want to be ya," I told her, waving good-bye as she left.

Brad got four pencils from Brina's desk and stuck them in his fist. I drew first. Mine was pretty long. Brina went next, pulling out a pencil that was shorter than mine but still respectable. Sully hesitated and then picked a chewed-up nub while Brad unfolded his palm. His pencil was so new it hadn't even been sharpened yet.

"I guess you're our sucker, Pete," Brad told Sully. Brad left the room to get some tunes for us to groove on while we were catching a predinner buzz, and Sully took off on his kitchen mission.

"So that's his first name," Brina said to me. "Pete. Peter Sullivan. It has a nice ring to it."

I scrunched up my face, thinking. "It's so funny, but I always just thought of him as plain old Sully," I said. "Like Madonna. Or Cher."

"Holy Mother of God!" we heard Aunt Rose scream from the kitchen. "What happened to your face?"

Mumble, mumble.

Seconds later, Grandma Ina appeared in the doorway of Brina's room shaking a flour-caked rolling pin. "Sabrina Maria Maldonati! Come downstairs this instant and explain to me why you almost killed this poor fellow!"

Brina trudged away to meet Grandma Ina's wrath, knowing there was no escape. Soon after Brina's verbal lashing began, Sully returned with a couple of bottles of vino, a corkscrew, and a platter of cheese and crackers. "I got everything." He smiled, waving the booty around.

"Uh, Sully?"

"What, Trace?"

"You actually forgot something."

He pointed to the wine, opener, and food and shook his head. "Don't think so."

"Are we going to slug it straight from the bottle, then?"

"Don't make me go back down there," Sully said, shaking his head and looking downtrodden. "It's getting uglier by the minute."

"Never fear, bro." Brad ran to the bathroom, rummaged around, and came back carrying the smallest, flimsiest Dixie cups I've ever seen.

"You are the epitome of class, Brad," I told him, uncorking the bottle and sloshing wine into the four shot-glass-sized paper cups.

Brina slunk back in the room just in time for our party. She had a white handprint on her ass, which set the rest of us off. "What's so funny?" she asked, looking around the room for clues.

I pointed to the telltale mark on the back of her jeans. "I can't believe Grandma Ina spanked you."

Brina just sat there with an uncomfortable look on her face. "She didn't."

"What happened, then?" I couldn't help asking.

"If you must know, Grandma grabbed my butt and told me men don't like 'fat in the can,'" Brina said, frowning. "Boy, I'm really looking forward to our meal after that comment."

Sully took the ice pack off his nose and examined Brina's posterior. "It looks pretty good to me," he said, absentmindedly thumbing through the slp letters that were still on the bed.

Brina got all red and huffy. "Hey! Paws off my property." She gathered up the notes and put them all back into the little box quicker than you could say "I sure as hell hope Mr. Perry isn't slp but I think he used to be an English teacher and those guys always teach poetry so maybe there's some bizarre possibility he actually is." Yikes.

"So who're they from?" Sully asked, leaning back against the wall and putting the ice back on his nose.

"A mystery man," Brina answered. "A very charming, poetic mystery man."

"You like this guy?" Sully asked Brina.

"Absolutely," she said. "There are some complications, though. . . ."

"Like?"

"It's just that I don't think I can be seen with him yet," Brina said. "There's a total age difference to consider. People would talk."

"How can you be such a snob?" Sully asked, shaking his head. "I'm sure your mystery man wouldn't be so quick to pour his heart out if he knew how concerned you were with what everyone else thinks."

"Kids!" Mrs. Maldonati yelled up the stairs before Brina could rip Sully's head off like I fully expected her to. "Suppertime!"

Mr. Maldonati stood up at the head of the table and clinked a spoon against his wineglass. "It's time now for a special Maldonati tradition," he said, clearing his throat.

Brad and Brina groaned in unison. "Dad, do we have to—" Brina started to say.

"Yes, we do," Mr. M. said, cutting Brina off before she could even finish the question. "Every Thanksgiving, we go around the table and share something we are especially grateful for this year. Then, we share a special wish we hope to be giving thanks for next year."

"I'll go first to give you an example," Mrs. Maldonati said. "This year, I'm most grateful to have two happy, healthy kids. And next year, I hope to be giving thanks that Brad is on the varsity soccer team and Brina is attending a good college." Mrs. M. started to sit down and then thought better of it. "Oh, and that she's quit snacking between meals."

Brina looked like she'd rather be the turkey at that moment. Being literally carved up had to be better than being verbally ripped to shreds in front of everyone.

"I am grateful to still be alive, period," Grandma Ina said, moving past the uncomfortable moment. "And next year, I hope to be thankful for more of the same."

Fair enough, I thought. On to Grandpa. "I am grateful I whipped the stuffing out of my dear son-in-law playing poker today," he said. "And next year, I'll hope to see the money he owes me." Everyone laughed. Mr. Maldonati is a notorious tightwad.

Next, Aunt Rose stood up and almost fell over. Obviously, she and Ina had been doing a lot more drinking than cooking in the kitchen. "I am thankful my boobs look as good as they do," she said. She turned to Sully and grabbed the bottom of her shirt, making it look like she was about to flash him. Sully stood up and knocked over his water glass—he was so freaked-out.

"Sorry about that," Sully said, mopping up the spill with one of Mrs. M.'s crisp white napkins. And to think, just a second ago it had been folded into the shape of a swan.

Aunt Rose continued on, oblivious to the scene she'd just created. "Next year, I hope to be grateful my husband has finally filled his Viagra prescription."

"I don't need any pills to get revved up," Uncle Mario grumbled. Then he patted his stomach and said, "I myself am thankful my gas has subsided for the time being. And next year, I hope to be grateful you haven't poisoned me with bad calamari like you did this year." He looked at Rose with daggers in his eyes.

"I didn't do any such thing, Mario," Rose said, her voice going up a few octaves.

"Break it up, break it up," said Mrs. Maldonati, motioning for quiet. "Bebe, you're next."

"I'm grateful I finally met a nice guy," Bebe said, blushing.

"You did?" said Brina. "That's awesome, Bebe. Who is he?"

"He's—" Bebe started to say.

"He's nobody you know," I said at the same time, praying Bebe would move on. She didn't.

"I thought maybe Brina would have known him since he works—"

"Really hard," I finished Bebe's sentence before she had a chance to. "In fact, he's a total workaholic," I explained to Brina.

Bebe looked at me like I'd gone off the deep end. "He told me he's done every day by four thirty," she said.

"Yeah, but what you didn't realize is that he gets there at six a.m.," I told her.

"How would you know?" Bebe asked me. Most days I'm still in total REM at that time of the morning.

"I've seen him."

"At six in the morning? Since when do you get to s—?" Bebe started to ask.

"Ssssss-tarbucks?" I said before Bebe could utter the word "school." "I go early every Tuesday and Thursday before trig tutoring."

"So your new boyfriend's a barista at Starbucks?" Brina asked Bebe. "Which one? Don't tell me. The dark, mysterious guy with the soul patch, right?"

"No. He's—"

I interrupted her again. "Why don't you just keep it under wraps for now, Bebe?" I said. "You don't want to jinx it or anything." I knew she'd agree to that line of reasoning, because the last time she'd talked about how much she'd liked a guy after their first date was the last time she'd ever seen him.

"You're right," she said. "I'll just move on to next year's wish, which is—"

Aunt Rose was the one who interrupted Bebe this time. "Wish for a ring!" she slurred drunkenly.

"Not just a ring," Grandma Ina piped in. "Wish for a wedding." She turned to Grandpa and said in a stage whisper. "Belinda never did marry, you know."

"OK, fine," Bebe said, still smiling. "Whatever you say." I wondered if she was really falling for Mr. Perry.

"Moving right along," Mrs. M. said. "It's your turn, Sully."

"I am grateful for the Dead," Sully said. We kids all cracked up. Upstairs, we'd been flip-flopping between retro stuff and new tunes. Sully was referring to the last song we'd listened to before dinner: "Hell in a Bucket" by the Grateful Dead. "No, really, I'm thankful you invited me here for Thanksgiving, because the alternative was going to Milwaukee to watch my brother's basketball tournament," he said. "And next year, I'll be grateful my nose is no longer the size of a football."

"He's grateful for dead people? Do you think he's one of those devil worshippers?" Rose asked Mario. "Maybe that's why he doesn't comb his hair."

"They're called dreadlocks, Aunt Rose," Brina explained.

"You can fix whatever the hell they are with some shampoo and a good comb," Grandpa muttered.

I was next in line. I'd been dreading this moment since the game was announced. It reminded me too much of being onstage. "I am thankful to have all you wonderful people in my life," I said. "And next year, I hope to have another rockin' person in my life. My dad."

Brina gasped, knowing I'd just stuck a knife in Bebe's heart in front of a tableful of witnesses. And Bebe just sat there, not moving a muscle. She was either too shocked, sad, or really freakin' angry to do anything.

Grandma Ina put her two cents in this time. "Poor thing is father-less," she told Grandpa.

"That's enough!" yelled Mrs. Maldonati. "On second thought, let's eat now. The food is getting cold. We'll finish this up later."

Bebe and I left the Maldonatis' loaded down with leftovers. I hugged the big wads of tinfoil to my chest, trying to warm up as we walked the ten long blocks home. Hoofing it had seemed like such a good idea when we thought of it in the morning, and it certainly seemed to have exhilarated Bebe on her little jaunt home to get the poetry book. Now, arms and stomachs full of food, it just seemed seriously misguided.

Bebe still hadn't said a word to me since the "grateful" game. I knew I had pushed things a step too far, and I also knew I should probably apologize. But seeing as I was too stuffed to eat even my words, we kept walking in silence.

"It's not like I haven't given you roots," Bebe finally said after the third block. "That's why we've never moved, why you've known the same people your whole life."

"I know," I said. "And I appreciate that, but—"

"But nothing," she interrupted. "Your dad isn't part of our lives, and he hasn't been for eighteen years now."

I scrunched down farther into my coat. The tinfoil package with the stuffing in it plopped to the ground. "If you won't tell me who he is, can't you at least tell me *something* about him?" I asked her, scooping it back up.

Bebe sighed. "OK. Here goes. Your dad was all that and a bag of chips—talented, hot, smart, wildly popular. He saw something special in me that all the other girls who chased him around couldn't offer. The rest is history."

"So what went wrong?" I asked her. The leaves covering the sidewalk made a crunch, crunch, crunching noise as we walked.

"We were young," she said, shaking her head. "I guess it just didn't seem like the right time to be pinned down."

Now it was my turn to sigh. "I could understand that if it wasn't for one little thing. You were pregnant. If there's any time to be pinned down, it's when you're having a baby together."

"Trace, I know it seems confusing, but somehow it made sense back then," she said. "And besides, I have no regrets. I have everything I could ever wish for—a great daughter, a great career. . . ."

"The only thing missing is a great relationship, right, Bebe?"

Silence except for the loud leaves. "Mr. Perry seems pretty great," she finally said. "I think I could end up really liking him, Trace."

"But can you imagine loving him?" I asked, afraid of the answer. The thought of having Mr. Perry as a permanent fixture in our lives was just too weird, especially if he was the one writing my best friend secret love notes. Talk about sticky situations.

"I can't imagine loving anyone as much as I loved your dad."

"Was his name Steve, too?" I asked quickly, trying to trip her up. It always worked for me in Simon Says. "Or maybe Bruce?"

"I'm not falling for that one, Trace."

"It was worth a try."

"Anyway, it looks like you have company," Bebe told me, nodding toward Zander, who was sitting on our front doorstep with his tie undone and dress shirt rolled up to his elbows.

"Aren't holidays a bitch?" Bebe asked him as she unlocked the door.

"You have no idea," Zander told her. "The Ritz-Carlton is no picnic on Thanksgiving."

"You poor, deprived baby."

"C'mon in," I said, pulling Zander to his feet. "I'm sure we can get over the trauma of it together."

"Night guys," Bebe said, retreating to her room to leave us alone.

Zander and I headed for the library, where I told him the very limited scoop I'd dragged out of Bebe. The most significant clue, I thought, was the "all the other girls who chased him around." If that didn't make it sound like my dad was a rock star, I don't know what did.

"That's great, baby. One step at a time." He put his arms around me and said, "You know what?"

"No, what?"

"I'm still hungry."

"You are?"

"Yeah," he said. "For you."

"Yum."

"I'm going to eat you all up," he said, growling and pretending he was getting ready to pounce on me.

"Will you two keep it down?" Bebe called from upstairs. "I'm trying to sleep."

"I will not keep it down," I said quietly, grabbing Zander's cheeks—not the ones on his face—and pulling him close. "I have every intention of keeping things up."

"Now, that sounds like a plan," he said, pushing me up against the wall and burying his face in my neck.

I've heard that kissing burns a lot of calories. If that's the case, I must have worked off my entire Thanksgiving meal over the next hour.

Later, when we were just lying on the couch wrapped in the yellow afghan my grandmother had made me a few years back, I asked Zander, "Would your parents let you take off for a couple of days during Christmas break?"

He propped himself up on his elbow. "That depends on where I was going and who I was going with," he said. "What'd you have in mind?"

"Me. And the East Coast. Maybe we can shake some skeletons out of the closet together," I said. "Bebe's closet, that is."

"Where would we stay?"

"At my grandparents' house, at the Jersey Shore. That's where all my mom's stuff from high school is. Maybe we'll find an old letter . . . or phone number . . . or, I don't know, *something* that will lead us in the right direction."

"Your grandparents would let you have a boy sleep over?"

"Well, not in the same room or anything. But otherwise? Sure."

"Sounds great. Like a romantic vacation for two," he said. "Or should I say four? Me and you, plus your grandparents."

I winced. "Did I mention Brina really wants to come? I could tell her no. . . ."

"Who am I to break up a great friendship?" Zander said, laughing. "And anyway, I think it'll be fun to watch her self-combust when we go out."

"It can be pretty amusing," I said. "If nothing else, she'll certainly be an interesting fifth wheel."

Zander nodded. "Trace, there's something I haven't been able to get out of my head the past couple of days."

"I know," I groaned. "Me, too. I'm so sorry Bebe played 'Pour Some Sugar on Me' twice last time you were here."

"I wasn't talking about that, but now that you mention it . . ." Zander laughed, starting to sing the mind-numbingly inane chorus.

"Don't get me started," I told him. "If you'll believe this, when I was little, I thought it went, 'Wipe a booger on me.' "

"I have absolutely no problem believing that," Zander said, pulling me close again. "The thing I really can't get out of my head is your list. I keep thinking that with everything we know right now, Mr. Springsteen might really be the one."

"Well, my dad sure isn't Billy Squier," I said. "So where does that leave us?"

"Sitting in neutral until we go on our double date plus one with your grandparents."

# CHAPTER

## 8

When we got back to school after Thanksgiving break, my already good spirits went through the roof. Thanks to our vacation plan and Bebe's confessions—however minimal—I felt like I was finally on my way to finding my dad.

Everyone else seemed hyperhappy, too. Except Brina, that is. She was moping and slogging her way through the season. Ever since the Rob-buh debacle, she hadn't had a date. Not even a one-night stand. A girl like Brina needs a little adulation here and there or she starts believing her mother's bogus claims.

"Maybe I'll go on the grapefruit diet," she said with a pathetic sigh.

"Why when you've already got two perfectly enormous ones hidden underneath your T-shirt?"

Brina let out a hurt little yelp and punched me in the arm. "That's not funny," she said. "But you know what is? Even slp has given up on me."

I couldn't believe he would just blow her off after all those tantalizing letters. "What did he say about the note you left him?"

Brina grimaced. "You knew I'd never send him a goddamn Emily Dickinson poem!"

"Well, then, what did you expect?" I asked her, all exasperated. "That he'd just keep adoring you forever with no encouragement at all?"

"Yeah. I guess that is what I thought," she said, scuffing her shoe on the old marble floor.

I took her by the shoulders and tried to shake some sense into her. "You know unrequited love sucks. So requite it! Write him a note. Right here, right now. What do you have to lose?"

"My pride," she said, looking embarrassed. "You really think I should?"

"I really do," I said. "And instead of a poem, why don't you take it one step cooler? Write back in lyrics."

"That's brilliant," Brina said, brightening. "Any ideas?"

"Try this one," I said, handing her the latest Heather Horton CD. "It's my new favorite."

Brina flipped through the liner notes, running her finger along the words like she was speed-reading. An instant later, she was scribbling madly. "So, what do you think?" she asked, handing me a sheet of notebook paper when she was done.

What did I think? That she was insane. It wasn't a love note she had written. It was more like a sex-crazed stalker note. It read:

> *Now baby, I'm not looking for love*
> *I'm looking for some action*
> *And some traction in your hooves*
> *So I've got push*
> *In order to go in and out*
> *In and out and in and out of love with you*

"That's . . . uhhh . . . great," I told Brina. "But isn't it a bit much?"

"Naaah," she said. "I actually think it's just enough. Nothing like the promise of some serious nooky to get slp back in gear again."

I had to admit, it was pretty ballsy of her. And pretty funny, now that I'd had a little time to get used to the idea. If slp didn't like it, it just proved he had no sense of humor.

"How's this for another idea?" I said. "You burn a CD with the song on it and I'll design a great label. It'll make an amazing Christmas present."

"I am totally going to do that," Brina said, jumping up and down. "Steven will love it!"

"For the millionth time, it is not Mr. Perry."

"That's how much you know," she said. "Today he came by my locker to give me Purdue's viewbook."

"So what?"

"So it was obviously an excuse. He must know I'd never go to school in Indiana," she said. "Plus, there's the bumble bee factor. He would definitely realize black and gold are all wrong for me."

I didn't have the heart to tell Brina that Bebe and her beloved Steven were going out again tonight for the third time this week. And it was only Tuesday.

The next day, armed with her CD and the sexy stalker note, Brina and I marched up to the abandoned locker next to hers.

"So what should I do?" she asked, examining the locker this way and that.

I grabbed the handle and pulled. "Open it up and put the stuff in, brainiac."

"No shit, Sherlock," she said. "I was just trying to figure out how we should let him know it's in here."

I thought for a second and then unveiled my undeniably brilliant plan. "You have lipstick in your bag?"

She rustled around in her fake-fur purse and came up with a tube of MAC. "Here," she said, handing it to me.

I uncapped it, scrawled *slp: Look inside!* on the locker, and tossed the lipstick back to Brina.

"Subtle," she said. "Real subtle."

I stepped back and surveyed my work. It looked like a murder scene. "Gosh, that's a little creepy," I said. "What color is it, anyway?"

Brina turned the silvery little case over and read the label. "Vampire State Building."

I smiled. "One thing's for sure. It'll definitely get his attention."

But it was hard to tell if we actually did catch slp's attention, because Brina still hadn't heard from him by the next week. She was in a piss-poor mood, and I knew she was regretting reaching out to him. Even if it was in a kind of funny, kind of scary, kind of sarcastic way.

"Well, it's not like you liked him anyway, right?" I said, patting her shoulder.

She shrugged my hand off. "Right. It was all a big joke. Just like my life."

Oh, jeez, I thought, bring on the drama. I'd be soothing her bruised ego all Christmas break at this rate.

Still frowning, Brina spun her combination and tugged the locker open with a jolt. A second later, her whole face lit up. She turned to me holding a tiny locket on a fine silver chain. There was a note attached.

"Let me see!" I begged her.

Brina cradled the jewelry in her outstretched palm. " 'I like to walk right there beside you / Always try to match your pace,' " she read. " 'But I don't want to rush things / Maybe you should slow down for me.' " She looked at me with her eyes wide.

"Brina, this guy is freakin' amazing," I told her. "You should go out with him even if he looks like Urkel and hangs out at *Star Trek* conventions."

She hugged me and said, "Trace, I've been thinking. Lots of poets have that smokin' long-haired, tattooed thing going. Probably poet wannabes, too. So that means there's a possibility slp's really hot even if he's not Mr. Perry, right?"

I detached myself from her death grip. "That's what I love about you, Brina. You're about as deep as a puddle."

The morning Zander, Brina, and I left for our East Coast drag-the-skeletons-out-of-the-closet tour, my alarm went off at six a.m. It blasted thunderous waves all over my room, and I started having nightmares about surfing a tsunami. When the noise didn't stop, the dream did.

I groped around my nightstand haphazardly, located the SNOOZE button, and slammed it down hard. A second later when I realized what day it was, I started rushing around like I'd been shot out of a cannon, taking all of about ten seconds to pull on my clothes, brush my teeth, and run my fingers through my hair. Then I ran down the stairs two at a time, grabbing my backpack and a Pop-Tart on my way out.

As I headed toward the door, I noticed Bebe drinking a cup of coffee in semidarkness at the kitchen table. I was surprised to see her conscious so early in the morning. Usually, she gets up late and doesn't say a word until she's had a full pot.

"Did you stay up all night?" I asked Bebe.

Mr. Perry came shuffling out of the bathroom in his robe and slippers. "I'll take that as a yes," I said, embarrassed for us all. "Good morning, Mr. Perry."

"I think if we're gonna keep meeting like this," he said, "you might as well call me Steve."

"OK, Mr. . . . uhhhh . . . Steve."

"Have it your way, Trace," he said, laughing. "I am now Mr. Steve to you. Outside school, of course."

Bebe took a slurp of coffee and let me have it. "Trace, just answer one question before you leave. Why the sudden urge to go see your grandparents? Usually you leave skid marks after our two weeks at the shore with them."

Good point. "I missed his silent but deadly burps?" I improvised. Grandpa's forever laying two fingers across his lips and exhaling hot, smelly air and then asking, "What smells like pork?" It's a real knee-slapper after the tenth time in one day, let me tell you.

"Sweet," Mr. Steve said, trying not to laugh.

But Bebe wasn't buying it. "Anything else I should know about?"

Yes, I thought. I am planning to dig up your secrets, Bliss, and find my dad. "No, of course not," I said.

More suspicious looks. "Uh-huh. Be safe, call me every day, and keep Brina out of trouble," Bebe said. "Oh, and don't do anything I wouldn't do."

Like that would be so hard—no getting pregnant. I thought I could handle it. "Wouldn't dream of it, Bebe."

The doorbell rang. It was Brina. She tried to come inside, but I pushed her back out and closed the door behind us. "I just wanted to wish Bebe a happy New Year," she said.

"Bebe's still asleep," I lied.

"Oh," Brina said. "I thought I saw her in the kitchen window."

"That must've been me," I lied again.

"Whose car is this?" she asked, running her finger along the Mini

Cooper as we walked down the driveway. "It kind of looks like that hot car Steven drives."

"It's a loaner," I lied a third time, proud of my quick thinking. Then I realized Bebe's Bug was parked right in front of it.

"But—" Brina started to say.

"It's a long story," I told her, and left it at that. I didn't know how much longer I could keep the charade up.

Brina, Zander, and I touched down in Newark a few hours later. My grandparents were waiting for us at the baggage claim, holding up a pillowcase done up in glittery rhinestones that read *Trace and Friends, You the Shizzy!* I could barely stifle the giggles that were bubbling up from my stomach as I wondered when they'd gone all gangsta rapper on me.

"Wow, Grandma," I said, hugging her, "that's quite a reception."

"Yo, my new BeDazzler is . . . pee-hat," she said, turning to hug Zander and Brina, as well. "Grandpa be givin' it to me for my birthday and it's totally . . . uh . . . hyper." The best part of my grandmother trying to be 50 Cent or whoever she was going for, other than the fact that she got every phrase just wrong enough to make it hilarious, was that she was so damn sincere about it.

"I think you mean 'phat,' honey," Grandpa said, opening his jacket up to reveal a ribbed wife beater with *phat daddy* BeDazzled into it. You just had to give it to those two for cuteness.

Grandma patted his tummy and smiled. "You're not fat, boo," she said, a look of concern crossing her face. "Or is that 'boop'?"

Grandpa consulted a little pamphlet he extracted from his back pocket. " 'Boo.' It means someone close to you, like a boyfriend or girl-friend."

"And that's you, boobie," she told him. "Let's boing, kids."

We all looked at her, not quite getting where she was going with that one. Grandpa referred to his trusty pamphlet again. This time, I was able to make out its title: *Rappin' with the Younger Generation*.

"It's 'bounce,' schnookie," he told her. Grandma looked like she was about to cry.

"When we found out you and your home fries were coming to visit over Christmas vacation, Trace, we took a class at the senior center to make sure you were feeling us up—"

"I think that's just plain 'feelin' you,' Mrs. Tillingham," Brina gently corrected her.

"See? I just can't get it right. And now you're going to think I'm a winkster."

"Wanksta," Zander whispered in my ear, eyes twinkling with unvoiced laughter. "This is going to be even more fun than I thought."

"Grandma, you don't have to talk differently on account of us," I told her, patting her shoulder and thinking how sweet it was she and Grandpa had gone to all that trouble. "You're off the hizzle just the way you are."

Grandma looked pleased as punch, as they used to say back in the day, and Zander started coughing to cover his snickering. I just shrugged, smiling back at him so hard my cheeks hurt. Grandma didn't need to know that my friends and I never used hip-hop lingo like "off the hizzle." I much preferred to let her think she was cooler than words.

Things were pretty quiet in the car as we drove to my grandparents' house in Red Bank—with the exception of Grandpa's frequent gaseous interruptions, that is. Since last summer, his punch line had evolved into "What smells like bacon?" Zander laughed along like it was the funniest thing he'd ever heard; actually using the correct term for a change, Grandma commented that Grandpa had "the dragon," aka bad breath. Poor Brina had to roll down her window, I assume to combat the smell and car sickness.

Still, we made it to their modest ranch house in the burbs relatively intact, considering. And we were no sooner over the threshold when Grandma started buzzing excitedly around us, desperate to show off our "diggity-dogs," whatever they were. As it turns out, Brina and I were assigned to the mildewy guest room with the pompommed bedspreads. My grandparents had obviously taken great pains to update our digs in anticipation of our arrival, because there were now posters of rappers all over the walls and a humongous boom box on the nightstand that looked like it was left over from the early eighties. Probably was. Where Grandma had gotten the idea I was into rap, I'll never know, but she seemed pretty obsessed with the whole thing.

"So what do you think?" she asked us, practically jumping up and down by that point.

"It's awesome," Brina said.

"Plush," I added, flipping through the cassettes Grandma had carefully stacked next to the tune box. Let's see, there was Vanilla Ice, Milli Vanilli, Snow, and Marky Mark and the Funky Bunch. Stuff even Bebe must've been too embarrassed to admit she'd bought way back when, preferring to leave her musical indiscretions in some old shoe box in the attic instead of toting them along to her new home in Winnetka. The dated rappers with less than zero street cred were in weird contrast with the real ones staring us down from the walls.

"Don't you just love that Dog Snoopy?" Grandma said, pointing to the wall next to my bed. "He's so . . . beauty-licious."

I couldn't believe she could possibly have a crush on Snoop Dogg, but I let both the implication and the misspeak fly. "Absolutely, Grandma," I told her, and changed the subject. "So Zander's staying in Bebe's old room?"

"Oh, no, honey," she said, flinging open the door of my mom's former digs. "We kind of converted it into an exercise area." Inside, a brand-new treadmill, recumbent bike, and free weights sparkled a little hello at us. I was still marveling at the weird extreme makeover my grandparents had given themselves over the past few months when Grandma dropped a real stinker on Zander.

"Here's your room, Z-man." It seemed he was going to have the supreme pleasure of camping out on the plastic-covered floral couch in the den.

"It's positively ghetto fabulous," Zander told her, plunking his bags down next to the sweaty monster of a sofa.

"Is that good?" Grandma whispered to Grandpa. He consulted his pamphlet for a second, then smiled and nodded. A wave of relief flooded her face.

"I hope you kids don't mind, but Grandma and I have our break-dancing class at the senior center today and we've got to get going or we'll never learn how to do head spins."

"No problemo, Grandpa," I said, relieved to be able to laugh about this whole scene so far with my friends without having to do it behind my grandparents' backs. "We'll just hang out and relax."

"I was thinking maybe you kids should take a nap," Grandma said, acting like we were still in preschool. "Because we've got everything all planned out for the rest of the time you're here. No doubt, you are going to go all wigwam."

I couldn't begin to imagine what those two hepcats had in store for us, but it was sure to be frightening. I was beginning to dread the next few days, and regretting that I'd dragged my friends halfway across the country on a wild-goose chase. If my grandparents hadn't told me anything important about my dad in the past seventeen years, why in God's name had I thought they'd start now?

Once those wild and crazy sexagenarians took off, we collapsed on the couch laughing. It crinkled and stuck to any exposed skin, making us crack up even more.

"I am going to be a pool of sweat sleeping on this thing," Zander said once he caught his breath.

"Too bad they decided to get all healthy on you," I told Zander. "Bebe's room actually used to be pretty cool. I always loved looking at her photo albums, and one time I even discovered a secret drawer where she kept all her notes and letters from high school." I was so lost in the reminiscence I barely recognized the supreme opportunity we had in front of us.

It was Brina who pointed it out to me. "*Chica,* how long did your grandparents say they'd be gone?"

"About an hour and a half. Why?"

Brina walked over to me and knocked on my head. "This is our one and only chance to find out something juicy about your dad, sweetness. Your grandma said she's got us all booked for the rest of the trip. So let's find out where they stashed Bebe's stuff and see what skeletons start jumping around."

I could practically feel my blood pumping through my veins—I was so ready to do this thing. "You're right. Everything must be in the attic. Let's go."

The only way to get there was to remove a smallish square part of the ceiling in the guest room closet, pull down a rickety old ladder, and somehow squeeze your body through the ridiculously tiny hole without killing yourself. Good thing none of us had much bulk, though I was pretty curious to see how Brina's curves were going to survive the test.

I made it through the opening without a hitch and flicked on a light so my compatriots would be able to see when they joined me. Wads of dust flew up with every footstep I took, filling my nostrils to the brim. A second later, I was showing off my talent for sneezing uncontrollably no less than eight times in a row. It drives Bebe bonkers. As if it weren't an involuntary reaction. Like I was doing it on purpose.

Zander clambered up next. He had a bit of a rough time figuring out how to maneuver his shoulders though the hole, but finally did this thing where he kept one shrugged around his ear and the other slumped down his side. I gave him a little kiss on the head as the top of his body popped through. "So glad you could make it," I said.

"The Z-man always finds a way," he said, hoisting the rest of himself up into the cramped little space. "This is it, Trace. I can just feel it in my bones."

I shot him an evil grin. "I love feeling your bones," I told him. "Jumping them, too."

Brina's head appeared next in the attic. "You promised, no sex talk with me around," she said. "I haven't scooped a guy in so long I'm going crazy."

"Maybe I could be of assistance," Zander said, grabbing one of Brina's hands and trying to help her the rest of the way up. After some struggling, the upper half of Brina's bodacious body finally made it through the little hole.

With that, a big green monster made an appearance in the pit of my stomach, kicking at all my internal organs until I felt like I was going to throw up. "The hell you will." I was going for lighthearted, but ended up sounding more like a shrew. I know it's lame to be jealous of something your boyfriend said kiddingly to your best friend, but when your best friend looks like Brina it's hard not to get crazy.

"Don't worry, boopie," Zander told me. "You're the only shorty for me."

I heaved a little internal sigh of relief as I joined the effort to pull Brina through to the other side. But no matter how hard Brina tried, or what Zander and I did to help her, Brina could not get her booty to clear the circumference of the attic entryway.

"Great. My ass has embarrassed me to a new low," Brina said, slamming her hand down on the attic floor. Dust flew everywhere, covering her hair, face, and shoulders. "Just bring me a box to sort through here."

I had to bite the insides of my cheeks to keep from dissolving into wild laughter. All whitish gray with dust, Brina looked like a bad replica of a bust you might find at a flea market alongside the velvet Elvises and the paintings of dogs playing poker.

"Don't you dare look at me that way," Brina said, screwing up her face at me. "Just bring me some clues."

While I'd been busy trying not to bust a gut over Brina's appearance, Zander had been hard at work finding Bebe's old stuff. He placed a box labeled *Desk* in front of me, one marked *Bookshelf* in front of Brina, and took the one that said *Bureau* for himself.

"Let's rock," he said, glancing at his watch. "We only have about an hour before those darn winksters get back."

"What would happen if they caught us up here?" Bust-o-Brina wanted to know.

"Grandma for sure would get all weird," I said, opening the top to my box and sifting carefully through the contents. "She still hasn't accepted the fact that Bebe got knocked up that summer. Wants to think it was some divine act of God instead of a hot 'n' horny one."

I picked up Bebe's yearbook and started reading the inscriptions her classmates had scrawled throughout. There was the same old, same old.

*Stay as sweet as you are! Don't ever change.*
*You're a great writer. Have fun at Fairfield.*
*Do bongs!*

And then there was something else entirely.

*Remember the time we TPed Jon's house? Let's do Bruce next time!*

Next to that entry, an addendum in Bebe's distinctive scrawly handwriting declared: *Been there, done that. And hope to do it again, as often as possible.*

"Look here, Z.," I said, pointing to the "Jon"—whom I assumed to be Bon Jovi—and "Bruce"—whom I assumed to be Springsteen—references. I took it Bebe had been talking about more than just childish pranks with the Springsteen one.

"That's funny, but it doesn't prove anything," he said. "She could easily have been kidding. Teenage bravado and all that, as my mom would say."

"What? What?" Brina screeched, wiggling around in her mole hole.

"Just that Bebe and her friends made a habit of decorating Bon Jovi's house with toilet paper. Possibly Bruce's, too," Zander said, putting Brina out of her misery.

"Or maybe she was doing something else with Bruce," I added. "Something more interesting. And naughty."

"Naughty, schmaughty," said Zander. "Keep moving. We're on a deadline here."

We were all so absorbed in being amateur detectives, we must've lost track of time. Because the next thing we knew, Grandma and Grandpa were busting back through the door singing "U Can't Touch This."

"Shit," I whispered, looking up at my friends in horror. I really did not want to have to explain this whole thing and then watch Grandma get all bummed out, not to mention go blabbing to Bebe about our little caper.

"Put everything back where you found it," Zander urged us in a low voice. "And let's get outta here."

I was about to shove Bebe's yearbook back into the musty old box when something went sliding out of the back cover and escaped to the dusty floor below.

"Can you grab that, Z.?"

Zander bent down to pick up what turned out to be a picture and handed it to me without looking. "Here you go."

I almost threw the thing back into the box without checking it out, but then thought better of it. I stared down at the photo and rubbed my eyes. There was no way this could possibly be happening. "Score," I whispered, giving Zander both a thumbs-up and a deer-in-the-headlights kind of look.

"What is it?"

"Only the key to my universe," I said, as mesmerized by the picture as the little girl from *Poltergeist* was by the TV screen.

"Yoo-hoo, home fries," Grandma called. "Dinnertime!"

"Where could those peeps be?" Grandpa mused, seemingly opening and shutting every door in the house. His footsteps were getting louder, and clearly we were the next scheduled stop on his search.

I stuffed the revealing picture into my back pocket and tapped Brina's head. "Get moving, girl."

She wiggled and wriggled, but couldn't seem to make any progress in getting herself unstuck. I pushed on one of her massive boobs, but that only made her cry out in pain. And punch me in the shins. "Hands off the merchandise, groper," she hissed.

"Oh, this is so cute, boopie," a muffled-sounding Grandma said. "The kids are playing hide-and-seek."

"Now you just come on down here, Brina," Grandpa hollered up the rickety old ladder. "We'll help you find the other two."

"Your grandfather just tickled me in the ribs," Brina whispered, writhing uncomfortably. "The hornbag."

"Sure thing, Mr. and Mrs. Tillingham," Brina called back, finally popping back through the other side of the hole. "Let's check out the basement. There are lots of good hiding places there."

As soon as their footsteps faded back down the hall, Zander and I bolted from the attic—but not before I had a chance to show him my great find.

"Whoa." He whistled through his teeth. "So we were on the right track all along."

"Looks that way," I said, sliding the picture back into my pocket and scrambling down the ladder.

Zander followed quickly, and after we replaced the little square ceiling tile, we both made a big to-do over running to the plastic couch and screaming, "Ollie ollie umption free!"

"Darn," Brina said, sauntering into the room and snapping her fingers. "You beat me again."

"Don't worry, honey," Grandma said, patting Brina's still-white head until the room was totally cloudy with a chance of a dust storm. "You guys can play some more after dinner."

Grandma crooked her finger and led us into the dining room. The table was set with a horrifying display worthy of *Fear Factor*. All that was missing was some live maggots, Madagascar hissing cockroaches, and a blender.

Brina, the major suck-up, gasped. "Oh, Mr. and Mrs. Tillingham. It all looks so wonderful."

"It certainly does," added Zander, vying with her for the biggest-ass-kisser award.

"Since you poor kids are so far from the ocean in Winnetka, we thought we'd treat you to a bit of the Jersey Shore." Grandma smiled.

Grandpa pointed to three bowls quivering with gelatinous sea creatures. I quivered along with them—in fear. "We've got crab salad, lobster salad, and scungilli."

Unable to postpone the inevitable, I plopped some stuff from each bowl onto my plate and said, "Speaking of the shore, Grandma, do you think we could borrow your car tonight so I can show Brina and Zander around a bit?"

"I don't think so," Grandma said, frowning at the idea. "We all need to hit the hay early so we'll have enough energy for our big day tomorrow."

"I can't wait to find out what's in store for us," I said, rolling my eyes at my friends. Still, I was so pumped up at my find, a little thing like being sent to bed before *Letterman* wasn't going to bring me down.

Until I bit into something crunchy and picked a shell out of my mouth, that is. After that, I was officially one hundred percent grossed out. I laid my napkin over the scoops of shellfish and buried my dinner at sea.

Soon enough, everyone else had had enough of the fishfest, too. "Thank you, it was delicious," Brina said, folding her hands in her lap and plastering another fake smile to her face.

After we'd cleared all the dishes, Grandma and Grandpa chased Brina and I into our room and Zander to the couch. "Nighty-night," said Grandma, who had forgotten to even try to be gangsta by this point.

"Sleep tight," Grandpa added, blasting us with one of his famous hot-air burps. Then he slapped his knee and laughed. "What smells like squid?"

# CHAPTER
## 9

I tugged on Brina's hair as we were brushing our teeth in the bathroom. "Check this out."

I handed her the picture I'd discovered in the attic. Brina examined it, flipping it this way and that before freaking out. "Oh, my God, this confirms it. I'm actually best friends with Bruce Springsteen's daughter!"

I was ready to explode with excitement, but was trying to keep it all in perspective. "Well, it definitely keeps him on the suspect list."

"More like guilty as charged, I'd say."

I took a deep breath before broaching my biggest fear. "But it could also be the other guy in the picture, right?" I asked Brina, unable to meet her eyes. I just couldn't bear to think that my mom had kept my dad from me this long if he was someone so boringly normal and unfamous.

Brina snorted. "Look at how Bruce and Bebe are lost in each other's eyes, Trace," she said, pointing at them. "Look at what Bebe wrote, for God's sake."

I stared at the picture again for the millionth time since I'd found it. Bebe was flanked by some random guy and none other than Mr. Springsteen himself. Random man had his arm snaked around Bebe's waist, but it was the Boss's darling twinkly eyes and off-center grin she was gazing up at. I flipped the picture over and read the words inscribed on the back again for the trillionth time since I'd found it: *The love of my life. August 1986.* Brina was right, I decided. Random man was just a friend for sure.

Since it was ridiculously early—not to mention the fact that I was still reeling over my amazing discovery—there wasn't a shot in hell that I was going to be able to fall asleep. Especially after I'd counted back and realized August 1986 was the month and year in which I'd been conceived. I decided to beseech my best friend for some time alone with my honey instead.

"Brina, would you mind trading places with Zander for a bit?"

Brina groaned. "Trace, unlike you, I really am tired. Can't you two fool around in the morning?"

"What, with Grandma and Grandpa taking pictures and calling me a garden ho or bumble bee-atch?"

"Oh, all right," she sighed, looking at her watch. It was only nine o'clock. "You've got a half an hour."

Brina plopped down miserably on the couch as I took Zander by the hand. We tiptoed into the bedroom and shut the door quietly.

"Danger turns me on," he whispered, throwing me on the bed. "But are you sure your grandparents are asleep?"

"Didn't you hear the wall-rumbling snoring when you went to brush your teeth?"

"I thought it was thunder," Zander laughed, pulling me on top of him. "Or maybe farts to go along with those awesome burps your grandfather blows all day long."

"Gross," I said, cringing at the mere thought of being subjected to Gramps's gas from down below, too.

We quickly got down to the business of love, but were interrupted a few minutes later by the sound of shuffling slippers in the hallway. "Please, please tell me that's Brina coming to claim her bed back," I whispered.

No such luck. "Are you OK there on the couch, son?" Grandpa's voice boomed. Thank God it was dark and he hadn't turned on any lights.

Brina cleared her throat. "Yes, sir," she said, in a fake tenor.

"You have a cold, Zander?" Grandpa asked. "Your voice sounds funny."

"Allergies," Brina said, in an even lower and faker baritone.

"Hmmpph," Grandpa snorted, shuffling on over to our room. He knocked and opened the door a crack. "You girls all right in here?"

"We're fine, Grandpa," I said. "Just a little sleepy."

"How about you, Brina?"

I threw my hand over Zander's mouth and tried to change my voice. "Just dandy, Mr. Tillingham."

"You sound like you have allergies, too."

Zander was silently laughing so hard the bed shook. As soon as we heard Grandpa shuffle back to his room and shut the door, Brina came bounding in. "Get out of here, Zander!"

"Brina, just give us ten minutes more."

"No."

"You promised," I said with a little whine in my voice.

"Fine, but you owe me big-time," Brina said, stomping back to that sticky plastic-covered couch.

I woke with a start much later and stuck my nose up against the clock. Five forty-five a.m. I snuggled farther into Zander's back until I realized what had happened. "Z.," I whispered, shaking him. "You gotta get on the couch before my grandparents wake up."

He looked at me bleary-eyed and fell out of bed. "No problem," he mumbled.

Zander practically sleepwalked to the den and started to lie down on the couch with Brina still on it. "Just a sec, bub," I said, poking Brina in the shoulder. "Honey, it's time to go to bed."

" 'Kay," Brina said, stumbling into our room. She threw herself on the bed and pulled the covers over her head. "Night."

The two were passed out again in a matter of seconds. But I was wide-awake by this point, so I wrote Grandma a note, strapped on my Brooks, and headed out for a run. Having been one hundred percent faithful to my marathon training thus far, I wasn't about to let things slide just because I was on the road.

Outside, it was crisp and clear—perfect for the twelve miles I was planning on doing over the next couple of hours. Here and there, a blast of arctic air would slap me in the face, but for the most part I felt invigorated. As I watched the sun dance around on top of the bare trees, I let my thoughts wander from potential papa Springsteen to Zander to Bebe to college. I couldn't ask for more right now, I thought. From there on in, I relaxed and enjoyed my run.

The resulting peace that washed over me was shattered the minute I got back to Grandma's house. Brina and Zander both jumped like I'd caught them doing something immoral or illegal when I walked in. Possibly both.

"Go on, Zander. Tell her," she said. I made a mental note: Do not leave these two alone again. Ever. Even with Grandma and Grandpa as chaperones.

"No, you tell her," the Prince of Darkness replied.

"No, you," she countered right back.

I crunched down into the plastic-covered couch, trying not to think about what might have happened on it while I was gone. Zander plunked himself down next to me, draping his arm around my shoulder. I quickly shrugged it off.

"Guess where your grandparents are taking us today?" he said.

"To the senior center to learn to moonwalk?" I pretty much hated my friends being the two musketeers with me starring as the third wheel, so my sarcastic self was back at it again.

"Not even close," Brina said, not noticing the edge in my voice. "We're hitting NYC. More specifically, Broadway. Your grandparents want to buy discount tickets for *The Lion King* at some place in Times Square."

Much as I love music, I am in no way, shape, or form a musical-theater lover. So I didn't exactly savor the thought of being held captive all afternoon for endless Disney sing-alongs. "Oh, Christ. I'm sorry," I told them, feeling semi-bad even though I still didn't like the way they were grinning and poking at each other.

"You know what else is in Times Square?" Zander asked me, practically sweating with excitement now.

"Will you just freaking tell me already?" I hissed, sick of their annoying little tryst.

"MTV," Brina said, frowning over my completely uncalled-for snake routine.

"Home to *Total Request Live,*" Zander said, grabbing my hand and looking intently into my eyes.

"And?" I said, not quite getting where they were going with the whole thing. "So what?"

"And so we're going to very nicely blow your grandparents off while they enjoy the afternoon matinee of *Lion King,* and hit *TRL* with these," Brina said, reaching under the couch and pulling out three T-shirts.

"Here's mine," Zander said, lifting up the one that was BeDazzled with *Miss Your Bliss?*

"And here's mine," said Brina, showing me a shirt that sparkled with *Then Find Your Bliss!*

"Finally, the pièce de résistance," said Zander, holding my T-shirt, which said *You + Bliss = Me 4ever!*

I stared at Zander, then at Brina, then at the shirts again. What were they up to? "Thanks for the effort, but I'm totally confused," I told them.

"When I woke up, I turned on MTV," Zander explained. "And they were showing clips of kids waiting in line for *Total Request Live.* Everyone was waving posters around and wearing personalized T-shirts on national TV."

"So I thought, today that's gonna be us," Brina said, too excited to let him finish. "Maybe someone with information about your dad will see these and call in. Who knows? Maybe Bruce himself will call in and fess up."

I was warming up to this idea, even if it was concocted under semi-questionable circumstances. Plus, I'd always wanted to see the MTV studios up close and personal. "But how are we going to convince my grandparents to go to the show without us?" I whispered before heading off for a glass of water.

"I've got that part covered," Zander said, so chock-full of confidence I had to believe he had it all under control. "No worries."

In the kitchen, the smell of seafood hit me like a rotten water balloon. It was a pretty unpleasant reality slap, to say the least. "Hey, Grandma," I said, hugging her little body to mine while I held my breath. "I hear you have a big day planned for us."

" 'I just can't wait to be king,' " she warbled, sliding a seafood omelet across the table at me. I spied a few tentacles that had escaped the egg part and almost puked.

"That's from *The Lion King,* right?" I said, inching away from the platter o' grossness. "What fun."

Grandma pushed the plate even closer to me. There was no way I was going to touch that rancid thing. "You kids are going to love it."

"I'm sure we will," I said, backing away from the table and running toward my room. "In fact, I'm going to get dressed right now so we're sure to be on time."

Later that morning, after we somehow got out of eating the leftover fish eggs, my grandparents loaded us back into their decades-old Country Squire station wagon and soon had us hurtling down the highway. Once we got to the PATH station in Hoboken, Grandma and Grandpa immediately hit the restrooms.

"Are you sure none of you has to go potty before we get on the train?" Grandma yelled, leaning her head out of the doorway. "It's a pretty long ride, you know."

I stared at my shoes, Brina examined her fingernails, and Zander ran his hands through his bed head. Not one of us acknowledged we'd even heard her. Eventually, she gave up and went inside to do her business.

"I'm never eating again," I told Zander and Brina after Grandma had disappeared behind the door. My intestines had been rumbling all morning. "The recycled seafood is really starting to take its toll on me."

"Just be grateful *that* wasn't on the menu." Zander gestured toward an enormous woman in a muumuu and hiking boots who kept dipping her fingers into a jar of Vaseline and then licking the clear goo off her hands with obscene pleasure.

"It probably tastes better than our breakfast did," I said, looking away. The combination of probable food poisoning and watching someone eat petroleum jelly was definitely not agreeing with me.

Brina, on the other hand, was riveted, analyzing the homeless lady's every move like a sportscaster for the Sicko Games. "Oh, look, she's digging out crust from under her fingernails and using it as topping for her Vaseline. Ooh, now she's putting it all in her hair. Just look at those shiny strands. Maybe they'll turn into superconditioned dreads. . . ."

I pushed Brina forward, trying to get her to move in the direction of our train's platform. "Let's go, please."

But Brina kept staring over her shoulder at the wacko woman as we headed far, far away. "On the bright side, I'll bet she's never constipated."

"Brina?" I said.

Brina looked at me, probably hoping I'd want to delve further into the habits of People Who Eat Vaseline. "What?"

"Shut up, already."

Zander walked over to a map and pointed to a red dot representing the Ninth Street station. "Looks like I might be spending a lot of time here next year."

"Really?" I said. "Funny, I don't remember Ninth Street in New York being anywhere near Stanford University."

"It isn't. But NYU is, and it has one of the best film schools in the country," he explained, as if I had any clue he was interested in film-making.

"How are you going to break it to your dad that you're blowing off his alma mater?"

"I might not have anything to explain," Zander said, shoving his hands deep into his pockets and slouching uncomfortably. "My application got deferred to regular admission. They'll review it again in the spring."

I hugged him tight. "I'm so sorry."

"Don't be. Either way, things will work out. So, where'd you apply, Brina?" he asked, taking the college spotlight off himself and placing it directly onto her.

Brina stared around the station and said nothing. I grabbed her face in my hands and forced her to look at me. "Sabrina Maldonati. Please tell me you've done something about your future."

"I'm going to get right on it when I get home," she said, still refusing to make eye contact.

I threw my arms up in disgust. "Don't expect to come flying out to see me every weekend because you have no social life of your own at Lake-Cook Community College," I said. "It'll be your own damn fault."

"You're right. I'm turning over a new leaf today," she said. "I'm going to pick up an NYU application once we're in the city."

"Not so fast, kimosabe," I said, grabbing the sleeve of her black leather jacket.

"What?" she asked, trying to look innocent.

"NYU is practically Ivy League, girlfriend," I said. "Your high school record wouldn't even get you into the kindergarten T-ball league."

"Fine," Brina said. "That's just fine." I could only hope Brina would figure her life out before she was stuck at home next year with her crazy mother on her ass all the time about the way she ate, looked, and acted. It was a fate worse than hell as far as I was concerned.

It didn't take long for Zander to put his plan into action once we got to Times Square. He stepped in front of Grandpa in line at the discount-ticket place and valiantly said, "Mr. Tillingham, please allow me. My parents let me visit only with the promise that I would treat everyone to a special day out."

Grandpa harrumphed and hemmed and hawed, but finally gave into the Z-man's pressure. He actually looked secretly pleased he wasn't going to have to shell out hundreds of dollars for our afternoon in Manhattan. "Are you sure that young man's family can afford such a thing?" Grandpa asked me as Zander crawled slowly to the front of the queue.

"Never fear—the guy's got mad flow," I told him, busting out the rapper lingo again to throw him off the track that things might be getting a little fishy, and not due to the repulsive meals Grandma had been feeding us. "Tons of dead presidents."

Grandma reached for her ever-trusty *Rappin' with the Younger Generation* pamphlet and scoured it. "Everything's chilly, bra," she told my grandfather a second later.

When Zander rejoined our group, his face was full of regret. "The good news is that you and Mr. Tillingham are going to the show," he told Grandma. "The bad news is they didn't have enough tickets for all of us."

"That's the wacky," Grandma said, right back to her misquoting ways.

"Well, just sell them back, son," Grandpa told Zander. "We are most definitely not going to the play without you."

"No reason you should miss out on the fun because of us," replied Zander, giving me a discreet wink. "Anyway, I have a thought. Maybe us kids could get some homework done while you two attend the show. I noticed there's a branch of the New York City library right over there—"

"Where?" Grandma said, squinting around at the surrounding buildings.

"Right there," Zander said, gesturing randomly. "We can camp out there and get a lot accomplished in the time you'll be gone."

Grandpa narrowed his eyes, trying to figure out if there was a catch somewhere. "I thought you kids were on vacation."

"Seniors never get to relax until we have our college acceptances in hand," I told my grandparents. They nodded, and I was suddenly very hopeful they just might agree to this crazy little plan.

"Well . . . ," Grandma said, looking at Grandpa for approval. "I *have* been dying to see this show for so long. . . ."

"You stay put in that library and promise not to go anywhere else," Grandpa said gruffly, caving under all our pressure. "We'll meet you in front of the theater at four o'clock, no later."

"Have a marvelous time, Mr. and Mrs. Tillingham," Brina added for good measure. She sounded so fake, I thought we'd be caught for sure, but no. My grandparents were already hailing a cab.

"I hope I have time to run to the potty before the curtain goes up," I heard Grandma say as she disappeared inside the taxi. That lady obviously had mad flow, too—though hers had nothing to do with money.

We ran across the street to MTV's offices, and my heart sank as I realized the crowd of kids we'd been eyeing were already lined up for *TRL*. I knew from Bebe that studio audiences are usually much smaller than they appear on television, and if the same held true for *TRL*, I guessed only a quarter of us, if that, would actually get in to see the show.

We plunked ourselves down at the end of the line behind a skanky girl who couldn't have been older than fifteen. She was treating everyone to her very own private walk down *TRL* memory lane.

"And that's me with Carson," she was saying, flipping to the first page of a fake-fur-covered photo album. "Since then, I've come back when OutKast was here, and the White Stripes, too."

"How did you do it?" someone asked the skank.

"Looks, brains, courage," she said, clearly loving the attention her veteran status was bringing her on these streets. "You've got to impress Courtney, the girl who decides who gets in and who doesn't. She'll ask you trivia questions, have you do a trial shout-out, see if you have anything interesting or out of the ordinary to say. You have to ace it on all levels to be chosen."

Just then, a collective gasp rippled through the crowd. The blond and beautiful Courtney had just appeared outside and was separating us into two groups: people with advance reservations and those of us without them. She corralled the lucky ones inside, then came back to make a disheartening speech to the rest of us. "We've got a capacity crowd, I'm afraid. Probably only three more of you will get chosen to participate in today's taping."

A few kids wandered off dejectedly, but most of us stayed riveted to the sidewalk, hoping for one of the coveted spots. "I can see I haven't scared many of you away," she said, laughing at her own joke. "I'll be out in a while to talk to a few of you." Then she left us again, ignoring the throng of teens trying to bribe her with everything from money to jewelry to baked goods.

The next half hour passed so slowly I could almost hear the seconds ticking by one at a time. Once, an intern came out and walked up and down the line, examining us and making notes on a clipboard. Brina, Zander, and I took off our coats and froze in the subzero temperature, hoping he'd notice our *Bliss*ed-out BeDazzler T-shirts, but he disappeared without so much as speaking a word to anybody.

"This is a total waste of time," I complained. "I don't think they even noticed us."

Brina cocked her head toward the front of the line, which Courtney was making her way through once again. "Oh, they noticed us all right," she said. "It's totally going to work."

Against all odds, Courtney stopped directly in front of us and scrutinized our chests. Brina's more than anyone else's, I might add. "What's with the Bliss thang?" she asked, looking pretty intrigued.

"Her mom was a groupie. Went by the name Bliss," Brina said, cocking her head at me. "Never introduced my friend to her dad, so we're trying to find him. He might be a big star from what we've been able to piece together."

"I'll tell you what," Courtney said, rereading the Ts. "We'll let your friend do a shout-out about it." She pointed a slender, manicured finger at me and said, "You get one sentence. Make it good."

Then Courtney turned back to Brina. "And you're our lucky fan of the day. Once your friend's shout-out is taped, c'mon inside," she said. "We'll save you a seat in the first row. You'll get a lot of camera time there." After sprinkling her very own version of fairy dust on us—exposure on national TV—Courtney spun around and disappeared back into the studios.

My feet were frozen to the ground in fear. Brina, on the other hand, was so excited she could hardly contain herself. She dug around in her backpack, things landing all over the sidewalk around her. Eventually, she hit pay dirt: her little makeup bag. Brina started taking every beauty product known to man out of it.

"Did you hear that? I'm going to be in your shout-out *and* the first row of *TRL*! My face is gonna be plastered all over the world!" Brina's version of heaven, my biggest nightmare.

I was really sweating by this point. I had never actually thought our plan would work, and now I had to face the consequences. "I don't think I can do this," I said, my heart palpitating at the thought of not only having to compose the perfect sentence in the next few minutes, but then having to deliver it on TV.

"Are you saying you're giving up?" Zander asked, taking my hand. "You're done with Dad quest?"

"No way," I said. "I want to find him more than ever."

"Then take a chill pill, Trace," Brina said as she went back to her million-step beauty regimen.

"I don't think I can. You know how I am about being onstage."

Zander took my hand and stroked it. "You're not on a stage, sweet cheeks. You're on a street. There's no point in freaking out. Just say, 'If you knew and loved Bliss way back when, you should get to know and love me—your daughter—now.'"

I nodded, considering his words. They conveyed about as much as you could in one sentence, and I thought I might be able to get it all out of my mouth without throwing up or stuttering. "OK, thanks," I told him. "But could you write it all down, so I don't choke once the camera's on?"

"Sure thing," he said, scratching the words onto a flowery little notepad that had fallen out of Brina's bag.

Just then, a couple of scruffy-looking guys walked down the line and stopped right in front of us. One carried a large handheld camera, while the other tried to tame the sea of cords attached to it. "You the groupie chick?" the guy with scraggly black hair and acne asked me, scratching his five o'clock shadow.

"Yeah, I guess so," I mumbled, not knowing whether I should correct him that it was actually my mom who held that title. I decided against it.

"Let's go over your shout-out before we actually get it on tape, OK?" He pointed the camera straight at my face and held up three fingers. "Here's how we'll do it: Three, two, one, then I'll point at you and you're on. While you're speaking, I'll pan across the shirts so everyone gets a good look at each of them. So go ahead."

"Uh, OK," I said, shuffling my feet and clearing my throat. "If you knew Bliss—"

"No, no, no," the cord guy reprimanded me. "All shout-outs start with your name and where you're from, and they all end with a 'Woo!'" He shook his head in disgust at what a *TRL* reject I was.

I took a deep breath and tried again. "Hi, I'm Trace from Winnetka, Illinois, and if you knew and loved Bliss way back when, you should get to know and love me—your daughter—now."

Both the cameraman and his assistant stared at me. They were really bummed out now. "You forgot the 'Woo!'" said the camera guy. He turned to his assistant. "They always forget to 'Woo!'"

"I swear I'll be much better once you start taping," I pleaded with them. "I perform really well under pressure."

"You get one last chance," said the camera guy. "Screw it up, and you're done."

Zander, Brina, and I lined up in a row. After a three count, I delivered my lines perfectly, along with a halfhearted "woo." I breathed a sigh of relief.

"Now all we have to do is wait," Zander whispered in my ear.

"Ha! Maybe that's all you have to do, but right now I'm expected inside the studio. Ta-ta, suckers!" Brina bounded away, looking so happy I thought her head might explode. I hoped at least her boobs would.

Zander and I retreated to a little pizza joint next door. There was no one else in the place, so we asked the guy behind the counter to switch the channel to MTV. "No problem," he said, sliding a slice and a Coke in front of us both.

We scarfed down the 'za and watched as Brina's face showed up again and again on-screen. Yea for her, I thought, this is probably the highlight of her life.

Just then, *TRL* went to commercial and my shout-out came on. I cringed at the sound of my voice and the close-up on my face. Zander sat there and beamed at me. "That was awesome!" he said. I was so mortified I put my head on the table and refused to move.

While I was busy drowning in embarrassment, *TRL* came back on. Carson was saying, "There are a few people on the line who may know something about this whole Bliss deal. Caller one?"

I finally lifted my head up. Zander looked at me and laughed. "What?" I asked him.

"Hot red-pepper flakes on your left cheek," he said. "Parm on your right."

I rubbed my face free of pizza toppings. "Do you think there's any way it's Bruce?" I asked.

Zander was nice enough not to immediately reject the idea, but a moment later any illusions I harbored about Mr. Springsteen actually admitting he was my father on *TRL* were shattered. Instead, a scratchy male voice told Carson, "I think I've found my Bliss—the chick with the long dark hair in the first row."

Carson ran over to Brina with the mike. "What do you think of that?" he asked her.

Brina did her famous hair flip and giggled. "It's absolutely blissful." Yuck, I thought, realizing too late she'd never get over being on *TRL*. And that meant I'd be hearing about it for the rest of my life.

"Let's try caller two," Carson said, as unflappable as ever. "See if she has something more interesting to say."

"Yeah, this is Trixie from Winnetka, and I just want to tell Trace her mother is gonna kill her if she sees this."

I practically choked on my pizza crust. I never considered that anyone who knew Bliss would actually be at home during the middle of the day watching *TRL*. The key thing I forgot was that Trixie was in a total midlife crisis, and tuned in every day with her four-year-old.

"Are you going to narc on her?" Carson asked Trixie.

"Nope," she said. "Just a friendly warning. And by the way, Good Charlotte rocks! Bye, Carson."

# CHAPTER
## 10

The next morning, Grandpa had magically turned into an alarm clock. A very loud one. "Get up, you lazy heads," he bellowed. "I have a big surprise for you today. And it's a doozy."

I rubbed my eyes and rolled over, hoping whatever it was would allow us to sleep at least three or four more hours. "That's great, Grandpa," I mumbled.

Grandpa pulled the covers off of me. "You are meeting a real, live dignitary today. So put on your fanciest clothes and let's get on the road."

I flopped my body out of bed and riffled through my suitcase. A second later, I held up a pair of dark denim Sevens and a sheer black T-shirt for his approval. "This is about as good as it gets."

He sighed and shook his head. "Well, OK. I'm sure Father Joe has seen kids wear worse."

Brina popped her head up from her pillow. "We're going to church? But it's only Thursday!"

Grandpa blew a seafood quiche burp her way. "No, even better. We're going to meet with my Jesuit friend at Fairfield University."

I jumped back in bed and pulled the covers over my head. "No need, Grandpa. I hate to break it to you, but I'm going to school in California."

"Not once you see my alma mater."

I shook my head vigorously. "Even after that, I'm afraid."

Grandpa stood his ground. "Care to make a wager?"

"Nope," I said. "My New Year's resolution is to stop stealing money from senior citizens."

"Good, Father Joe will love to hear all about your high moral standards. Let's go, kids. Time's a-wastin'."

We all reluctantly got scrubbed and ready for a supremely dull day with an old priest and my gassy gramps.

"Yesterday was obviously the high point of this vacation, Trace," Brina whispered as we got back in the car for yet another road trip. "And today will undoubtedly turn out to be the low one."

A couple of hours later, we pulled into the campus and Grandpa proudly pointed out everything there was to see. It took all of about three seconds.

"Isn't this place the shizzle?" Grandpa asked, staring at us in the rearview mirror.

"It's great, Grandpa," I said in a flat monotone. I was tired, bored, and achy from sleeping on the crappy bed at my grandparents' house. And I just wanted to get home and regroup so I could figure out what to do about the picture I'd found. The gears were totally spinning in my head—I had so many ideas I wanted to put into action.

"So you'll think about attending next year?" he asked, like a vulture preying on some poor distracted bunny.

"Not a chance," I said, snapping back to life before he had a chance to devour my serious reservations and spit back out an honest-to-goodness Fairfield freshman.

"Just wait until you meet Father Joe," Grandpa said, as insistent as ever that this rinky-dink school was the place for me. "You'll for sure be convinced after that."

Grandpa parked the car and led us through the heavy oak doors of Bellarmine Hall. Snowflakes swirled around our feet as we stomped our boots on the doormat.

"These Fairfield people must be really into hunting," I said, eyeing the large deer head mounted above the fireplace in the reception area.

"Very funny," Grandpa said, snorting his disapproval. "That's actually our mascot."

"You're a Beheaded Fairfield Deer?" I asked, peering back up at the unlucky animal.

"A deer doesn't have antlers," he not-so-patiently explained.

"So you're the Fairfield Moose?" It seemed an unlikely candidate for a mascot for a school in Connecticut.

"No, we're the Stags."

"Fags is more like it," Brina whispered in my ear.

I glared at her. Even if I wasn't coming here next year, that didn't mean Brina had the right to knock it. Especially since she wasn't going anywhere farther than the local community college the way things were looking now.

Before things dissolved into a bitch fight, a dignified-looking man in a priest's collar ran up to my grandfather and hugged him like mad. Next thing I knew, the guy was hugging the rest of us with the same kind of enthusiasm. "Hey, Joe!" Grandpa kept saying over and over, slapping the guy on the back in great wallops. "How long has it been?"

"Too long," Father Joe replied, smiling like an angel and ignoring the fact that he was probably going to have bruises from Grandpa's overly enthusiastic back pounding. "Far too long."

Father Joe turned his attention to me, holding me at an arm's length and taking a long look before grabbing me in another embrace. "And you must be Tracey," he finally said. "Your grandfather has told me so much about you. And it's such a pleasure to meet you."

"And you, too," I said, pulling back and smiling at this sweet man.

"I hear you may be joining us next year," Father Joe said, making small talk as he led us to the faculty cafeteria.

"I just might do that," I said, wondering if lying to a guy in a priest suit gave me an immediate pass into hell, or if I'd have a chance to explain how I simply hadn't been able to bring myself to hurt his cute little feelings.

Grandpa grinned and chucked me on the shoulder. "I knew you'd come around."

At the cafeteria, we were joined by a couple of students named Caitlin and Pat. Father Joe had recruited them in the hopes that they'd give us a better idea of the wild and crazy life of a Beheaded Moose. He shouldn't have wasted their time, I thought.

We were all chowing down on some pretty decent food—the best we'd had since touching down in Newark two days ago, with no seafood in sight, praise the Lord—while Father Joe regaled us with funny stories about when he and my grandpa were Fairfield students way back during the crustacean period or whatever prehistoric era it was. I was pretty surprised to realize I was actually having a good time.

Just as we were all finishing up, Father Joe excused himself. "Well, everyone, it looks like my time is up. I've got a meeting in five minutes."

Grandpa wiped his mouth with a napkin, tossed it on his tray, and delivered a frightening speech. "Kids, I've been worrying that this snowstorm is a bit much for the old station wagon to handle," he said. "But don't worry. I've arranged for us all to camp out in Father Joe's room tonight."

Zander, Brina, and I looked at each other in complete horror. Brina recovered first and plastered a big smile on her face. "Wow, won't that be a blast?" she said.

Caitlin practically choked on her Jell-O before coming to our rescue. "Mr. Tillingham, would you mind very much if Trace and her friends stayed at my beach house tonight? I'm sure it would give them a better picture of what college life is like."

I held my breath and nodded furiously. Who cares if I knew next to nothing about this girl? Anything had to be better than having a slumber party at a priest's house.

"Well," Grandpa said, looking like he couldn't quite believe we'd rather bunk with people our own age, "if they really want to."

"Oh, we do," I said, squeezing Caitlin's hand under the table. I turned to her and mouthed, "Thank you, thank you, thank you."

"I guess I'll just mosey on over to the library for a while, then," Grandpa said.

"Here's my phone number and address," Caitlin said, handing Grandpa a piece of loose-leaf. "We'll see you in the morning."

"I'll be by at eight o'clock sharp," Grandpa said, wagging a finger at us. "Don't make me wait."

"No problem," I said as he walked out of sight.

Caitlin and Pat got up from the table right after Gramps and Father Joe did, and the rest of us followed suit.

"Hide the trays under your jackets," Pat whispered. "This weather is too good to waste."

"What the hell?" Zander said under his breath.

"Just do as you're told," I said. "Those two just saved us from a night of pin the nail on the cross, remember?"

The five of us semi-inconspicuously shoved the bulky cafeteria trays into our coats and ran outside. A second later, Caitlin and Pat were halfway up Bellarmine Hill, whooping like maniacs.

"Huh?" Zander said, still not getting it.

As soon as our new friends reached the top, they whipped out the trays and came flying down the steep incline on their pseudosleds. It looked like a blast, so I started running uphill as fast as I could, leaving Zander and Brina eating my dust. Thirty or so tray rides later, everyone was whipped, cold, and totally content.

"That rocked, you guys," I told Caitlin and Pat. "I'm having more fun today than I've had in my entire senior year so far."

I looked at Zander's expression and backpedaled. "Except for all those great times with you, Zander."

Now Brina looked hurt. "And you, too, of course, Brina," I added.

Caitlin put her arm around my shoulder and squeezed me tight. "So come here next year and let the good times roll."

I looked away, embarrassed that we were taking up all her time when I had no intention of ever becoming a Beheaded Deer. "That probably won't happen, but I'm sure it would be fun."

"It would," Caitlin said. "I guarantee it."

After we were all sledded out, Pat pulled the campus shuttle around and picked us up. "No one's around today anyway. So I'm gonna blow off my regular runs and drive you guys down to Caity's house."

"Great, we get to ride around in the sped bus," griped Brina.

"Stop being such a cynic," I said, pinching her. "Just because this isn't *TRL* doesn't mean you can't have fun."

She scowled back at me but did as she was told. While I was busy not speaking to that crabby friend of mine, I tried to make small talk with our saviors. "So, how did you end up at Fairfield?" I asked Caitlin.

"I actually transferred here from Phoenix State sophomore year," she said. "It was weird, because I was positive PSU was the place for me. I mean, who wouldn't want to go to a college where there's year-round great weather, plus wave pools and taco stands on campus? Fairfield seemed totally lame in comparison."

"I wonder if there's still time to apply to PSU?" Brina mused, getting all excited at the thought of it.

"I wouldn't if I were you," Caitlin said, shaking her head. "All the freshman lectures were huge and taught by graduate students. And if you weren't in the right sorority, forget about having a social life."

"Didn't pledge well, huh?" Brina said.

"Actually, I did," Caitlin said softly. "I just didn't like excluding other people because of it."

I really like this girl, I thought. I've always considered all that cliquey stuff the worst part of high school, and have steadfastly refused to align myself with any single group. That way, no one could think a catchphrase like "jock," "brainiac," or "goth" defined my entire existence.

"Are you happy with how everything turned out?" I asked.

"Absolutely. I only wish I'd spent my freshman year here, too," she said as Pat pulled up to her house.

"I'll catch you guys later," he called after us. "Be sure to tell everyone the party's at the Stone Pony tonight."

"The Stone Pony?" I asked Caitlin as she wrestled to get her key in the nearly frozen lock. "As in the bar in Asbury Park?"

"Nope. All the student beach houses have names," Caitlin explained, finally prying the door open and escorting us in. "Pat and his rugby buddies are Bruce Springsteen fanatics, so theirs is called the Stone Pony. I swear, those guys know every ridiculous thing there is to know about that man. They go to all his concerts. Make an annual pilgrimage to Rumson to camp out in front of his house. Basically, they're insane."

My heart started to race. I'd just have to corner Pat tonight and see what he had to say about my little secret.

"What's the name of your house, Caitlin?" Brina asked.

"Home Away from Home," she said, shaking snowflakes out of her hair. "HAH! for short."

"Sounds just about right," Zander said, plunking himself down on the couch, putting his feet up on the coffee table, and flicking on MTV.

By eleven o'clock, the Stone Pony was wall-to-wall kids and the party was rockin'. Unfortunately, I was having a hard time cornering our host. Every time I got remotely close to him, he'd go do a keg stand or start making out with one chick or another. I had almost given up hope that I'd ever have a chance to pick his brain when I found myself standing next to him in line for the bathroom.

"Can I ask you something?" I said, feeling a little shaky and nervous. After all, this guy might have some brilliant ideas about how to go about proving my dad's true superstar identity.

"Sure, Trace," he said.

I looked around at the other people in line, trying not to lose my nerve. "In private?" I asked. Pat nodded while some drunken dickhead made a crack about how sixteen would get Pat twenty. As in I was jailbait and was planning to let Pat violate me in some way, and then he'd have to spend some time in the slammer. As if any of that might happen.

Pat took my hand and we pushed our way through throngs of kids until we were in his room. He got all comfy on the bed while I paced. "You're going to think I'm totally weird, but I was wondering if you could help me find my dad." The sea of words came spilling out of my mouth in a jumble. I was kind of surprised there wasn't some sort of bizarre alphabet soup left floating on the bedspread in the aftermath.

"Sure thing, baby," Pat said, pulling me down next to him and wrapping a beefy arm around me. Oh, shit, I thought. This guy really did think I wanted him, and that I was using a lame excuse to get into his pants. I pulled the picture from my back pocket just before Pat swooped in for a kiss. "Check this out," I said, popping back up off the bed.

"No freakin' way!" he yelled, standing up to high-five me. "You've met the Boss? In person? That fucking rocks, dude!"

Though I'd never really thought about it before, I guess I do look a little bit like Bebe did at my age. "Actually, no," I said, totally bursting his bubble. "That's my mom in the picture with Bruce."

Pat flicked on the overhead light and examined the photo more closely. "Oh, cool," he said. "She's with the lead singer from that Springsteen cover band, too."

"She's with who?"

"The dude from Born to Run," Pat told me. "They're like that Neil

Diamond tribute band Super Diamond. Totally reverent about the whole thing."

Now, there was an interesting piece of information. I had kind of ig-nored the other guy in the picture after Brina and I collectively decided he was nothing more than Bebe's conduit to Bruce—I'd preferred to concentrate on the two lovebirds instead. "You know this guy's name?" I asked, more interested now that I realized the dude might hold the key to Bebe's secrets.

"Hmmmmmm," Pat said, tapping the side of his cheek. "I always hear people refer to him as the Boss-alike—he's such a carbon copy of Bruce."

Think. Think! I mentally urged Pat. This Boss-alike guy might be able to get Mr. Springsteen to own up to being my dad. I stared into Pat's eyes, trying to will him into coming up with a name. A moment later, he snapped his fingers.

"If I remember correctly, it's Mac. Mac Donald," he said, sounding unsure. "No, that doesn't sound right. Maybe it's Mac Donnelly."

OK, I thought. Now I have a possible witness to interrogate. I couldn't wait to get home and Google the guy and his band.

"Or is it Mac Donohue?" Pat mused.

So I'd have to try Born to Run plus all three names: the unlikely Mac Donald, Mac Donnelly, and Mac Donohue. At least I was headed in the right direction.

"Do you happen to know where this guy is from?" Since Pat wasn't even sure about the Boss-alike's real name, I wasn't expecting him to have the answer, but thought it was worth a shot, anyway.

Pat cocked his head. "I think they're based out of San Diego now."

"Now?" I asked. "Where were they before that?"

He smiled and slung his arm around me again. "New Jersey, of course."

We walked out of the bedroom arm in arm, and I stood on my tip-toes and kissed Pat's cheek in gratitude just before he took off down the hall. And that, of course, was the exact moment Zander spotted me. It seems he'd been searching high and low for quite a while.

"Hey, Z," I said, hoping he'd missed the suspicious-looking scene.

"You really took to this place quickly, didn't you?" he said, practically spitting the words through his teeth. OK, so apparently he'd seen everything and jumped to conclusions.

"It's not how it looks."

"How stupid do you think I am?"

I grabbed his hand and held on tight, even though it was clear he wanted no part of me. "I don't think you're stupid at all. Pat's a big doofus, and he did try to hit on me, but nothing happened," I said, a hint of desperation creeping into my voice.

"And that's why you kissed him on the way out of a dark bedroom? To thank him for hitting on you and being a big doofus?" Zander finally broke his hand free from my vise grip.

"No, no, no," I said, shaking my head and wishing I was a little less buzzed so I could explain everything more clearly. "I took him aside to show him the picture of Bebe because he's such a Springsteen fanatic. I thought he might have ideas about figuring out if Bruce is my dad or not."

"And?" Zander crossed his arms and tapped his foot impatiently.

"And he actually knew who the other guy in the picture is, along with where to find him," I said, still a little awestruck by the whole thing. "Now all I have to do is interrogate the guy and voilà! I'm bastard chick no more."

"Cool," said Zander, seemingly ready to forgive and forget now. "Good work, Trace."

We rounded up Brina, who had attached herself to the brawniest, dumbest rugby man alive, and relayed my discovery. Everyone was in a celebratory mood: me, because I had one more lead in the search to find my dad; Zander, because he was now ninety-nine percent sure I hadn't cheated on him with sweet but dopey Pat; and Brina, because she'd finally ended her scooping drought and was making out happily with Mr. Rugby Man.

Around midnight, Pat and his buddies organized bat races on the beach. Zander and I somehow got separated and ended up on opposite teams, pitted against one another. True to form, Brina refused to participate, preferring to hang on to her dude's arm and watch us make fools out of ourselves.

"You're going down," Zander said to me before it was our turn to chug. Apparently he wasn't completely over my imagined indiscretion quite yet.

"Not if you do first," I said, winking at him and trying to diffuse any leftover hurt feelings.

We both slammed our beers equally fast and twirled ten times around the bat together. Zander kept his equilibrium despite the dizziness and ran straight across the finish line to seal his team's victory. I, on the other hand, ended up stumbling into the freezing waves.

"I kicked your ass!" Zander was whooping when I came up soaked to the gills.

"Give her a break," Pat said, wrapping me in a towel like a knight in shining armor. I tried to shrug him off so Zander wouldn't get mad again, but Pat steadfastly stuck by my side.

"Sorry," mumbled Zander, patting my back and adding, "But I did whip your butt."

"Whatever," I said, my teeth chattering nonstop.

I sloshed my way back up the beach. After she high-fived me, Caitlin grabbed my hand and led me to her house a few doors down. "You look like you could use some warming up," she said once we were inside, offering me some cozy sweats and a cup of tea.

"You're right," I said, shivering uncontrollably. "Thanks." I turned around and peeled off my wet, frozen things and replaced them with her warm, fuzzy ones. "Caitlin, what's your favorite thing about Fairfield?"

She started ticking reasons off her fingers. "Cool people, living at the beach, being close to New York City, small classes," she said. "And other special stuff, like the outdoor mass during parents' weekend. My father, especially, wouldn't miss it for the world."

I sighed. Just another thing I'd never share with my dad.

"You don't have to go to it, of course," Caitlin added quickly, probably thinking I was anti-organized-religion.

I don't know why, but I started spilling my guts to her. She poured us cup after cup of steaming tea while I blabbed on and on about Bebe, my nonexistent dad, and how Brina was always in the spotlight and how I felt so damn hunchy next to her.

"Trace, I want to change my answer," Caitlin told me after I was done purging my soul. "My favorite thing about Fairfield is that it just feels like home."

I had to admit, she had a point. If this was the true Fairfield—traying, beach parties, bat races, and staying up half the night with potential lifelong friends—I could certainly think of worse places to end up. I fell asleep wrapped in the comfort of a warm blanket and kind words, thinking I might have to give more serious consideration to my college choice.

But when I woke in the morning to the ten-below gusts rattling the rafters, any fleeting thought I might have had about actually attending Fairfield flew out the window. Sun and sand, I thought. That's where I'll be spending my next four years.

I shook Zander and Brina awake. On our way out, I wrote a note thanking Caitlin and Pat for their hospitality and left my e-mail address in case either one wanted to look me up in the future.

"Yesterday was so much fun, wasn't it?" I said as we hopped in Grandpa's car.

"If you like the clean-cut, boring variety," Brina said, rolling her eyes.

"It's my favorite kind," I said, feeling defensive, though I wasn't quite sure why.

"Moving right along," Zander said, interrupting our little catfight. "Let's decide what kind of a rockin' New Year's Eve we're going to have tonight."

"Can't we just stay in?" I whined. "I hate New Year's." And I have good reasons. Number one: Last New Year's Eve, Brina threw up on my shoes. Number two: The one before that, Reece cried on my shoulder all night because stupid Stu the wrestler had broken up with her. Number three: The one before that, Brina made out with my boyfriend at midnight. She claimed she was so drunk, she thought he was someone else. It was a likely story.

"Get your party shoes on, kids," Grandpa said, beaming at us in the rearview. "Because we're all going to the senior center's multigenerational New Year's party tonight, and it's gonna be a doozy."

"Oh, my God, things are going from bad to worse," Brina muttered under her breath.

# CHAPTER
## 11

All day, Zander, Brina, and I tried to figure out a way to get out of the party. We considered feigning stomach poisoning from the cafeteria at Fairfield, but later rejected the idea when we realized Grandpa had eaten the exact same meal. We were still in the midst of a serious brainstorming session when Grandma called us to leave.

"It's only five o'clock, Grandma," I called back. "We don't have to go yet, do we? I mean, the party probably won't get cooking until after ten, right?"

She popped her head inside our rapper room. "Didn't I tell you?" she said, flitting about in her surprisingly cool Lucky jeans, Candies, and off-the-shoulder top. "The party is from five thirty until nine thirty. Some of the older and younger folks need to get to bed way before midnight."

So much for our conspiracy. We all reluctantly got dressed and piled back into the Country Squire.

"I am totally whipped," I complained to no one in particular.

"See? That's why we have the early-bird hours," Grandpa explained. "So people like you can still enjoy the party."

Inside the sterile confines of the senior center, a DJ who looked like he was about a hundred years old was spinning tunes. Though we tried to sit it out, being cynical and making snide remarks about everyone out there shaking it on the dance floor, we finally caved in to Grandma's pleading and Macarena-ed like maniacs. After that, we moved on unashamedly to the Chicken Dance, the Electric Slide, and the Hustle. It was actually hot, sweaty, crowded fun. Surprise, surprise.

"I take it back, Zander," I said. "I don't hate New Year's anymore."

He smiled and leaned against the wall, pulling me back with him. "Told you so."

Brina took one look at us pawing each other and moved on to greener pastures. "I'm on the prowl. See you lovers later!" She vamped over to the other side of the room. When I looked up a minute later, she had a crowd of admirers trying to impress her. Granted, they were all still in diapers, due to either extreme youth or old age, but it was still better than watching us make out, I'm sure.

At 9:20, the DJ announced that it was almost time for the normally dreaded countdown to the New Year. "I better head to the bathroom now if I want to get back in time for my smooch," I told Zander.

"No problem," he said.

I threaded my way through the crowd, only to find that practically every little girl and old lady in the place had the same idea as me. I sighed and did the only thing I could—crossed my legs and waited my turn. Frustrated, I checked the clock, my watch, and the position of the moon every few seconds. For the first time in my life, I actually wanted to be in the mix when it hit midnight—well, fake midnight at this party—and this lousy line was probably going to keep me from getting there.

Finally, an open stall. I hovered over the seat, thigh muscles burning, and finished as fast as I could. On my way out, I paused just long enough to run my hands under the water and check my hair. But maybe I should have washed with soap. Or put on some lipstick. Or read some of the graffiti. Because the minute I got outside the ladies'-room door, my right foot slid out from under me and I landed— SPLAT!—in a puddle of Chunky Puke soup. A little girl was still heaving next to it and crying into her grandmother's skirt. "But I only had one bag of gummy worms, Grandma. Usually it takes me at least two packs before I throw up."

I wanted to cry, too. The moment I had been waiting for just wouldn't be quite as romantic with me smelling like Eau de Vomited Neon Night Crawlers. Sighing, I pushed my way back into the bathroom and began wiping globs of colorful gel balls off my clothes. I even put a quarter in the vending machine and bought a cheesy spray deodorizer. I spritzed the offending parts of me and sniffed. I smelled like a new car that had been barfed in.

I'll just have to make the best of it, I thought, and plastered a smile on my face. I started winding my way back through the crowd as the countdown started. "Ten, nine, eight, seven, six, five, four, three, two . . ."

Just as everyone yelled "one," I made it back to where Zander was standing. It just so happened he was whispering something in Brina's ear at the time. Nope, I said to myself, I will not get jealous. I repeated it over and over in my head, like a mantra. I will not get jealous, I will not get jealous, oooooommmmm, oooooommmmm, oooooooommmmmm.

And I was doing a great job at keeping my cool until I heard Brina ask him, "Do you think Trace found out about our little thing?"

"I hope not," he said, and hugged her.

"Found out about what?" I asked, not sure I wanted to hear the answer.

"The three blow jobs I gave him when you were out running," Brina said, laughing.

"Yeah," Zander added. "We filmed it all for that new video series, *Friends Gone Wild*."

"Fuck you," I said to him, so entirely sick of the whole flirty-flirty thing those two had going. Admittedly, knowing my dad walked away without a backward glance didn't help much, either. Even if he was a rock god, that didn't give him the right to abandon me and my mom.

"Give me a break, Trace," Brina said. "We were just kidding."

"And fuck you, too," I told her, heading toward the door.

"You're going all bunny boiler on me again," she said, grabbing on to my sleeve. "Don't embarrass yourself."

I shook her off and kept going. "What part of 'fuck you' didn't you understand?"

"I'm not making up any excuses for you, Trace," she said. "This time, Zander's gonna find out the truth about your awful jealous streak."

"Have fun flirting with my boyfriend," I said over my shoulder. "Be sure to tell me how he is in bed. We haven't quite gotten to that point in our relationship yet, but I'm sure you will before the night's over."

"That's not fair," she said, looking hurt.

"Says you," I said, slamming through the exit. I knew I was going to have to just sit there until my grandparents and friends came out, but I was stubborn enough and pissed off enough to do just that.

"You are going to feel like such a jerk when you find out what you're blowing a fit about," Brina said.

"I doubt it," I called after her as she headed back inside. I actually would, later, but for now I was content to stew in my overreaction.

I didn't speak a word to my friends the entire car ride back to the house. When the g-rents tried to find out what was wrong, I pretended I'd been the one who'd gotten sick, not the little girl. And they believed me, mostly because I totally reeked by that point.

Back at the ranch, I stormed into the bedroom and slammed the door just to spite Brina. I couldn't even think straight. Sleep eluded me, though I pretended to be completely passed out when I heard Zander and Brina tiptoe in the room about a half an hour later.

"Don't worry—she'll come around in the morning," I heard Brina say. She was so wrong it wasn't funny.

I stared at the clock until it was six a.m. Then I packed up my things, woke Grandma, and told her I had to catch an earlier flight than my friends because I just remembered I had a big paper due at school on Monday, and called a cab. I ignored all offers of a ride and attempts to dissuade my foolishness.

At Newark Airport, I took out my journal and spent the whole flight composing an embarrassingly bad poem. The sum total of my efforts was contained on one measly page where I had scrawled lines, crossed them out, and rewritten them until I was semisatisfied with the finished product. It read:

Trying to be cool
Thinking that you're friends
All you're really doing
Is hurting me again
Trying not to care
Never even thinking

Go and do it all again
Never even blinking
Trying to get away with it
Being so abrupt
Having no compassion
Needing to grow up
Why hurt the person closest to you
By playing little games
Putting on your phony act
When inside, you're all the the same
All I can say
Is leave me alone
Both your hearts
Are made of stone

I reread my piss-poor work once more before we landed. I realized I was no Emily Dickinson. In fact, I realized I wasn't even on slp's level. He could always find just the right words to fit the occasion, even if they were someone else's.

When I dragged my body through the door three hours later, everything was still quiet in my house. Thank God, I thought. There was no way I wanted to talk to Bebe yet. I dropped my pack in the laundry room, and was tiptoeing my way upstairs when I *thunk*ed to a halt.

"We've got to stop meeting like this," Mr. Perry said with a grin.

"Have you been here all week?" I asked him, yawning.

"No," he said. "Actually, Belinda stayed at my place a couple of days. I needed to feed the fish and get my messages."

"Mr. Per—" I started to say, and then caught myself. "I mean, Mr. . . . Steve . . . Perry?" My tongue was getting all tangled up.

"I thought we were going for plain old Mr. Steve, since you can't seem to go whole hog and just call me by my first name."

"Right, Mr. Steve," I said, wanting so badly to ask him the question that had been rattling around in my head for days now—the one about whether he was slp, and if so, why he was spending every second of free time with my mother.

"What's up, Trace?"

"Nothing, nothing," I said, my balls shriveling up and running home to their mamas. "I just wanted to know how your week was."

"Honestly?" he said, his eyes practically twinkling. "It was my best Christmas vacation ever."

"That's great," I said, moving past him. "At least one of us had fun."

Before he could try to delve into what had happened on my trip, I ran up to my room. Closing the door behind me, I plunked myself down at my computer and typed in *www.borntorun.com*. I was rewarded with a guy selling Springsteen memorabilia and mobile homes in Alabama. I tried the *.net* extension. Nothing—the domain name was for sale.

I changed my tactics and typed in *Born to Run tribute band*. That led me to a bunch of pasty boys from Liverpool, England, who liked to pretend they were born in the U.S.A. None of them resembled Bebe's friend Mac Whoever-He-Was in the least bit.

Next, I tried *Bruce Springsteen tribute* and came up with pages upon pages of bands with names like Candy's Room, Tramps Like Us, Greasy Lake, and Spirits in the Night. And to think, just last week I didn't even know people like the Boss-alike existed, and today I was learning they were a dime a dozen.

Switching gears again, I Googled the name *Mac Donnelly*. No one who was even remotely involved in a Springsteen tribute band or appeared to be Bebe's age came up. I struck out again with *Mac Donohue*. Desperate, I tried *Mac Donald*. You can only imagine how many times our redheaded, striped-jumpsuit-wearing friend Ronald appeared.

Just before I was about to click off the computer, I took one last look at the Spirits in the Night band Web site. Clicking a recommended link brought me directly to backstreets.com, the Boss's unofficial Web site.

Surfing around, I quickly discovered that the "Loose Ends" section was where rabid fans went to find anything and everything related to Bruce. I figured I kind of counted as being possibly related to him, so I dashed off a posting requesting that Mac Donnelly (or possibly Donohue or Donald)—or anyone who knew him—contact me to help return something important that Bruce had misplaced the summer of 1986. I neglected to say that something was me.

Satisfied with my amateur sleuthing, I pulled down the shades, un-plugged the phone, turned off the computer, and threw the covers over my head. I was seriously considering hibernating until it was time for college to start when I fell asleep.

I woke up later wondering where the hell I was. Everything was pitch-black. I squinted at the alarm clock, finally making out that it was ten-something p.m. through glued-to-my-eyes contacts. January first was almost over. Next year, I vowed to trust my judgment and stay home.

"Mrowwooww." My stomach was complaining about the lack of food, so I tiptoed back down the stairs again, hoping Bebe had already gone to bed for the night. No such luck. She was sitting at the kitchen table, staring at what I *thought* was my BeDazzled pillowcase with *You the Shizzy* on it.

"This isn't funny, you know," she said, glowering at me in the dark. It almost looked like she had cat eyes. "And you had no right snooping into my business."

Uh-oh, this sounds bad, I thought. I went for the "Who, me? I'm in-nocent" routine. "I have no idea what you're talking about," I told her.

"This," Bebe said, holding up the pillowcase. "I found it in your backpack."

"What do you care if Grandma's gone BeDazzler crazy and talks like a retarded rapper?" I said, almost yelling now. "And why the hell were you snooping in my things?"

"For your information, I was being nice, doing your laundry," Bebe said. "Wait a minute. . . . Are you saying your grandmother made this? I'm gonna kill her!"

"For making a gaudy hip-hop pillowcase? You're nuts," I said, snatching it away from her.

"Look again, honey," Bebe said.

I stared down. Bebe, Bruce, and the Boss-alike stared back at me. " 'Who's Yo' Daddy,' " I whispered as I read the rhinestone lettering.

"That's what I'm talking about," Bebe said.

If I didn't think I was in such big, fat trouble, I would have laughed. "I am SUCH an asshole," I said, smacking myself on the forehead as I realized this is what Brina and Zander were talking about at the party last night, not sexual favors.

"Yeah, and so are your two best friends," Bebe said. "They've been ringing the phone off the hook all day. Wanted to make sure you got home all right."

"I'm just fine and dandy for a girl who's been lied to her whole life," I said bitterly.

"Just who do you think you are?" Bebe asked, her voice shaking.

"A near adult whose mom doesn't have the guts to tell her the truth," I said, disgusted with the whole mess.

"And you're nothing but a spoiled, disrespectful child who doesn't deserve such a long leash," Bebe said. Then she delivered the kicker. "You're grounded."

"Ha!" I snorted. I'd never been grounded in my whole life, and I didn't intend to start now. "That is such a joke, Bebe." A horrible thought popped into my head and I smirked, going for it. "In fact, *you're* such a joke. You were the lamest groupie ever created, and you're an even lamer mom."

The second I said it, I wished my comeback lobe had stayed in its coma. Bebe looked like I had physically hit her, and I couldn't have felt worse if I had. Eventually, she asked me, "Whoever said I was a groupie?"

"You? Your book jackets?"

"Oh, that," she said. "That's just a marketing thing, so people like you with very little imagination can have a nice, neat little label to hang on me."

Mr. Steve popped his head in the kitchen. Bebe and I continued to glare at each other. "What's going on, girls?" he said, looking from me to Bebe and then back again. "Want me to make some hot chocolate?"

"I was just on my way out," I said, not even taking the time to get my backpack or keys as I headed toward the front door.

Bebe followed me. "Trace, where are you going?"

"To sleep at my boyfriend's house." I don't know what gave me that idea, but now that I had said it, it sounded as good as any.

"Don't be stupid," Bebe said, grabbing the sleeve of my pajamas.

"Condoms take care of that kind of stupidity," I told her, walking outside to the front porch. "But I guess you didn't know that when you were my age." I couldn't believe how mean I was being to her—but I just couldn't seem to stop myself, either.

"I deserve more credit than that, Trace."

"Why?" I said, practically spitting the words out now. "You were stupid enough to keep my father from me my whole life. Why shouldn't I think you'd be stupid about birth control, too?"

I took one last look at Bebe's shocked face and ran away as fast as I could in the pink bunny slippers Brina had gotten me as a joke for Christmas. A cop car drove by, and I ducked behind a big oak tree. I figured I could probably get thrown in the loony bin for being in the streets wearing fleece pajamas and kiddie slippers at eleven o'clock at night.

Ten minutes later, I was staring at Zander's house trying to remember which window was his. I counted three in and threw a few pebbles at it. Nothing. I picked up a bigger rock and chucked it harder. Psych! His window was opening. Only . . . wasn't the guy in there a bit too small to be Zander? Oh, crap, I'd woken up his little brother. I jumped in the bushes and ducked.

"See, I told you. The Penguin is not here," I heard Zander saying. His brother was hysterical at this point, apparently convinced Batman's archenemy was trying to get into his room.

"Hey!" Zander yelled, sticking his head out the window and peering around. "Who's there? I'm calling the cops right now!"

I stood up and put my arms in the air. "It's just me, Zander," I said, feeling very, very embarrassed.

"Trace, why didn't you just ring the bell? It's a lot easier than getting your ass shot out of the bushes, which is what I intended to do next."

"I didn't think your parents would go for it," I said, hanging my head. "Not to mention I wasn't thinking very clearly after the huge brawl I just had with Bebe."

Zander laughed. "My mom and dad are out of town until tomorrow. Meet me at the back door."

I walked around the house and Zander led me up inside.

"You haven't seen the third-floor den yet, have you?" he asked me.

"Nope," I said.

It turned out to be more like an adult playroom with a pool table, Pop-A-Shot, Ms. Pac-man, Centipede, pinball machines, a humongous flat-screen TV, love seats with cup holders just like at the real movie theater, and a whole karaoke setup complete with a stage to perform on.

"And you bother leaving the house because . . . ?" I asked him, staring out the huge picture window at Lake Michigan.

"To meet cool people like you," he said, taking hold of my hand. "So tell me what happened. Why did you leave us hanging at the g-rents' house?"

"I heard you and Brina talking, and I assumed . . ." I trailed off, feeling like a fool. I just couldn't face dredging up the past twenty-four hours again.

Instead, I wrapped my arms around Zander's neck and kissed him passionately. He must have liked my answer, because he picked me up and plunked us both down on the love seat, where we continued our major lip-lock. This went on and on, progressively getting more intense until I started to think, What the hell? Why not just go for it? I practically told Bebe I was going to do it anyway.

"Do you have . . . any . . . you know . . . ," I whispered in his ear.

"Any what?" he asked, not getting my drift.

"In your wallet . . ." I trailed off again, hoping I wouldn't have to spell it out for him.

Zander sat up, flicked on the light, and looked straight at me. I covered my face with a pillow, completely mortified. I couldn't believe it. My virgin sacrifice was being completely, totally rejected. And I really *was* a virgin, unlike Brina's who-knew-when-she-actually-lost-it variety.

"Your motives aren't exactly pure right now," he told me.

"Obviously," I said. I mean, duh. Having sex is just about the antithesis of pure.

"I can't believe I'm even saying this, but sleeping with me because you're mad at your mother and disappointed we haven't found your father yet—isn't quite the motivation I was hoping for." Zander tried to pry the pillow off my head, but I wasn't letting it budge.

"What is, then?" I asked him, my voice muffled.

"I always thought it was supposed to be about two people who care about each other, wanting to make each other happy." Zander's voice was low and reassuring. "With no ulterior motives."

Maybe, just maybe, I'd remove the upholstery from my face before I turned twenty-one. I felt Zander get up, so I lifted the corner of the pillow up just a bit to see what was going on. He was standing in front of the big picture window, his head lowered over the neck of a guitar. His back was to me, and the moonlight made it look like he had a halo. Come to think of it, he had really earned one for not jumping my bones when he had the chance to. Zander strummed a few chords and started singing a John Mayer tune—the one about candy lips and bubblegum tongues.

When the song was over, Zander put his guitar down and sat back down on the couch. I peeked out from behind the pillow and saw him grinning down at me.

"But I never said we couldn't fool around." He threw the pillow on the floor and wrapped himself around me. Snuggling under the warmth of the blanket, we didn't come up for air until much, much later.

"By the way, nice slippers," Zander told me when we were all kissed out, not to mention various other verbs.

"You liked them enough to bite them off my feet, mister," I said, happiness bubbling up inside of me. I couldn't believe I had tried to seduce Zander in this goofy getup, and was more than grateful he'd put it all into perspective. Someday, we'd do it up right, complete with lingerie, mood lighting, and handpicked tunes. For now, though, I had some serious business to attend to—making peace with my mother.

"C'mon," he said. "I'll take you home."

The sun was coming up by the time Zander drove me home. As we pulled in the driveway, I noticed Mr. Steve's Mini Cooper was nowhere to be found for the first time in months.

"Remember, Trace. Bebe probably feels as bad about this as you do. Be gentle with her."

"Thanks for everything," I said, giving him a quick kiss on the cheek. "I'll call you later."

I walked quietly through the front door. Bebe was still seated at the kitchen table in the same spot where I had left her the night before. I pulled a chair up next to her and ate my words as best I could.

"I am so sorry about what I said last night. It wasn't right and it wasn't fair."

Bebe looked up from her cup of coffee. Her eyes were so puffy she was barely recognizable. "I'm sorry, too, Trace," she said in a hoarse voice. "Sorry for ruining your life. When you're eighteen, you don't expect something that happens one night to have an impact on the rest of your life."

Even though I'd always admired Bebe for taking the high road—as in not scraping her uterus free of me while she still had a chance—the all-encompassing impact of her decision hadn't hit me until this moment. "You were so brave to keep me, Bebe," I said, taking her hand in mine. "I probably haven't thanked you enough for it."

Bebe smiled, though she still didn't look the least bit happy. "I never considered for a second having it any other way," she said.

"Are you ready to tell me what really happened?" I asked, scared of what I might hear.

She took a deep breath. "Trace, it was so long ago."

"An explanation," I said, feeling stronger and more determined by the minute. "You owe me at least that much."

Bebe ran her fingers through her already messy hair. "I was in love with your dad, so naturally we did the things young lovers do—"

"I don't want to hear it," I sang. "Lalalalalalalalalala." My mom's sex stories. I mean, how gross can you get?

Bebe let the tiniest laugh escape from her mouth and I thought, She's gonna be OK. Thank God. For a minute there, I thought I'd sent her over the edge.

"The condom broke—"

"Let's just skip the naughty parts and move on," I interrupted, looking at Bebe in what I hoped was an encouraging, c'mon-spill-your-guts kind of manner. "How did you go from being in love to never being in the same room again?"

"After an awesome concert at Giants Stadium, I told your dad I had something really important to tell him. Something that would change his life," Bebe said, eyes misting over. "I had spent a whole week trying to figure out the best way to break the news I was pregnant to him. I wanted to soften the blow as much as possible because I knew it was going to take some serious rearranging for us to be together."

I was hooked. This was a great story. Then I remembered I already knew the ending, and it wasn't a happy one. Still, I needed to know the truth once and for all. All of it. "Why was that?"

"Like I told you on Thanksgiving, we were going in different directions."

"No way is that enough information for the open and honest conversation we're supposed to be having," I said, putting my foot down both literally and figuratively.

Bebe stared down into her coffee some more, then sighed deeply before plunging ahead. "OK, you win. Here's what really happened. I was headed off to college and he was planning a tour of Europe. We hadn't uttered the *L* word yet, but I was pretty sure he felt the same way I did. So being young and naive and, quite frankly, stupid, I started my confession with those three words."

"And then what happened?" I said, breathless by this point. I could just picture the scene: Bruce and Bebe under the stars of a now-empty stadium as she declared her love to him.

"And then the bastard totally freaked out," Bebe hissed, slamming her hand down on the tabletop so hard that coffee sloshed over the sides of her mug. "He went completely white, mumbled a bunch of unintelligible shit, and then finally spit out something about how we were getting too serious and needed to pursue our dreams separately. That he wasn't anywhere near ready to think about settling down, even though he loved me more than he ever believed possible. The guy actually had the balls to suggest we make a pact to meet back in four years to pick up where we'd left off."

"That was obviously before you told him you were pregnant," I said. "Surely he changed his tune once he found out?"

Bebe got up from the table and walked over to the sink. "Not really."

My eyes bugged out. "You mean he left and never looked back?"

"Sort of."

"Bebe, you're being totally evasive again," I said, staring her straight in the eyes. "Spit it out."

"This is so mortifying to admit," she said in a voice so low I could barely hear her. "But I kind of was never able to tell him."

"What the hell do you mean?" I said, my heart pounding so hard I thought I might pass out.

"Trace," she said, pleading with me now. "He practically sprinted away after I admitted my feelings for him. I was more pissed off and hurt than I'd ever been in my entire life."

"So you're saying you neglected to tell him you were pregnant because you were mad at him? Way to get back at the guy, Bebe," I said, balling up my hands into fists and shoving them deep into my pockets so I wouldn't be tempted to slug her. I could totally sympathize with all those convicts who claim they never meant to commit whatever heinous crime had landed them in jail.

Bebe's tears fell on the place mat in front of her, looking like tiny indoor raindrops. "Trace, it's not like it seems. After about a week of nursing my wounds and hoping he'd call, I realized I'd just have to suck it up, swallow my pride, and go tell him in person. But when I got to his place, I found he'd already packed up and left without even saying good-bye."

"Ever heard of using the telephone, Bebe?" What did she think I was, an idiot? How hard could it be to find an international superstar?

"This was before cell phones and e-mail and instant messaging, Trace. His phone was disconnected. He'd moved out of the summer place he'd been renting. I sent a whole handful of letters to his old address hoping they'd get forwarded to him in Europe, but I never heard anything back."

"Surely there was some way you could've contacted the guy, Bebe," I said, refusing to believe she'd been that easily deterred. "And if not, you could've gotten his management or lawyers or someone on his staff to pass the news along to him."

"What the hell are you talking about?"

I rolled my eyes at her. "You're telling me you couldn't find Bruce freaking Springsteen just because he was on tour? It's not like he went into hiding after you spilled the beans about being in love with him."

Bebe nearly fell off her chair laughing. "What in God's name gave you the idea you were Bruce Springsteen's daughter?" she asked, practically gasping for air. "Other than some seriously deluded fantasies?"

"You always mention his name every time you discuss my dad," I mumbled, feeling pretty stupid. And let down, for that matter. "And because on the back of the picture I have of you two together, you wrote *the love of my life* and dated it with the month and year I was conceived."

"Did you ever notice there was someone else in that picture, too, Trace?" Bebe was picking at the edges of a napkin now, leaving a trail of paper shreds in her wake.

"The Boss-alike?" I whispered, my eyes unable to focus on anything. My worst fear had just bitch-slapped me in the face, and the room was swirling around uncontrollably. "You're telling me my dad is just some loser who's obsessed with another man?"

Bebe shrugged, not knowing quite what to do with that one.

"So what's your excuse for not finding Macky-D, then?" I taunted Bebe. "Donnelly or Donald or Donohue or whatever his name is? Why didn't you drop the bomb on his parents or friends or whoever?"

"Believe me, I thought of that. I called every Donohue in northern New Jersey with no luck. What was I supposed to do?"

"Try harder," I hissed, kicking the table leg with my foot. My toes went numb and it just served to piss me off more. "And keep on trying until you found someone who could lead you to him."

"I tried as hard as I could," Bebe said, staring at me defiantly. "Your dad and his buddies had just graduated from college that summer, and all headed off for Europe together in one big pack once they'd made enough money painting houses. See? No employer to track down names and addresses from. And I had no clue where the other guys' parents lived, not to mention what their last names were. Eventually, I hired a private detective, but all that got me was a five-hundred-dollar bill I couldn't afford to pay. And after a while, I just gave up. It was almost easier that way. I'd already been hurt enough."

I stood up and shoved my chair back from the table. It was all I could do to keep myself upright—I was shaking so much. "All my life, I've wondered what I did wrong. Why I wasn't good enough to be loved by my father," I said, choking on my words. "And now you're telling me he doesn't even know I'm alive. That's the worst crime of all, Bebe."

She nodded. She must have known what she'd done was unforgivable. I stalked off to my room and packed my bags, vowing never to come back.

# CHAPTER 12

Brina picked me up an hour later. Together, we dragged my suitcases out of my house and into hers. The Maldonatis were nice enough not to ask any prying questions, though I'm sure Brina had given them the lowdown.

"I set up the air mattress for you in Sabrina's room," Mrs. Maldonati said as I walked in. "I usually have breakfast ready by seven. Let me know if you're on a special runner's diet or anything."

I hugged her, grateful to have such good friends in my life. "Thanks, Mrs. Maldonati, but there's no need to go to any trouble for me. I just appreciate your letting me stay here."

She smiled and brushed away some nonexistent lint off my shoulder. "We love you, and so does our daughter. You're practically family."

Brina had cleared out a drawer and part of her closet for me, so I started putting my stuff away. She sat down at her desk, pulled out the ceramic heart, and handed me a piece of notebook paper.

"I wanted to tell you yesterday, but you were still mad at me. . . ." Brina said.

"Let me guess. The mail slot again?" I asked her.

A huge smile spread across her face. "Yup. Slp's better than ever."

I unfolded the note and read:

*I like the way you roll the dice*
*Always put my bets on you*

*But I can't gamble my life away*
*Maybe you should take a chance on me*
*slp*

"It's kind of like a challenge, isn't it? Like, come and get me if you dare," I said. "I love it!"

"The only question is, how should I go get him?" Brina asked me. "You have to be more understated with an older man."

"Brina, there's something I've been meaning to tell you about that." I felt more confident than ever that Mr. Steve was on the up-and-up. He and Bebe were acting like two crazy kids in love, so I couldn't imagine why he would be writing to Brina at this point. In fact, I had a wholly different idea about who slp might be.

"I know what you're gonna say, Trace, but let me make a confession first," she said. "Steven winked at me a couple of times before Christmas vacation and once he even told me he liked my outfit."

I ignored her complete and utter misconceptions about Mr. Steve. "Brina, what I was going to say is, don't you think it could be someone our age? Or even younger?"

Brina screwed up her face like she'd just eaten my grandmother's seafood potpie. "Junior meat? Perish the thought," she said.

Little did she know the guy I suspected was slp wasn't a junior. He was actually sophomore meat. I decided that wouldn't go over well right now, so I filed the thought away for later and changed tactics. "Listen, I know for a fact it isn't Mr. Perry."

"How could you possibly know that?"

"Because he's dating someone seriously."

"Says who?"

"Says me," I said. I couldn't quite bring myself to tell Brina about Bebe and Mr. Steve's relationship. I was afraid my new bunkmate might boot me because I'd been keeping it a secret for the past two months—and the last thing I needed was to be completely homeless. "Just promise me you won't do anything crazy. I guarantee you'll feel like a total fool if you do."

"The only one crazy here is you."

"Brina, just think about it logically," I said. "Even if it was Mr. Steve—which it's most definitely not—you couldn't possibly do anything about it until you graduate anyway. You'd get him fired, and you don't need a poor, unemployed, very-much-older-than-you boyfriend on your hands."

"Good point," Brina said. "I'll give it until the end of June, and not a moment later. Then I'll let him know I know, and we can come out of the closet."

"You don't even know the guy," I said, making a face at her.

"I know him well enough to know I could fall in love with him."

"Oh, please," I said, rolling my eyes. Brina knew Mr. Steve so *little* she had no idea he and my mom were all cozied up in bed right now.

"And what's with this 'Mr. Steve' business?" she asked.

"Just being goofy," I lied.

Later that week, Brina found me at my locker and punched me playfully in the arm. She looked flushed and was grinning like an idiot.

"I think I know who slp is," she whispered.

"Me, too," I said, surprised but happy that she seemed so into it. "So are you going to go for it?"

"Absolutely. Stu is so dreamy."

"Stu?" I said, bewildered. We were obviously not on the same page like I thought we were. "The same Stu we both love to hate?"

"Make that one of us," Brina said. "I don't hate him anymore."

"Why not?" I asked her. "I could give you a thousand reasons why you should." Even as I said it, I realized that as much as I disliked Stu, he was Brina's type times three, personifying every rotten quality she liked in a man. Arrogant? Yup. Cocky? Every inch of him. Lacking in the brains department? Stu was so brain-dead he couldn't even qualify for dumb as a post. He was more like dumb as toast.

"Don't even start," she said. "We just didn't understand him before."

"What's not to understand?" I asked, doing my favorite impression of him. "Duh, where's the keg?"

"Do you know what his nickname is?" she asked me.

I took a wild guess. "Asshole?"

"No," she said, scrunching up her face at me. "The Lion. Get it? S-L-P. Stu 'the Lion' Purcell."

"I don't think Stu would waste his time writing anonymous love notes." Not only was Stu a total A-list jock, but he had a horrible love-'em-and-leave-'em reputation. He had dated the entire cheerleading squad and most of the gymnasts this year alone. "In fact, I'm not even sure he knows how to write."

"That just proves how little you know about Stu," Brina said, shoving her hands on her hips. "I think he got sick of the meaningless hookups and wants something more from a girl. And that girl is me."

"Whatever you say."

It was so classic, Brina believing she was going to change a guy who so obviously had no interest in being changed. But my opinion didn't matter anyway. By the end of the day it was a done deal.

I walked to Brina's locker after my last class only to find her and Stu involved in a major lip-lock. I ended up following them home like a little lost puppy, walking three steps behind as they gazed into each other's eyes with lust. I wanted to puke.

When we got to Brina's house, I thought I'd try to diffuse their love-fest. "Hey, you guys want a snack?" I asked them.

"Oh, yeah," Stu growled, riffling through the refrigerator and cabinets. He resurfaced with a jar of maraschino cherries and a can of Reddi-wip.

"Feeding time!" Stu said, winking at Brina. He sprayed a glob of whipped cream onto a cherry and dangled it by the stem from his mouth, grabbed Brina around the waist, and pulled her close. She licked the whipped cream off the cherry, then popped it off the stem and rolled it around on her tongue. Stu spit the stem out in a hurry—on the kitchen floor, no less—and the two of them took turns sucking the cherry from each other's mouth. It was like a cheesy porn flick.

"Uggghhh," I muttered, and walked out of the kitchen, which they had long since forgotten I was in anyway. I headed upstairs and I stuck my head into Brad's room. He and Sully were there, cranking tunes and making a vague attempt at homework.

"Mind if I join you?" I asked.

Brad looked up and smiled, clearing a space on his bed for me. "There's always room for you, Trace."

"So where's your partner in crime?" Sully asked, stretching his long arms above his head and turning around in his chair.

"Downstairs devouring the biggest jock idiot in our class," I said. "It was too embarrassing to witness, so here I am." I flipped through Brad's CDs, finally settling on some Nickelback. Thought it would help us all let off some steam.

"Who's the lucky guy?" Sully asked me.

"Stu Purcell," I said. "Brina even thinks he might be the mysterious note writer."

Sully buried his head back into his history book. "There's no way it's him," he said. "That guy can't even spell his own name."

Looking at Sully's sad expression, I knew my suspicions had been right on the money. I was looking straight at slp. And boy, was he gorgeous—not to mention way smarter than that loser in the kitchen. I would just have to find the right time to convince Brina this one was worth breaking the rules for. Now was not that moment.

"Try telling Brina that. She won't listen to me."

"It won't last more than two weeks," Sully predicted, making long swipes in his textbook with a yellow highlighter.

"Let's hope not," I said, winking at Sully. "For all our sakes, right?"

He blushed a deep crimson. He knows I know, I thought. I decided it would be in all our best interests just to keep my mouth shut and see how everything played out.

The nonmeddling me lasted about two hours. That night when we were in bed, Brina couldn't stop talking about Stu, Stu, and more Stu. If I started discussing a specific class, she'd say how much Stu liked (or hated) that subject. If I mentioned my dad, suddenly Stu's dad was the next topic. After a while, I was convinced if I talked about anything in the universe—necrophilia! Ashtanga yoga! rutabaga farming in the Netherlands!—Brina could somehow make it have something to do with Stu.

"Brina, no offense, but can we stop talking about Stu?"

"Trace, that horrible jealous streak of yours is showing again. You have Zander. Now let me have Stu."

"You're welcome to him," I said. "I just think there's a guy out there who likes you more, would treat you better, and is completely right for you."

"You told me I had to wait until the school year is over to go after Steve, remember?"

"I'm totally not talking about Mr. Perry," I said, ready to drop the bomb. "It's Sully, Brina. Slp is Sully."

"Sully?" Brina said, laughing. "His initials are pls, remember?"

"Whatever. Chalk it up to dyslexia. It's him."

Brina was quiet. Finally, she said, "Ewwwwww. You really think so?"

"I know so," I said, disappointed by her reaction. "Brina, how can you even put the words 'ewwwwwww' and 'Sully' in the same sentence?"

"It's easy. Ewwwwww, Sully. Still in diapers. Too young. Sophomore meat. Not Stu."

With that, she dismissed the subject and went back to Stu-ifying me. My eyelids starting burning and I must have dozed off, because the next thing I knew, she was shaking me and asking, "Is that cool with you, Trace?"

"Hmmmmm? What? Oh, sure," I said, rolling over and closing my eyes again. I had no idea what she was talking about, but agreeing seemed to be the best way to get her to stop blabbing about Stu.

"Great. I knew you'd understand," she said. "Sleep tight."

I mumbled good night, already halfway back into my coma.

When I shuffled downstairs the next morning in my pink bunny slippers, Mrs. Maldonati and Brad were already at the kitchen table. I wondered briefly where Brina had gone so early in the morning.

"Are you doing all of your interviewing this morning, as well, Trace?" Mrs. Maldonati chirped brightly.

I was still half asleep, my head just barely bobbing above the teacup. "What?" I asked groggily.

"You know, the instant-admissions college fair," she said, bustling around the kitchen and cleaning every already-spotless crevice.

"Mmmmmmmm," I said, trying to be noncommittal. Had I been awake enough, I would have had to pinch myself to keep from laughing. First of all, as far as I knew there was no such thing as an instant-admission interview. And second, there was certainly no college fair like that at Northshore—today or any other day. The fact was, most college application deadlines had come and gone more than a month ago.

Mrs. Maldonati sat down next to me and touched my leg. "Something's fishy here, isn't it, Trace?"

"I don't think so, Mrs. Maldonati." I stared down into my tea, hoping the conversation was over.

It wasn't. Mrs. Maldonati pinched my cheeks in one birdlike hand, forcing me to look at her. "I smell a rat," she said. "Tell me what's going on."

"Nothing, Mrs. Maldonati," I said. "No seafood, no rodents. No wildlife whatsoever."

She dropped her hand long enough to dial Northshore's guidance office. "Yes, Mr. Perry, could you tell me which colleges are participating in the instant-admissions fair today?" She paused, turning beet red. "Yes, I see. No, I'm the one who's sorry."

Mrs. M. slammed the phone down and glared at me. "And I know someone else who's going to be very sorry when she gets home."

I have to tell Brina, I thought. She needs to come up with a good alibi or she's going to be grounded for life.

I ran to school as fast as I could. When I arrived at Brina's locker, panting and out of breath, I found her in much the same state, though not due to exertion. Brina and Stu were so seriously intertwined, it was hard to tell where she ended and he began.

I tapped on Brina's shoulder. "I need to talk to you."

Stu intervened, his beady little pigeon eyes staring back at me. "Not now. Can't you see I'm busy?"

I thought he might have mistaken me for one of his many gymnasts, so I tried again. "You are in deep doo-doo, Brina."

Stu glared up at me again, even more annoyed by this second interruption. "Can you tell your friend to beat it?" he said to Brina, sucking away at her beautiful neck and marking his territory like the dog he was.

Brina waved me away with a smile. "I'll catch you later," she said.

I retreated, pausing for a second to look back over my shoulder. Those two were locked into another appalling PDA. Two weeks would seem like an eternity at this rate. Oh, well, I thought. I tried. It was no skin off my butt that Brina was gonna have her ass handed to her later.

When I got back to Brina's house after school, all hell had broken loose.

"In the future, can you please be a good little friend and just keep your mouth shut?" Stu snarled at me as he was leaving. "Mrs. Maldonati just kicked me out. Told me to come back some other time."

"Poor baby," I said, slamming the door in his face. It was incredible to me that Brina couldn't see past his muscles and into the black hole that occupied his skull where his brain should be.

I ran up the stairs but stopped short at Brina's closed bedroom door. I could hear Mrs. Maldonati bitching inside. A few choice words like "liar," "lazy," and "irresponsible" wafted out through the walls.

Brad was in his room with his ear plastered to a glass he was holding against the wall. He waved me in. I crouched beside him, waiting to hear the scoop.

"This is awesome. Brina is sooooo busted," Brad whispered. "And so grounded."

Mrs. Maldonati burst out the door and stormed downstairs. A few seconds later, I started hearing thunk after thunk against the wall. When I finally got up the courage to find out what was going on, I saw that Brina had used every college catalog she'd ever received for pitching practice. The books now lay in a useless heap on the far side of Brina's room.

"What do you do for an encore?" she asked, giving me a fierce look.

"What did I do?"

"Don't play dumb with me," she said, practically growling now. "It's your fault I'm in this mess." She threw Antioch's viewbook straight at me. It missed my left knee by inches.

"It's my fault you didn't finish any of your applications on time?"

Brina looked at me like I was as stupid as Stu really is. "No. It's your fault I'm grounded," she said. "You really blew it."

"I blew it?" I said, pointing at my chest. "You're the one who blew it. I tried to warn you at your locker, but your leading man told me to buzz off."

"Why are you pretending you have no idea what happened here?"

she asked me. "Last night you promised to cover for me, and this morning you chirped like a little birdie."

"Ohhhhh," I said. So that was what this was all about. "I didn't even hear you. I was half asleep."

"All you had to do was say so." She threw another catalog at my feet. I picked it up. Valparaiso this time. "You really screwed me. Now I can't see Stu for a whole week."

"That's a gift, not a punishment." I couldn't help it. The words slipped out of my mouth before I could lap them back up.

Brina freaked out and threw four catalogs at me at once. I ducked just before they hit me in the head. "You know what, Trace? You've overstayed your welcome," she said. "Go home and leave me alone."

"You're kicking me out of your house for not backing up your incredibly stupid lie? What were you going to do, fake admissions letters and pretend to go to college next year?"

"Something like that," she said, and kicked the door closed. A second later she opened it back up just long enough to throw my stuff out into the hall, and then slammed it in my face again.

I gathered my stuff and went downstairs. "Do you think you could drive me home, Mrs. Maldonati?"

"Sure thing, honey. Just let me get my keys."

"I want to thank you for making me feel welcome," I told Mrs. M. as she looked for her purse. "I really appreciate it."

"And I really appreciate the fact that you didn't lie to me, Tracey," she said, wrapping her birdlike wings around me. I could feel every bone in her body. It was like hugging Mr. No-Skin, the skeleton in biology class. "Brina could use more friends like you."

"I don't think she feels that way right now," I said, hoping our fight would blow over quickly, though I wasn't counting on it.

"She'll get over it," Mrs. M. said, giving me another one of her hummingbird hugs as we pulled into the driveway right next to Mr. Steve's little car. "And listen. I know your mother's a little unconventional, but I do believe she means well. Don't forget that."

I dragged my stuff back inside, feeling like a frigging nomad. Leaving everything in the front hall, I plunked myself down in an overstuffed chair in the library and curled my legs under me.

I wondered how something so right could turn out to be so wrong. All my mom wanted to do that summer was have some fun before college started and look what happened instead. She got pregnant, became a single teenage mom, had her heart broken in a million little pieces. Much as I didn't want to give it to her, I realized Bebe needed my support, not my anger. So maybe I couldn't forget what she'd done. But maybe, just maybe, I could forgive her.

As if she'd read my mind, Bebe walked into the library and gave me a huge hug. "I missed you," she said, burying her face into my hair.

I hugged her back, hard and tight. "I missed you, too." And I meant it. Who knows what I would have done in Bebe's position? Possibly the same thing.

"I'm so sorry for everything," Bebe said, smoothing my hair like she always does when I'm upset.

"Me, too."

"So can we just move on?" There was a hint of desperation in her voice.

"Seems like the only thing we can do," I told her. "We've reached an impasse."

What I didn't tell Bebe was that there was no way I was giving up my search. I was merely taking her out of the picture. If I didn't expect her help, I couldn't get frustrated when she wouldn't give it to me.

Every day, I checked my e-mail for a reply from Macky-D, as I had taken to referring to him. But the lame response that trickled in over the next few weeks was like having my fingernails pulled out slowly, one by one. I had gotten back only four backstreets.com replies, none of which brought me any closer to solving my mystery.

A couple were polite "Sorry, can't help you, never heard of this Mac guy" kinds of responses. Some were encouraging, wishing me luck. One even said I sounded hot and then went on to list every sick thing he wanted to do to me.

Funny thing was, even as I was drowning in this "so close yet so far" quicksand, Brina had basically died and gone to heaven. Not only had she and Stu survived her grounding, but it ended up throwing massive fuel on their romantic fire.

"What are you doing this weekend?" Brina asked me on our way into the cafeteria for lunch.

"I thought we were hanging out at your house tonight," I said.

She shook her head. "Did I forget to tell you? Stu asked me to the Decades of Fun dance," she said. "We're going in wild seventies disco outfits. Why don't you bring Zander along and we'll all go together?"

"I'll pass," I told her. I was still a little miffed about being unceremoniously booted out of her house over a misunderstanding, as well as unceremoniously booted out of her life for a guy as dumb as toast. Stu had been so all-consuming lately, I only got to see or talk to Brina when he wasn't available.

I rolled my eyes when I saw Stu approaching our table. Brina stood up to greet him, and he grabbed her butt. "Hey, babe."

"Stu-u-u! I told you, not in public!" she giggled.

"The Lion needs his meat!" Stu growled, pretending to bite her fanny.

Ugh. I couldn't believe this total Neanderthal had stolen my funny, cynical best friend and turned her into nothing more than a freakin' hamburger patty. As they walked away arm in arm, I banged my head against the table. "Please let the Lion rip her heart out and eat it soon," I whispered to myself. "I can't take much more of this."

That night, I spent a very boring evening alone, clicking through channels trying to find a show that would take my mind off things. At about ten, I gave up in disgust and went to bed.

Shrill ringing shattered my slumber a couple of hours later. I fumbled around my nightstand, looking for the phone. I finally found it on the floor, pressed the TALK button, and croaked, "Hello?"

"Trace?" It was Brina. "You were right. Stu is a total idiot."

"Tell me about it," I said, giddy at the thought of having Stu out of our lives once and for all.

"Let's just say Stu's not exactly a poet. Or even a poetry lover," Brina said. "In fact, he didn't even recognize the verses from the slp notes when I quoted them to him during a slow dance."

"So that pretty much confirms he's not the one," I said, stating the obvious.

"Yeah, that's what I thought, too," she said. "But I wanted to make sure. So I asked him what his favorite poem was."

I couldn't wait to hear the answer. "And?"

"And Stu said the only kind of poetry he can stand is limericks. He's especially fond of 'There once was a man from Nantucket.'"

"Good God," I said, appalled once again by Stu's lack of brain cells. "So does this mean Stu is in, out, or somewhere in between?"

"Trace, he's so five minutes ago," Brina said, taking a deep breath. "I'm sorry I let him come between us. I got a little carried away, thinking he was my slp in shining armor."

"Happens to the best of us." Hey, I thought, I'm getting really good at this forgiveness thing. First Bebe, now Brina. Who next—my dad? "Was the dance fun otherwise?"

"Not really," Brina said. "I didn't even leave with my dopey ex-boyfriend."

Now that was not surprising in the least. "Pulling a Country Day Cotillion on me again?"

"It's February. Even I'm not that crazy," she said. "Actually, I hopped a ride with Sully and his date."

"You mean slp and his date. And Sully's not old enough to drive," I pointed out.

"Nope, but Brenda Kaplan is," Brina said.

"Whoa. She's a total hottie. And a senior, too. Go, Sully!" I hollered. He really must have been making a name for himself at Northshore if he was going out with Brenda Bedhead.

"Brenda Kaplan hot? She's so trashy," Brina snorted. "And so not Sully's type. He could do so much better."

"So much better, meaning with you?" I asked, baiting her.

"Dream on, Trace. I won't date a guy who has to pick me up on his tricycle," she said, sounding as convinced as ever. "Even if maybe, just maybe, he's the one who's been writing me incredibly sweet notes all year long."

"OK, have it your way," I said. "Miss out on an awesome boyfriend just because he was born a few years later than you wish he had been."

"Moving right along. Steven bought me one last chance to get into college next year," Brina said, ignoring my Sully comments. "At Mount St. Agnes, outside of LA. I'm interviewing for their High Potential

Program in a couple of weeks. It's basically a stomping ground for smart screwups. Wanna come and check it out with me?"

Now let me see: southern California in February or freezing, gray, windy, miserable Chicago? "I am so there," I told her.

"Good, 'cause Bebe already said yes and my mom already booked your ticket," she told me. "Brad and Sully are coming, too, to check out UCLA."

"Are you going to jump slp's bones there, where no one is looking and your mom is the one providing the transportation?"

"Once and for all, no," she said. "I like him as a friend and that's it."

"Have it your way."

"Hey, Trace?"

"What?"

"Do you really think it's him?"

"Yup."

"I'll just have to let him down easy in California, then," Brina said. " 'Cause it's never going to happen between us."

"Too bad," I told her. "Because Sully's about as primo as they come."

# CHAPTER 13

The day I was leaving for California, I trudged down the hall toward my locker after last period only to see a little vase of flowers, two plates with Oreos on them, two empty Dixie cups, and a carton of milk. Oh, and a pair of shoes that on second glance were attached to Zander's feet.

"This little going-away party is very cute," I said, plunking myself down cross-legged next to him. "And also kind of embarrassing."

"Yeah?" Zander poured himself a drink and took a gulp. A milk mustache appeared above his lip. "I hadn't noticed."

"Hey! Where are your manners?" I asked, holding up my empty cup.

"Equal rights, baby. Do it yourself," he said, looking at me kind of funny.

"What?" I asked, rubbing my nose and running my tongue along my teeth simultaneously, hoping no boogers or Oreo remnants were hanging out there.

"Nothing," he said, still staring.

"Did you lace these with pot or something?" I asked him. "You look stoned."

"Nope."

"Then what?"

"Trace, don't you ever read while you eat?"

"Sure, sometimes. But I was lacking material here, plus I would rather talk to you—" While I was blathering on and on, Zander turned the milk carton around so I could see the back of it.

"Oh . . . my . . . God!" I screamed. Everyone in the hall turned and looked to see what all the commotion was about. "Just a spider," I told them.

"So what do you think?" Zander asked me.

"I think you're crazy and amazing. How did you get Bebe, Bruce, and the Boss-alike on the back of this carton?" I asked him, looking for tape or glue. There wasn't any.

"I thought your mission could use a little kick in the ass," Zander told me. "So I pulled a few strings at O'Brien Packaging. It pays to be the CEO's son sometimes."

I took a closer look at the "Have you seen me?" ad Zander had created for me. It read:

> Lost: Mac Donnelly (possibly Donohue or Donald), aka the
> Boss-alike. Boyfriend of Bliss, father of Tracey. Missing for
> 18 years. Reward for information leading to his discovery.
> Call 1-800-ESTREET.

"How . . . what . . . when?" I was speechless, and didn't know whether to freak out or slobber all over Zander. It was the sweetest, most wonderful thing anyone had ever done for me. Also totally risky. I mean, what if Bebe was drinking milk one day and caught a glimpse of this carton? She'd go ballistic. And as it was, things were just starting to get back to normal.

"You ain't seen nothin' yet. Just wait until you hit the Wilshire Boulevard exit on your way to UCLA," he said. "And Trace? Just remember this when all those surfer dudes try to steal your heart away."

"This is just what I needed," I said, wrapping my arms around Zander and kissing him with Oreo-laced lips. "I love you."

The statement hung in the air for what seemed like days. I wanted to turn back time, rewind my words, and get back to the light 'n' fluffy fun we had been having a minute ago. Zander cleared his throat and gave me an awkward hug back. "Uh, yeah. Have fun. Call me when you get back."

"You got it," I said, going to give him a good-bye kiss. He turned his head at the last second, and it landed on his cheek.

By the time Mrs. Maldonati came to pick me up later that afternoon, I had worn a hole in my bedroom carpet from pacing so much. Why did I have to go and say that? Zander seemed totally wigged, and I hoped I hadn't scared him away forever just like Bebe had scared Mac away forever in the exact same way. On the long plane ride out to California, I finally decided there was no way that could happen—not because of three little words—and that a weekend away was probably what we both needed to let it slide and move on.

We got to the all-suite hotel in Laguna Beach at around ten o'clock local time—midnight to us. Not surprisingly, we were all keyed up and no one had any interest in hitting the hay except Mrs. Maldonati.

"Don't stay up too late, kids," she told us, shutting the door to her room. "Tomorrow's another day."

Sure, tomorrow was another day, but I didn't want to waste any precious time while I was actually in La-la Land. Already, the swaying palm trees and crashing surf had me feeling totally relaxed and happy. Besides, we had all weekend to play before Monday's college visits and I intended to have a blast.

"Let's go check out the pool," I whispered to the rest of the gang. Everyone grabbed a suit and sneaked out of the room as quietly as possible.

"Be back before midnight!" Mrs. Maldonati yelled as we ran laughing down the carpeted halls.

It was a little chilly outside but the hot tub was warm and inviting, sending waves of steam into the cool night air.

"It's calling our names, Pete," said Brad to Sully.

"Yeah, now all we have to do is find some chicks to join us. No offense to you guys," Sully said, nodding at me and Brina.

"None taken," I said.

Brina and I walked into a cabana and changed into our suits. "How does this look?" Brina asked when she turned around.

I was speechless for a minute. "Great," I said when I finally found my voice. I looked down at my athletic two-piece, suddenly feeling very plain-Jane-y. Though I could actually do stuff in my suit—like move without exposing key body parts—it was clear I wouldn't be getting hit on in it. Not with Brina standing next to me in that thing.

In fact, people's eyes might pop out if she wore that to the beach tomorrow. I could just hear it on the evening news: "Today, thousands of eyeballs were found rolling in the surf on Laguna Beach. No one's quite sure what caused this strange phenomenon, but witnesses say the source of the optical exodus was a skimpy bathing suit worn by a Chicago tourist. Anyone missing an eye is urged to contact the station to ensure its safe return."

As we walked back to the hot tub, Sully whistled long and low.

"Stop ogling my sister," Brad said, punching him in the shoulder.

"I was just being appreciative."

"Since when do you have such bad taste?" Brad asked Sully, looking disgusted.

"Since he started dating the Bedhead," Brina said.

"Hey! That Bedhead was nice enough to drive you home when your meathead started macking on the only gymnast he hadn't sampled yet," Sully shot back.

I looked at Brina. "You never told me that part."

"That's because I didn't know about it," she said, staring out at the ocean.

Sully unsuccessfully tried to remove the foot from his mouth. "I'm sorry, Brina. I assumed . . ."

"Never mind, Pete," Brina said, shaking it off like a trooper. "Let's get this party started. Truth or dare." She pointed at Brad.

"Truth."

"What's your middle name?"

"You already know my middle name," he grumbled.

"Yeah, but I thought everyone else would like to share in the mirth."

"Salvatore, all right?" he said. "The second two-thirds of my name make me sound like a little Italian man with hair growing out of his ears. Bradley Salvatore Maldonati." He laughed despite himself. "Now you, Brina."

"Truth."

"Your moment of embarrassment now," Brad said, pointing at her. "Middle name, please."

"Everyone already knows mine, thanks to Grandma Ina at Thanksgiving, remember?" she said. "Maria. So if you're a hairy little Italian man, I'm a big-boned washerwoman. Strong like bull. Your turn, Trace."

"Truth."

"OK. Same question."

"Mine is really bizarre," I said. "And it doesn't exactly fit me."

"Like mine does?" Brad said.

"All right, already. It's Rosalita."

"As in 'Jump a little lighter'?" Sully asked.

"Uh . . . I don't know," I answered. "I have no idea what you're talking about."

"It's an old Bruce Springsteen song," Sully said, serenading us with the chorus of "Rosalita (Come Out Tonight)."

Brina and I stared at each other, our mouths hanging open. "The Boss-alike strikes again," I said.

"Bebe must have really loved him," Brina said, practically swooning.

"Totally," I said, relieved my mom wasn't crazy enough to name me Rosalita without a damn good reason. "Now you, Sully. Truth or dare?" I asked him.

"Truth again."

"Let's make this thing go full circle. Your middle name is?"

"Liam," he said.

Brina perked up. "That's a great name," she said. "Peter Liam Sullivan."

Sully and Brad looked at each other and laughed so hard I thought they might explode. They would calm down for a split second, only to go into hysterics again the next.

"Just what is so funny?" Brina demanded, completely pissed off now. This made the boys laugh even harder, and Brina get even madder. She jumped out of the hot tub and wrapped a towel around herself.

"Where are you going?" I asked.

"For a walk," she growled. "Alone."

"C'mon, Brina. Nobody's laughing at you," Sully said, hopping out of the tub. My God, he had a gorgeous body, complete with six-pack abs. If I were Brina, I would have attacked him long ago.

"No, Brina," Brad teased. "We're laughing *with* you."

"Yeah, right," she said, stalking away toward the beach.

Sully caught up to her and draped his arm around her shoulder. "I'm coming along as protection," he said. "You can't wear that micromini bathing suit alone in the middle of the night. You'll get attacked by some psycho."

"And this way you can attack me instead?"

Sully frowned and took his arm off her shoulder. "Don't flatter yourself," he said, walking back toward the hot tub.

Brina turned around and sucked it up. "Sully, you're right. I need a bodyguard. I'm sorry for being such a bitch." She hooked her arm around his. "I'd love the pleasure of your company."

"Well, that's all she wrote," I said. "I'm going to bed, Brad. See ya in the morning."

"I'm coming up, too," he said, reaching his arms over his head and letting out a humongous yawn.

I heard the bedroom door creak open at six a.m. I popped my head up and smiled at Brina, the dirty rotten stay-out. "OK, spill it."

"There's nothing to spill," she said, sitting down on the bed and rustling around in her suitcase looking for jammies. "We walked; we talked; we swam."

There was a knock on the wall from the next room. "C'mon, Brina, tell her the truth."

She banged back, laughing, "That is the truth and you know it."

"But you know you want me," he said.

"Oh, yeah. You're my number one fantasy man," she said, crawling into bed.

I rolled over to look at her. "This is how you let him down easy?"

"Look, I made it clear we're just friends," she said. "I don't need to go and embarrass the guy by spelling everything out. We're totally chill."

"I think you like him," I said, hoping it was true. "You do, don't you?"

"Don't think so," Brina said, sticking her thumb in her mouth and sucking it like a baby.

"Then you just don't know it yet," I told her, rolling back over and facing the wall. "You were just flirting like crazy."

She hit me over the head with her pillow. "I was not."

"You're my number one fantasy man, Sully, ol' Petey, ol' boy," I said, doing an imitation of her. "I want to lick whipped cream off your ripped abs. I want to massage your pecs. And just wait until I kiss your hard, manly—"

Sully peeked his head in our door. "Sounds good, Trace. You name the time and place."

"I'll let you know," I said, embarrassed at being caught.

"I'll be waiting."

Once he was gone, I said to Brina, "I just might take him up on that sometime." I wouldn't—or should I say couldn't, not with Zander waiting back home for me—but I wanted to gauge Brina's reaction.

I got none. "Shut up and go to sleep, Trace."

"No problem, lover girl."

It was nearly noon before any of us got out of bed. Mrs. Maldonati had already cleaned the tiny kitchen in our suite seven times by then, and finally went out for a walk by herself in disgust.

"Let's get out on the beach, girlfriend," I said, shaking Brina gently to wake her up. "Just look at all those guys we need to scope out."

Brad popped his head in our room, brushing his teeth. "And all dose girlsh."

"What did you just say, doofus?" Brina said, finally lifting her head off the pillow.

Brad spit in the bathroom sink and rinsed his mouth. "I said, 'And all those girls.' Let's get moving, Peter."

This sent Brad and Sully into hysterics again. Brina gave them a look and slammed the door to our room shut. She reappeared a moment later, wearing lots of makeup, that hypnotizing swimsuit, and chunky high platform sandals. "All ready to wow the boys," she said.

I surveyed my getup: Adidas flip-flops, the same athletic suit as the night before, and my hair swept back into a casual ponytail. "This should be fun," I muttered, envisioning a day of boredom while Brina toyed with every surf god on the beach.

"You look cool—don't worry," Sully whispered in my ear, putting his arm around me.

"Thanks for the encouragement," I whispered back. I was afraid I might actually start crushing on Sully myself. He was sweet and sexy, and knew how to make a girl feel good. Brina was so bananas to write him off just because he was a little younger than us.

"Let's hit the road," I said to my partner in crime. We hiked down the road to the beach lugging towels, sunscreen, trashy magazines, and a small boom box. I felt light and airy, springing down the street grinning at everyone who passed. Brina, on the other hand, was back to beached-mermaid status. Her sarong-and-suit getup looked great but made it hard for her to move faster than a turtle.

I was getting exasperated. "The sun's gonna set before we get there."

"Shut up," Brina said, giving me a sweaty, pissed-off look. "I'm doing the best I can."

Eventually we got to the beach and scoured it, looking for just the right spot. "Over there," I said to Brina. "That's it. Next to where the surfer dudes have taken up residence."

We dropped our stuff and got comfy. Brina arranged herself to look like a *Sports Illustrated* swimsuit model, leaning back on her arms with her legs crossed, tummy tightened, and boobs thrust forward for everyone to see.

"How do I look?" she asked me.

"Obvious," I said. In seconds, I was sure every guy on the beach would be circling around her and drooling.

"What's that supposed to mean, Miss Natural Beauty?" Boy, she was in a pissy mood today.

"Nothing," I told her. "Forget it."

We watched the guys hit the waves for a while until one wearing a blue O'Neill wet suit plunked his board and himself down. Next to me. "Hey, you surf?" he asked, patting my leg with a damp hand.

"I haven't, but I'd love to try," I said.

"Then I'd fully love to be your teacher. The name's Dusty."

"Trace." I stood up and shook the sand off of me. "Let's do it."

Brina couldn't stand the lack of attention. "How about teaching me, too?" she pouted, arching her back even more.

"You wouldn't last three seconds out there," Dusty said, taking one look at her and realizing she wasn't up for the challenge. "I'll get one of my crew to babysit you while Trace and I hit it."

Dusty waved a tall, dark-haired guy over and had a little conference with him out of hearing range. A minute later, Dusty introduced him to Brina. "Cody, meet your new best friend. New best friend, meet Cody."

Instead of slobbering in response to his good fortune, Cody looked bored. "You owe me, dude. Don't trash my board."

"Trace, I'm gonna let you in on the secret of surfing," Dusty said as he showed me a few moves on the sand. "But before I do, you have to promise not to tell anyone."

"I promise."

"OK, here it is," he said, looking around to make sure no one was listening. "Get up and stay up."

"Thanks," I said, punching him in the arm.

"That really is the secret, Trace. If you can do that, you're surfing."

"Can we get in the water now?" I said. "I'm totally psyched."

"Not until you start sounding like the real deal," Dusty said. "So you're amped."

"What?"

"Amped," he said again. "That's how we say it around here."

"OK, I'm totally amped," I corrected myself.

"Now you're talking."

Following Dusty's lead, I did the stingray shuffle into the water and paddled out into the waves. But as hard as I tried to stay on my feet my first hundred tries, I ended up taking doughnuts. Dusty said that was surfer lingo for getting eaten by wave after wave.

"Dude, keep trying," he said, encouraging me every time I wiped out. "Next time you won't get pitched for sure."

"I am not quitting until I get up at least once," I muttered, gritting my teeth. My competitive streak had kicked in big-time, and I was damned if I was gonna let the whole beach see me fail. I paddled back out behind Dusty and waited until just the right moment.

"C'mon, Trace," he called to me when it hit. "This one has your name all over it."

Dusty and his board went gliding along the water. Unbelievably, I was right there beside him. I was actually riding the wave—a real live surfer chick, stuck in the Midwest for only a couple more months until I could completely transform into my new persona.

"That was totally stylie, Trace," Dusty said when we reached the shore. I figured it was another one of those surfer sayings, along the lines of "That rocked."

"What a fantasy," I said, grinning like a complete idiot.

"My specialty," Dusty said, his eyes sparkling underneath those long blond bangs.

"Surf lessons or fantasies?"

"Both," he said, tucking a clump of wet hair behind my ears. "So how 'bout me and you go out tonight?"

"Awesome," I said, no hesitation. A little dinner couldn't hurt anyone, could it? I needed to eat, right?

"See you at eight, then," Dusty said, leaning over and giving me a salty kiss on the cheek.

"Cool."

I ran up the beach toward where I had left Brina. She was still in the same spot, looking sullen. "Did I just see you two kissing?" she asked me.

"Uh, no," I said. "He was just congratulating me for finally catching a wave."

"Right," she said, not believing it for a minute. "So, I take it you had fun today?"

"It was one of the most amazing experiences of my life."

"Sorry I can't say the same."

"What's wrong?" I asked, the smile fading from my face.

"What's wrong is either I've lost my touch completely or I'm a big flop in California," Brina said. "Not one single guy even talked to me. I was totally bored." She lifted her sunglasses and gave me a good staring at. "And you were gone a long time."

I was about to say something like "Welcome to my world" when Brad and Sully plunked themselves down next to us. "Any luck?" Sully asked.

"Yes," I said.

"No," said Brina at the same time. "How about you guys?"

"We struck out," admitted Brad.

"We batted less than zero," Sully said, laughing. "No surfboard, no play around here."

"That's why Trace is the only one who scored," said Brina. "She's now an official surfer chick, with her very own surfer dude."

Sully put his arm around me and whispered in my ear, "Told ya you looked great."

Brina gave us a disgusted look and started gathering her stuff for the turtle trek back to our hotel. "I am so outta here," she said. "California sucks."

Ain't role reversal a bitch? I thought, and hoped Brina could weather having me in the spotlight for once.

I met Dusty at Javier's, a crowded little Mexican joint, that night. "So how long are you here for?" he asked as we chowed down on a bowl of fresh-baked chips and guacamole.

"Just the weekend," I said, smiling. My sunburned cheeks felt too tight for my face. "We're actually heading up to UCLA Monday morning and then catching a flight home later in the day."

"Too bad," he said. "I would've loved to hang out with you some more."

"Maybe we can in a few months," I said. "I'm probably coming out this way for college in the fall."

"I hope I can last that long," he said, flirting like crazy.

When we were finished eating, Dusty paid the check and we headed down to the beach. The moon was nearly full, so everything looked sparkly and magical. After we'd walked a while, Dusty sat down and patted the sand next to him. "See that star up there?" he said. "It's the one Aquinnah and I always wish on."

Well, at least I didn't have to feel bad about having a hometown honey. "Your girlfriend, huh?" I asked him.

"God, no," Dusty said, laughing. "I wouldn't be here with you if I had a girlfriend, would I?"

"I guess not," I mumbled.

"Aquinnah's my five-year-old stepsister."

"Kids are great," I said, feeling like a total scum.

"Hot out here," Dusty said, pulling off his T-shirt and revealing a Chinese symbol tattooed on the top of his back.

I traced the outline of the writing. "What's it mean?" I asked, my heart ricocheting around in my chest.

"Peace," Dusty said, taking my face in his hands and kissing me. Oh, my God, it felt good. I wished there were no stupid rules about not sleeping with every guy you met, the minute you met them. Unfortunately, my conscience kept reminding me that there were. In fact, it was just barely letting me enjoy the very beginning of this sandy make-out fest.

Dusty laid us down gently in the sand, kissing me the whole time. His hand slithered up my shirt so expertly I barely noticed what was happening. The delicious shivers running up and down my body gave him away.

"Wait," I said, trying to talk and kiss at the same time.

"What?" he said, still going for it. "You have surf rash?"

"Yeah," I admitted. "And guilt rash, too."

Dusty sat up. "What's that supposed to mean?"

"I kind of have a boyfriend." All night, Zander's words about not falling for a surfer guy had been haunting me. And I figured he must be over the shock of my "I love you" by now.

"So what are you doing here with me, then?"

"I guess I feel like I have one foot stuck in the past and one stuck in my future," I told him. "So the present isn't even factoring in right now."

Dusty rubbed his temples. "You are really confusing me, Trace."

"Let's just say you've made it really easy to forget everything going on back home," I said. "I'm sorry if I led you on."

"I liked where we were going," he said. "But I think I'll live."

As we walked back up the beach to the main drag, I asked Dusty, "Where'd you get inked?"

"Place up the road," he said. "Why? You looking for some?"

"Oh, yeah," I said. "Let's do it." First surfing, then mashing on the beach, and now tattooing. I was turning into a regular risk freak out here. And I liked the new me—all except for the cheating part. That felt pretty crappy. I dug around in my purse looking for my cell phone. "Mind if my friends join us?"

"Why not?"

Ten minutes later Brina, Sully, and Brad met us in front of the Laguna Ink Spot. "I'm getting my belly pierced tonight," Brina said, totally fired up.

"I am getting a shamrock right here," Sully said, patting the top of his butt.

"And I want Popeye bulging out of my biceps," Brad said, rolling up his sleeve and flexing his nonexistent muscle.

"Hey, Paco," Dusty said as we walked into the Ink Spot. "I rounded up some blank slates for you to work your magic on."

"Who's first?" Paco grunted as he lumbered toward the front of the shop. Piercings and tattoos decorated his entire body. I wondered how much more there was underneath his clothes—not that I wanted to see or anything.

"Me!" Brina squealed, raising her hand. She picked out a belly bar with a pink daisy and brought it to him.

"Lift up your shirt," Paco said. Brina giggled nervously and did as she was told. Paco examined her belly, pulling the skin this way and that until he finally picked just the right spot to pierce.

"Lie down here," he told her, rubbing alcohol on her stomach and marking it with a pen. Then Paco took out tongs, fastened a rubber band around them, and clamped the skin above Brina's navel.

"Close your eyes, Brina," I said as Paco picked up a long, gleaming needle big enough to knit with.

"Why?" she said, panicking and starting to sit up.

"Lie down," Paco ordered again.

Brina squeezed my hand in hers so hard I thought it might explode into a million pieces. "If I die, tell my mother I love her."

"Is this chick really your friend?" Dusty whispered to me, making a face. "She's such a baby."

"She really is," I said, both claiming her as my friend and agreeing that she could be a big baby sometimes. Like now.

"Don't worry, Brina," Sully said, stroking her forehead until the needle poked through the top of the tongs. Brina didn't even flinch.

"It's all done," Sully said, helping Brina sit up.

"It is?" Brina looked down at her belly in wonder. "And I didn't even die!"

"It looks cute," I said, wishing I could pierce my belly, too. But after watching that? No way.

"You pick out your designs yet?" Paco grunted at me and Sully.

"Yup," we said at the same time. I pointed to a Nike Swoosh. I wanted to "Just do it," and that included everything from getting into a good college to finding my dad to doing some more mashing on the beach next year—with Zander, of course, when we were both at college out here.

Sully had chosen a Notre Dame leprechaun over the more simple shamrock. "You planning on going to ND?" I asked him.

"Oh, yeah, my family's gone there for generations," Sully said.

"So they'll have yet another Sullivan to look forward to in a couple of years?" Brina asked.

"Well, actually . . . ," Sully started to say, and then trailed off.

Brad started wildly motioning to the Popeye tattoo. "I'll have this one," he told Paco.

"You'll have nothing and like it, sweet pea," Paco said. "Come back when you're eighteen."

"Shit," Brad muttered under his breath, flopping down into a chair in the waiting room. He picked up a body art magazine and started leafing through it.

"OK, you two, head to the back room," Paco said, handing Sully and me our receipts.

"You coming, Dusty?" I asked him.

"Naaah. I gotta rock," he said. "Thanks for the fun night. E-mail me when you find out about college. And when you dump your homeboy." He gave me a quick kiss on the cheek and took off.

"He seems like a cool guy," said Sully as we watched Dusty head out the door.

"Oh, he is," I said, still not quite over our little scrumf on the beach. "But so is Zander, of course."

"You get a little when-the-cat's-away-the-mice-will-play action?"

"No," I said, not looking at him. "OK, maybe a little. But I stopped and told him the truth before things went too far."

"Agghhhhh," Sully said, wincing. "The kiss of death. Admitting you have a boyfriend."

Sully and I kept blabbing and flinching as the tattoo artists worked on us. I have to admit, Sully was way more stoic than me. "You are such a wimp," he laughed.

"My tattoo is on bone," I said, pointing to my ankle. "And yours is on fat. Any questions?"

"Fat, schmat," he said. "This thing is pure muscle."

"Well, it's not bone, at any rate."

Sully gave me an evil grin and winked. "Nope, for that you'd have to roll me over."

"Don't tempt me," I said, blushing. My hormones had gone into overdrive. I was just going to have to control myself until I got home to Zander, and that was final. Pretty much.

# CHAPTER
## 14

On Monday morning, Mrs. Maldonati woke us up at the crack of dawn. "We have to get on the road in an hour to make it everywhere we need to go today and still catch our plane," she said, turning the lights on full blast and opening the curtains.

"OK, Mrs. Maldonati," I said, throwing my feet out from under the blankets and standing up. "Owww!" I picked up the foot that now sported a Nike Swoosh, and hopped around. My ankle was throbbing so much it had its very own heartbeat.

"What's wrong, Trace?" Mrs. M. asked, concerned.

"Just twisted my ankle is all," I told her. "It's no big deal."

Brina rolled out of bed next. When she tried to pull her nightshirt from her body, it wouldn't budge.

"Gross! I'm oozing all over the place," she whispered to me.

"Get used to it," I said, clamping my hand over her mouth. "Paco said it's gonna be like that for at least six weeks. And you better keep it a secret from Mommy dearest or you are in serious trouble."

Mrs. Maldonati popped her head back in the door of our room. "Keep what a secret?"

"Brina's outfit," I said, jumping in front of her and the stuck-on nightshirt.

"Oh, no, you don't," said Mrs. M. "I brought this lovely dress for Brina to wear today." She held up a pink-and-green Lilly Pulitzer cotton sheath.

Brina took one look at the vile preppy garment and set her mouth into a grim line. "I am not wearing that," she said. "Not today. Not ever."

"Guess again," Mrs. Maldonati told her, laying the dress out on Brina's bed. "If you had applied to colleges when you were supposed to, you could have chosen your outfit. But things being the way they are, we're playing by my rules."

"I don't even want to go to Mount My Asshole," Brina grumbled.

"And you know what? They may not want you, either," Mrs. Maldonati said, pointedly ignoring the crude language. "Remember, Brina, beggars can't be choosers."

Brina curled up her lip but knew she had no choice but to put the horrible thing on. "A little privacy, please, Mom," Brina said, opening the door and waiting for her mom to leave.

"Oh, please," Mrs. M. said. "Let me help you into the dress."

"That's OK, Mrs. Maldonati," I told her when I saw the panicked look in Brina's eye. "I'll get her all zipped up for you."

Brina's mom looked at me, then Brina, and backed out of the room. "Yell if you need me," she said, closing the door.

"Please shoot me and put me out of my misery," Brina said, tears welling up in her eyes.

"Can't," I said, shaking my head. "You have a very important date with St. Agnes in two hours."

"St. Ass Wipe," Brina corrected me.

"Whatever," I laughed. "Now be a good girl and put this heinous thing on."

"Bradley, could you introduce me to your mother's friend?" Sully asked when Brina walked into the living room. With her hair pulled back into a pretty silver clip, the sleeveless Lilly dress, a white cardigan tied around her neck, and Kate Spade canvas sandals, Brina really did look like the quintessential Winnetka mom.

"Sure thing, Peter," Brad said, laughing so hard he fell off the couch.

Brina scowled at them both. "I'm ready to go, Moth-er," she said, drawing out the two syllables to let her mom know she was really annoyed.

We all piled into the car and drove about half a mile before Brina started whining in the backseat. "Mom, I need a latte. I won't be able to string two sentences together without a little caffeine boost."

"Brina, you know coffee is bad for the skin and makes you retain water," Mrs. Maldonati chided.

"So I'll be bloated and broken out for my interview," said Brina. "That should go perfectly with this vile outfit."

"Fine," Mrs. Maldonati said, pulling over at Starbucks. "But don't come crying to me when your stomach gets gassy like last time."

Brina shot her mother the most evil look you can imagine.

"Brina, don't worry," Sully said, hardly able to contain his laughter. "I was just reading in the *Insider's Guide* that coffee farts make a great impression in interviews."

It was all too much for Brina—the horrible outfit, the fart comments, the pressure of having one last shot to get into college—and she plopped herself down on the curb and started to cry.

"I'm sorry, Brina," Sully said, looking horrified. "I was just kidding."

"Screw you," she said. Sully shook his head and walked off toward Starbucks.

"You can't tell slp to screw," I said, trying to make Brina laugh before she totally melted.

"Didn't I already tell you about the Sully 'ewwww' factor? And that he totally knows we're just friends?"

"So far, all I've seen you do is flirt with him."

"You're completely wacked. It's called making polite conversation."

"You make polite conversation with somebody's aunt Irma," I told her. "You stay out until six a.m. on a beach flirting with hot men like Sully. And I still don't think he gets that you're just friends."

"You don't?" Brina said, looking worried.

"Nope. And the longer you wait, the more painful it's gonna be," I told her. "If you have to do it, do it quick. Like pulling off a Band-Aid."

"That's the only way?"

"Well, there is one other option you might consider."

"Anything would be better than your Band-Aid suggestion."

"How about giving the guy a chance?"

"Trace, give it up already. I just don't see him like that," she said, tears really flowing now. "This whole trip has been nothing but a downer. I just want to go home."

I handed Brina a wilted tissue I found at the bottom of my backpack.

"You're just nervous about your interview," I told her, patting her shoulder. "Give it your best shot. Then we'll go home."

She blew her nose into it with a great honk. "No."

"You have to."

Sully and Brad came out of the coffee shop carrying four lattes and various accoutrements—spoons, sugar packets, and stirrers. "Friends?" Sully asked Brina as he passed her a *grande* latte.

"Friends," she said, drying her eyes. "Just friends."

We doctored up our drinks and got back in the car. "What was that drama all about?" Mrs. Maldonati asked.

"Nothing," Brina, Brad, and I said at the same time.

"Gas," Sully said simultaneously, and we all cracked up.

"Don't you dare get anything on that dress," Mrs. Maldonati warned Brina. "It cost an arm and a leg."

"It's so ugly it shouldn't have cost more than a fingernail," Brina said. Mrs. Maldonati ignored her and kept on driving.

A few minutes later, we were tooling up the freeway. The caffeine must've kicked in on us kids, because we were all squirming and giggling and generally making a nuisance of ourselves. "Look, I made a tooth spoon xylophone," I told everyone, dragging it across my teeth. It sounded really, really annoying. I liked it.

"Guess who I am?" Brad asked, scraping his spoon on his teeth in rhythmic bursts. "Tooth spoon bass."

"I'll be tooth spoon drums," said Sully, and tapped two spoons in his mouth at once.

"I think I'll be—" Before Brina could join the band, Mrs. M. swerved onto the shoulder and stopped the car.

"Give me those spoons this instant," she screamed.

We reluctantly broke up and handed our spoons to Mrs. Maldonati, who rolled down the window and chucked them out onto the freeway. "Good riddance," she muttered. "My nerves are shot."

We rode in silence until I saw a sign for the Wilshire Boulevard exit—the place where Zander had told me to keep my eyes peeled. A second later, I sucked in my breath, unable to speak. I hit Brina and pointed out the window.

"What?" she said.

No words seemed to want to leave the comfort of my mouth, so I hit her and pointed again.

"Holy shi—" Brina gasped.

Mrs. M. turned around and smacked Brina on the head before she could finish the obscenity. "Sabrina Maria Maldonati!"

I opened my window and stuck my head out like a dog, trying to get a better look at the billboard we were whizzing by. It was a bigger—actually, a humongous—version of the milk carton missing-persons ad. Bebe, Bruce, and the Boss-alike were smiling at one another and all of LA while the copy pleaded for information about my dad.

I blinked my eyes and it was gone, lying behind us on the highway.

"I cannot believe Zander did that for you," Brina said, a huge smile on her face. "That was the nicest thing I've ever seen."

"I don't know whether to hug him or beat him," I said. "If Bebe gets wind of this, I am dead meat."

"Does she have a lot of friends out this way?" Brina asked.

"Some," I said.

"Enough chatter, girls. Here's the plan," Mrs. Maldonati said. "Tracey, Sullivan, and Bradley, I'm going to let you off at UCLA's main entrance. Boys, see that you meet the soccer coach at eleven o'clock like you're supposed to. Tracey, I trust you can keep yourself amused. I'll be back to pick you all up by three. Don't be late—we have a plane to catch."

I looked over at Brina. "Sullivan?" I whispered. "Is she going to start calling me Tillingham next?"

"Probably," Brina said, twirling a finger around her head. "She's nuts."

"Good luck," I said to Brina as I got out of the car. "Knock St. Ass Breath's socks off."

"I'll try," she said, looking a little pale. "Have fun."

"See ya, Trace," Sully waved as the boys took off for the sports complex. "We'll meet you back here this afternoon."

I walked around aimlessly for a while, just taking in the palm trees, beautiful architecture, and stunningly gorgeous student body. The only problem was, I felt like Bebe in Winnetka. Pale, brunet, and petite didn't quite seem to fit in here at tan, blond, leggy land. I rubbed my neck and felt a hunch coming on.

I decided a tour might help me get a broader perspective on the campus, so I made my way to the admissions building. Inside, there was a crowd of people milling about. I tacked myself on to the end of it. "Follow me," a willowy, golden-maned girl said with all the enthusiasm of a funeral director.

I tapped the kid next to me on the shoulder. "She's really making this exciting, isn't she?" I whispered.

"Shhh! I'm trying to listen."

I rolled my eyes. "Sorry."

I detached myself from the group in search of my own personal guide—someone along the lines of Caitlin and Pat at Fairfield—so I could experience the real UCLA. The one where I'd blend. But after a few attempts at being friendly, I gave up hope. Everyone seemed too busy or just plain uninterested in getting me psyched about coming to their school. Don't get me wrong—people were polite, almost to a fault. They'd listen and nod, then say, "I'd love to, but I've gotta run, maybe some other time," and take off. Maybe if my people called their people, I could have found someone willing to take me under their wing.

Dejected, I walked into an Internet café. I found an empty seat, ordered a Coke, and pulled up my e-mail. I deleted all the usual junk until I came to a message that made my heart jump up into my throat.

Subject line: Mac Donohue

I think I may be able to help you find the person you're looking for. If I can reach him, what should I say it was that Bruce lost that summer?
All the best,
Shamus

I picked up my Coke and spilled half of it on my pants—my hands were shaking so badly. I thought for a moment and then typed back:

Shamus,
I wouldn't want to spoil the surprise via e-mail. Trust me, it's pretty cool.
So if you can hook me up directly with Mac, I'd greatly appreciate it.
Trace

I hit SEND as a guy with a carefully crafted goatee and unwrinkled khakis sat down next to me. "What year are you in?" he asked me.

"Senior," I said, not really lying. After all, I was a senior in high school.

"Oh, great, you're of age," he said, shoving his business card into my hand. "Listen, I'm recruiting girls to dance at bachelor parties. Nothing illegal, just some good clean girl-on-girl fun and great money. What do you say?"

"I say, get away from me, loser."

"Actresses," he muttered, moving on to another live one. "You all think you're too good for the gig."

Three o'clock can't get here fast enough, I thought. I spent the next few hours daydreaming about meeting my dad. I also spent quite a bit of time mulling over what I was going to say to Bebe if she found out about the milk cartons and the billboard.

I rehearsed different scenarios in my head. The one where I came in and she was crying went like this: "Bebe, I am so sorry. I didn't mean for you to get hurt. I had no idea Zander would go this far." If she was angry, I thought I might say, "Bebe, if you had just been honest with me from the beginning, I wouldn't have been forced to go to this extent to find my dad. Now why don't you just come clean and we'll be done with it?" The one where she had committed suicide over the whole thing was the worst. In that case, I figured I'd simply have to throw myself over her dead body and beg for her and God's forgiveness.

Finally, my day at UCLA was over. I spotted Mrs. Maldonati's rental car and hopped in. The boys joined us a minute later.

"How'd it all go, gang?" Mrs. Maldonati wanted to know.

"It was awesome," Brad said, all excited. "Chicks, chicks, and more hot chicks."

"Bradley, that's not what I meant and you know it."

Brad laughed. "The soccer program was pretty good, too."

"Did you wow them?" I asked Brina.

"Oh, Trace, I just loved it," she said, positively glowing. For once, Mrs. Maldonati was beaming with pride at her. "And I think I aced the interview."

"That's great," I said. "I knew you could do it."

"You seem kind of freaked-out," Brina said. "Are you still worried about that foot-in-the-mouth thing with Zander?"

"No, I just got an unexpected e-mail," I told her. "Plus, UCLA just wasn't what I expected."

"It was all I expected and more," said Sully. "Beautiful campus, awesome sports program, and did we mention the chicks yet?"

"Poor Brenda," said Brina. "She's about to lose you to a California girl, isn't she?"

Sully shrugged. "We're kind of not seeing each other anymore."

"Oh, really?" Brina said.

"Really. So, do you think your boyfriend is gonna love the idea of you going to an all-girls Catholic school?" Sully asked, tossing the ball back in her court.

"Even though it sounds like every guy's fantasy, it wasn't anything like what you're thinking," she said, laughing. "Anyway, I don't have a boyfriend right now."

Sully eyed her. "What happened to your secret-love-note man?"

Brina made a big show of yawning. "I'm over him," she said. "He's a lot of yabba dabba and not a lot of do." I guessed this was where the letting-Sully-down-semieasy part was going to come into play.

I snapped back into reality. "What's that supposed to mean?" I asked her.

"It means I'm over slp. He's all talk and no action. Besides," she said, nudging me in the ribs, "there was too much of an age difference between us."

Sully stared at Brina for a second, and then closed his eyes and pretended to sleep. Brina snuggled into my shoulder and did the same. And I felt about as alone as I ever have in my whole entire life.

That all-alone-in-the-world feeling lasted just until we pulled onto my street. Camera crews littered the lawn. Spotlights were strategically pointed at the front door. And all my neighbors were lined up on the sidewalk, curious to find out who died or won the lottery or whatever.

"Just what is going on here?" said Mrs. M., almost to herself.

"I think Zander's plan is working," Brina said, pointing out the window.

186 / TRISH COOK

"Working?" I said. I couldn't figure out how Brina thought this scene was anything but bad. "All this means is I won't be able to go out again until I'm thirty."

"No, what it means is that your dad won't be able to stay a mystery much longer," she shot back. "Not with all these reporters hot on his trail."

Brina had a point. But at that moment, all I could concentrate on was getting into my house without the wolves tearing at my throat. I'd had enough national TV exposure for one lifetime already.

"Would you like me to walk you inside, Tracey?" Mrs. Maldonati asked as she pulled into a neighbor's driveway. Ours was full, with the Beetle, Mr. Steve's Mini Cooper, and a few television vans.

"Want me to act as a decoy?" Brina asked almost at the same time. I could see she still hadn't gotten over her *TRL* appearance just yet. Now she was looking for a permanent spot as an evening entertainment news reporter.

"I'll take it from here," I said, shaking my head. "Thanks, though."

I grabbed my gear, hopped over the neighbor's fence, and sneaked into the backyard unnoticed. My key slid into the lock silently, and I pushed the door open and tiptoed in. Somehow, I thought I could put off the inevitable—a showdown with Bebe—if I just stayed out of her way for the next year or so. I closed the door behind me until I heard the lock click.

"Don't move a muscle, bucko!" Bebe screamed as she flicked on the lights. "I'm armed and dangerous!"

I had to laugh. The only thing she was carrying was a bag of potato chips. What was she planning to do, salt some poor guy to death?

"Nice weapon," I said, nodding at the munchies. "Sorry I scared you."

"You and your boyfriend have a lot more than that to be sorry for," she said, ignoring my joke. "Like ruining my life."

I tried to soften her up. "You're way too tough to have a little manhunt spoil your entire existence."

"Good try, Trace," Bebe said, gesturing toward the front lawn. "Did you see all those vultures out there?"

"At least your agent must be happy," I said, trying to make lemon-ade out of the rather lemony situation. "It's good publicity, right?"

"It's a juicy story, and people can't get enough of it," Bebe said, flop-ping down into the overstuffed chair in the living room. "Unfortu-nately, it makes me look like a complete idiot, not to mention a total fraud. Who ever heard of a romance novelist who can't even figure out her own love life?"

"Your love life isn't a mess," I said. "Mr. Steve's here, isn't he?"

"Yeah, but the reporters don't know that," she said. "All they want to know about is Bliss and the Boss-alike."

"I wasn't trying to humiliate you," I told her. "Just trying to find him."

"Yeah, and now everyone else is, too," she said. Bebe clicked on TiVo and replayed *Entertainment Tonight*. Pat O'Brien appeared on-screen, saying:

> Now, here's a new twist to an age-old story. Boy meets girl, boy gets girl pregnant, boy takes off—and eighteen years later their daughter launches a multimedia campaign to find boy. This is the situation Belinda Tillingham, author of more than ten best-selling rock-and-roll romance novels, finds herself in these days. Belinda and her mystery beau split up before daughter, Tracey Rosalita, was born. Now Tracey is mounting her own search to find Daddy dearest. Neither Mom nor daughter was available for comment, but here's a look at Tracey's efforts so far.

*ET* went into a little montage then, showing first the milk carton, then my shout-out on *TRL,* then the billboard on the freeway, and fi-nally a shot from our front lawn. "If you know anything about Mac the mystery man, you're being asked to call this number." Pat reeled off Zander's toll-free one.

Bebe pressed STOP and looked at me. "Ready to give up yet?"

I shrugged and looked at my feet. "Not really."

"You might as well," Bebe said, flicking off the light. "If all these reporters can't find your dad, no one can." She walked out of the room, leaving me in total darkness.

Bebe and I spent the next few days playing dodge-the-TV-crews. We screened all our calls, because nearly every one was a request for an interview, a psychic claiming to know where my dad was, or a private detective looking to take on the case.

The whole situation had gotten so out of control, Bebe almost started to think it was funny. "Pretty soon they're going to ask me to be center square."

"They already did," I told her.

"Yeah, right."

I motioned toward the phone. "Check the answering machine if you don't believe me."

Bebe walked over and pressed PLAY. Sure enough, her agent was running down a long list of potential media opportunities—everything from a guest appearance on *Howard Stern* to *Conan* to any number of game shows, including *Hollywood Squares*.

"He's got to be kidding," Bebe said. "I thought that went off the air years ago."

"I think you should go for it, Bebe," I said. "Why not enjoy your notoriety? Play it up huge and get that next book out there as fast as you can. It's sure to take the charts by storm."

"Why should I take career advice from you?" Bebe asked, hands on her hips. "I shouldn't even be talking to you after what you've done to my life."

I walked across the room and hugged her. "You should take my advice because I love you, and I only want the best for you." In my head, I added, "And because maybe the Boss-alike will see you on *Howard* or *Hollywood Squares* and realize we're looking for him."

Hey, my motives could only be so pure at this point. I mean, I just wasn't ready to hang it up yet. Honestly, I didn't know if I ever would be.

# CHAPTER
## 15

Just like that very first day slp wrote his way into Brina's life, I looked up from my locker to see her careening down the hall toward me, clutching a piece of paper.

"Trace, he finally outed himself," she said breathlessly. "It's Steven after all."

How could that be? "What?"

"Just read it," Brina said, shoving the note into my hands. It said:

*Brina:*
*I like to sketch you in my mind's eye*
*Always see you as pure art*
*But neither pen nor ink can capture you*
*Maybe you could draw yourself closer to me*
*slp*

"The only thing this proves," I said, "is that maybe he knows we hit a tattoo joint last weekend."

"Wrong. It means he's finally ready for us to be together," Brina told me.

"How do you figure?"

"Steven and I just had a big long meeting about how I want to be an art major," she said. "And he's the one who set me up for the interview at Mount St. Agnes, which has a great art program. Don't you see, Trace? It all adds up."

"No, it doesn't. Want to know why?" As crazy as it might seem, I'd never gotten around to correcting Brina's mistaken belief that Bebe was going out with the Starbucks guy and not Mr. Steve. It was just that I couldn't even begin to figure out how to break it to her after so long. The more I waited, the more pissed off I knew she would be. And now here we were, six months later. How in hell was I ever going to explain this one? This must've been just how Bebe felt when year after year she neglected to tell me my dad didn't even know I was alive.

She shook her head. "I'm going to draw myself closer to him right now. And there's nothing you can do to stop me."

"Brina, no. Don't do it."

"Trace, it's completely crystal clear."

"Brina," I said, grabbing her by the shoulders. "It's Sully, remember?"

"Says you. Why would Sully write again after I pretty much faced him in LA?" A sad look spread across Brina's face and she added, "Gosh, I really should apologize to him for that later. But for now, I've gotta go meet my man!"

"There's something I need to tell you!" I yelled as Brina started running down the hall toward the guidance department. She ignored me. I finally caught up to her just as she was throwing her arms around Mr. Steve.

"You are an amazing man," she said, kissing him on the cheek.

There was only one way for this all to end: disastrously.

"Thanks," Mr. Steve said, trying to pry her arms from around his neck.

She clung on like a baby monkey. "And so creative," she said, pulling back to stare in his eyes now. "I like that in guys."

"Brina, have a seat," Mr. Steve said, finally succeeding at peeling Brina off of him. "Now, what can I do for you?" He had no clue what this was all about. I had pretty much known it all along, but was relieved to see it so clearly in his eyes nonetheless.

"You don't have to pretend anymore," she said, gazing up at him in awe. "I know it's you."

"Brina, I'm sorry," Mr. Steve said, more gently now. "I really don't know what you're talking about."

"The notes," she said, tears threatening to spill out her eyes. "The poems."

Mr. Steve knelt down in front of Brina. "Not mine. But whoever your note writer really is, I can tell you one thing about him. He has good taste."

Brina blushed until she was practically eggplant purple, and sniffled loudly. "Oh, sure."

"No, really," Mr. Steve said. "And you've got to give the guy credit. I probably would've been way too scared to write you notes in high school." He pulled a book from high on his bookshelf, flipped it open, and pointed to a picture.

"Who's this?" Brina asked. By this point, she was covered in itchy-looking hives brought on by the severe humiliation she'd just subjected herself to.

"Read the name," he said.

" 'Steven Lee Perry,' " Brina read, looking back up at Mr. Steve in surprise. "It doesn't look like you at all."

"I was kind of a late bloomer," Mr. Steve admitted. I looked over Brina's shoulder and laughed. Mr. Steve looked like a total geek, complete with braces, glasses, zits, and flood pants.

Brina stared down at the yearbook. "What's an AV aid?"

"I was the guy who wheeled the filmstrip machines around."

After what seemed like an hour of awkward silence, Brina finally said, "There's just one thing I still don't understand. What's a filmstrip?"

"I am so embarrassed," Brina said, hanging her head when we left Mr. Steve's office. "How could you let me do a stupid thing like that?"

"I tried to stop you," I said. "And anyway, Mr. Steve's a lot cooler than you might think. He'll never tell anyone what happened."

"Since when do you know him so well?"

"Since he's been hanging around my house every night."

"You and him?" Brina asked, her eyes growing a size a second.

"No," I laughed. "Bebe and him."

"Why didn't you tell me?" she asked, looking hurt. "Before I made a complete idiot out of myself, I mean."

"I tried," I said. "You didn't listen." It wasn't completely true, but she was too distracted to notice.

"Well, I'm listening now," Brina said, crumpling up the latest slp note and throwing it on the ground. "And you know what I hear? That slp is a big, fuckin' fake."

"Why do you say that?" I asked her. "It's a cute note. Not one of the better verses, but give Sully a break."

"Trace, get serious. This isn't from Sully," she said. "I finally got the joke. There is no slp. Just some prick getting his kicks by torturing me."

"I can't imagine that—" I started to say.

But Brina wasn't having any of it. "And to think, for seven months, I've looked forward to these notes," she said. "I even thought about me and slp falling in love for real."

I shot her a surprised look. "You did?"

"A girl can dream, right, Trace? But the thing is, I got totally wrapped up in the whole fantasy," she said. "So wrapped up, I didn't even look for anyone else."

I had to point out the obvious. "Well, you did venture into the Lion's den—"

"Stu Purcell? Only because I thought he was slp!" she countered. "Don't you see? Slp was playing me the whole time. He only wanted to watch me waste my entire senior year pining away for a goddamn fictional character."

"I think you've got it all wrong," I told her.

"No, I think slp got it all wrong," Brina said. "Nobody screws with me and gets away with it."

"If what you think is true, then he did get away with it," I had to break it to her. "It's not like you can get revenge on the Invisible Man."

Brina whipped out a permanent marker from her backpack. She waved it menacingly in my face. "Look out, slp, 'cause here I come." Then she turned and ran down the hall the other way.

I took off after her for the second time in an hour, yelling, "Don't do anything you'll regret!"

"The only thing I could possibly regret is being a doormat for one second longer!" she yelled back over her shoulder.

I was in a full-blown sweat by the time I caught up with Brina. She'd already started scrawling bold black words on the broken locker next to hers, and there was nothing I could do to stop her. When she was done a minute later, the useless door was practically screaming with venom:

> *No longer are you worth my time*
> *I realized that I'll be just fine*
> *Don't be surprised when you see my face, reflecting back without a trace*
> *You'll be reminded of these days of old*
> *Begging forgiveness for being so cold*

Brina stood back and cocked her head. Then she taped the silver locket slp had given her for Christmas onto the door and drew a noose above it. "That's more like it," she said, surveying her work.

"Satisfied?" I asked her.

Brina crossed her arms and stared at her masterpiece. "Very."

"So who'd you plagiarize this time?"

"My latest musical discovery—a great band called Forte," she answered, looking extremely pleased with herself. "You know what 'forte' means in Italian?"

I shook my head.

"Strong. A force to be reckoned with, just like me."

I smiled and hugged her tight. At least my spunky best friend was back with a vengeance.

I had been home for days, and still no sign of Zander. My calls went unanswered, my messages unreturned. Things couldn't have been any worse. That is, until Bebe slid three very thin envelopes across the kitchen table at me. The return addresses read "USC," "Santa Clara," and "Fairfield."

"Lake-Cook Community College, here I come," I groaned, my heart doing sick little flip-flops in my chest.

"I'm sure . . . ," Bebe said, groping around unsuccessfully for something to say, when the doorbell rang and Zander walked through the door. He could barely look at me, his gaze coming to rest on the envelopes in my hand instead.

"What do your letters say?"

Judging by the look on Zander's face, confronting him about why he hadn't called me—which is what I had been planning to do when I finally talked to him—seemed too scary. I stared down at the ominous envelopes and I stuck with the topic at hand. "I didn't even open them," I said. "What's the point? They're too skinny to be good news."

Zander took the letters from my hands and flipped through them one by one. "You never know. . . ." He trailed off, sounding much less convincing than I'm sure he intended to.

"Fine, have it your way." I ripped into the USC one and began to read aloud.

*Dear Ms. Tillingham:*
*We regret to inform you . . .*

My voice caught as I choked on the words. I looked up at Zander, tears in my eyes. "Told you."

Next, I tore open the Santa Clara envelope. "Blah-blah-blah, wait-listed. If a space becomes available, blah-blah-blah . . ." I tossed the two letters into the trash, thinking if I got rid of them quickly enough, maybe they would never have existed at all.

"This sucks," I said, putting my head on the table and sighing. The Fairfield envelope was still just sitting there, staring at me. It was such a slap in the face to be rejected by a school I wasn't even interested in, so I tossed it aside, not even opening it.

"Yep," Zander agreed. "And it's about to get even suckier."

"That sounds frightening."

"It kind of is," he said. "Can we go outside and talk?"

My stomach heaved and I felt like I might throw up my half-digested Balance bar. "Sure," I said, opening the door and following Zander outside.

"Trace, you know how much I care about you."

"Oh, Jesus, here it comes," I said, shaking my head. "Zander, if this is about the verbal screw up I made before I left, forget about it. I didn't mean it. It just slipped out."

"Trace, I think you did mean it," he said. "And I'm completely flattered."

I brightened about one iota. "Really?"

"Yeah, but here's the thing. The way it's looking now, we're going to be headed in different directions—" We really are all destined to repeat our parents' mistakes, I thought incredulously.

"So? We'll always just be a flight away," I said, hoping I didn't sound as pathetic and desperate as I was feeling. "Isn't that what we always said?"

"I don't want you to waste four great years waiting for me," Zander said. "Or vice versa."

"I wouldn't consider that a waste of time," I said, tears falling like rain down my face now.

Zander gathered me into his chest and hugged me tight. "Trace, I don't want us to hold each other back," he said. "We both need to pursue our dreams. So I think it's best for us to break up now, before either of us gets too attached."

"Sure," I said, sarcasm dripping from my voice. "Let's make a pact to hook up in four years and see where things go from there."

Zander pulled back and smiled at me. "Hey, now, there's a great idea."

"I was just fucking kidding," I said, heading inside. Before I slammed the door behind me, I stuck my head back out. "By the way, I cheated on you in California. And you know what? I should have screwed Dusty while I had the chance."

I ran up the stairs and flung myself on my bed, sobbing. It wasn't enough that two out of four colleges I'd applied to so far had dinged me. No. My boyfriend had to go and break up with me, too. What, did all guys read the same book about how to cut their girlfriends loose before college starts?

I heard a soft knock at the door. "You OK?" Bebe asked.

"Nope," I snuffled. "It seems I'm living your life."

Bebe gasped. "How far along are you?"

Just for a second, my tears turned into laughter. "I'm not pregnant!"

Bebe put her hand over her heart. "Oh, thank God. I had no idea how I was going to handle that one."

"What I meant was, Zander broke up with me using the same excuse my dad used on you. How exactly can someone say the reason they're letting you go is because they care too much about you?"

Bebe smoothed my hair out of my eyes. "Because they're scared to lose you after it's too late."

"Too late for what?"

"To forget about you."

# CHAPTER
# 16

While I was feeling crappy about my college prospects, Brina was one hundred percent pleased with herself about the public exposure of the whole slp sham. "I got him in the end, didn't I, Trace?"

I looked at slp's locker. A block of steel gray paint now covered the words Brina had inked in anger. "I guess so," I said, leaning back against the locker. I heard a little pinging sound, so I stood up and then leaned back again. Same thing.

I pulled the door open and found the tiny silver locket hanging from the grates inside, just like the first time Brina discovered it. Underneath the necklace was a note scrawled directly on the door in fine ballpoint pen.

*Brina:*
*I'm closer than you think, baby*
*Less than an arm's length away*
*We're closer than you think, baby*
*Only a heartbeat away*
*You'll find me just around the corner of your world*
*slp*

My hand started to shake as I touched the words. "Brina?"

Her head was buried inside her locker, so she didn't pick up on my freaking out and kept blabbing on and on. "You know how you told me Bebe is being all distant with you? Well, ever since we got back from

California, Sully is acting totally distant toward me." She popped her head out and looked at me. "And you know what? I miss him. I feel like I've lost my best friend."

I was still standing there with my mouth hanging open. Brina took that to mean I was upset. "Oh, Trace. Don't be mad—you know what I meant," she said. "You're still my best friend. It's just that I felt like Sully and I had a cool connection, and now it's gone."

As amazed as I was that Brina was finally, finally, FINALLY admitting she had some sort of feelings for Sully, I couldn't push aside my curiosity about the latest slp note.

"Let's get back to this discussion later," I said, pointing at the locker door. "Right now, you've got to see this."

Brina took a good hard look at the words. "You don't think . . . ?"

I nodded, my heart racing. "I do. I really do."

Brina took my hand and we started toward the end of the hall. She stopped short before we got there. "I can't do this," she hyperventilated. "What if it's a setup? What if slp's a total dork? What if it's—"

I peeked my head around the corner. "Sully," I whispered. "I was right all along."

"Sully?" Brina gasped when she saw him leaning against the wall. "You really are slp?"

He grinned. "None other."

Brina stayed glued to the ground. "Then I think you have dyslexia."

"What are you talking about?"

"Peter Liam Sullivan. That's pls, not slp."

Sully roared with laughter. "I can't believe Brad and I never corrected you," he said. "Pete's just a nickname. Short for Peterson. My name's Sullivan Liam Peterson."

Brina still hadn't moved. "Get it, Brina?" I said, tapping her on the shoulder. "*S-l-p.*"

"You . . . you . . ." Brina ran over to Sully with her arm wound up like she was going to hit him, but he caught her midswing. A second later she dissolved into him. Soon, kids began to gather around the two people who had recently melded into one. Everyone was trying to figure out just who was kissing whom.

Brina opened one eye and realized what a commotion she and Sully were causing. "Haven't you ever seen anyone rob the cradle before?" Brina scolded the crowd. "The show's over. Move on."

I turned to leave with the rest of the onlookers. A second later, I turned back around, unable to resist. "Hey, Sully, how did you know we'd look in the locker today?"

Sully managed to pull himself away from Brina for just a second. "I didn't. I've been waiting here after school every day for a week," he said. "Any more questions before I get back to kissing your best friend?"

I thought for a moment, then said, "Yeah. What was with the poem?"

Sully smiled at me. "It was actually the lyrics to my parents' wedding song," Sully said. "When Bebe figured out it wasn't an original work, I freaked and didn't write again for a long time."

"That's when I thought you'd given up on me," Brina said. "And I sent you the 'In and Out' note."

"Believe me, it was all I could do not to chase you down and admit everything after that," Sully said, smiling down at her.

She hit him, playfully this time. "Sex fiend!"

"True dat," Sully said, just beaming at her. "Now, speaking of lyrics. Your latest Forte locker creation was totally uncalled-for."

Brina brushed a stray dread from his forehead. "Yeah, I guess it was," she told him. "But I promise I'll make it up to you."

When I got home, I went straight to my room—I didn't even stop for my usual snack—and checked my e-mail. I took a sharp breath when I saw the mysterious Shamus's return address. I clicked it up and read it.

Subject: Our meeting

Trace,
I've attached the upcoming tour schedule for Born to Run, the band I manage and Mac plays in. Are you by any chance going to be in the area for any of the shows? I could put you on the guest list and we can talk afterward.
Shamus

I scoured the tour dates, not really believing there'd be any place we might possibly intersect. But lo and behold, Born to Run was one of the bands playing on the course of the Rock 'n' Roll Marathon. I typed back my reply with shaking fingers.

Shamus,
Cool! I'm actually running the Rock 'n' Roll Marathon. But I don't think I'll be up for hanging around afterward. Could we all hook up—me, you, and Mac—somewhere on Saturday instead?
Trace

Just before I pushed SEND, I added a P.S.:

P.S. Tell Mac he'll need to give me a password before I can tell him about the lost thing. How about we make it who he attended the Springsteen concert with in August of '86?

Satisfied I had foiled this guy if he was just some psycho trolling for a gullible girl to hack up and toss into a dozen different trash bags, I put on some mellow tunes, got my homework out of the way, and curled up with a good book I'd been meaning to get to for months. I didn't even bother with dinner.

At around nine, I tossed the book and checked my e-mail one last time before I shut down my computer. And there it was—an e-mail from Shamus saying he and the Boss-alike would meet me at the Pacifica Breeze Café in Del Mar at ten o'clock on Saturday morning.

I whooped with delight. I was finally going to meet my dad. And the funny thing was, I wasn't even mad at him anymore. After all, it wasn't his fault my mom was so lame she couldn't find him to say she was pregnant. It's not like he had rejected *me*.

I hunkered down under the blankets, even though I still was totally keyed up. At some point, I must've fallen asleep, because later on—I'm not sure how much—the phone shook me awake. I fumbled for it in the darkness, adrenaline pumping like it always does when I get a call in the middle of the night. "Hello," I croaked into the receiver.

"Trace, it's me," Brina said.

I cleared my throat, trying to get the frog out of there. "What a pleasant surprise. Is this the same Brina who was draped all over a certain gorgeous underclassman the last time I saw her?"

"That's me," she giggled. "Remember how I kept saying Sully was a baby, Trace?"

"Yeah. It was your favorite excuse for not even considering him as boyfriend material."

"Well, I feel the need to report back that he's no baby. Sully's all man." I could just picture Brina kicked back in bed, grinning like an idiot and waiting to give me the play-by-play.

I cut her off at the pass. "I don't need to hear all the gory details. Just tell me you two are deliriously happy together, and that's enough for me."

"OK. We're deliriously happy together," she said. "I just feel bad about all the times I dissed him this year, acting like I was too good for the guy just because he's fourteen months younger than me."

Leave it to Brina to find a way to make what she formerly thought was a huge deal into small potatoes. "You counted?"

"Yeah. I'm one of the youngest in our class, and he's one of the oldest in his," she told me. "He's getting his driver's license in the fall."

"Way to go, Brina," I said. "You and Sully. Perfect together."

"Trace, remember how I also told you I fantasized about falling in love with slp?" Brina's voice was almost a whisper.

"Yeah," I whispered back.

"I think my fantasy is coming true," she said, gulping hard. "I'm just having a little trouble getting the words out."

"A momentous occasion like this calls for a bold statement, I think," I told her.

"You mean, something like taking over the microphone during the morning announcements and broadcasting my feelings to the whole school?" Brina asked. "I can't. Even though I'm totally infatuated with Sully, I still can't get my mouth to admit it."

"Actually, I was thinking of something a bit more subtle," I said. "And quieter. More like something slp would do."

"I'm too overwhelmed by everything that happened today to brainstorm with you," Brina said. "So give me a hint about what you had in mind."

"Picture this: There's a big block of gray on the locker next to yours, and it's just waiting for you two to make some beautiful music together."

Silence. The clunking sound of the phone falling. Loud rustling noises in the background. "What in God's name are you doing?" I yelled, hoping the phone was close enough to Brina that she'd hear me.

Brina got back on the line a few seconds later. "Trace, I've been hoarding lyrics all year. By now, I've got something for every occasion. Lust, hate, sex, fear, hope, revenge. Even declarations of undying love," she said. "I just found the right one, by Heather Horton again. Meet me at my locker tomorrow morning at seven."

"Seven a.m. is like the middle of the night for me, Brina. But for you, anything."

The next morning, I dragged my silly ass out of bed and shuffled downstairs. Out of the corner of my barely open eyes, I noticed two envelopes—one big and one regular-sized—propped up against the coffeemaker.

I fingered them and tried to focus. One turned out to be the same skinny Fairfield envelope again—the one I'd never opened—and the other was a new package from UCLA.

I started to panic. What if I didn't get into any school at all? You might as well tattoo a big *L* on my forehead. I could just imagine the comments: Ever heard of a safety school, Trace?

I swallowed back the fear and went with the UCLA packet first. It looked more promising, being the larger of the two pieces of mail. I slid the cover letter out with shaky hands and scanned it.

*Dear Ms. Tillingham,*
*We're delighted to offer you admission to the class of . . .*

I stopped reading right there and did a little jig around the kitchen. They're delighted, I thought. UCLA is delighted to have me. What a relief. I would be living out my California dream after all.

When I stopped dancing, the remaining letter was still there, staring at me. Suddenly, it wasn't so scary anymore, like the monster in the darkness that turned out to be just clothes draped over a chair when the light flicked on. What the hell, I thought, and tore open the envelope.

> *Dear Tracey,*
> *Welcome to the Fairfield family. . . .*

I did a double take. What? For three weeks I'd tortured myself, thinking I'd been rejected, when all along this warm, sweet acceptance was waiting for me. I couldn't believe I'd wasted so much time being miserable. And thanks, Fairfield, for wanting me, I thought, but I'll be in sunny LA.

I looked up to see Bebe leaning against the doorway. I don't know how long she'd been standing there, but she'd obviously seen enough to know this was a happy occasion.

"So it's UCLA all the way, Trace?"

"Absolutely." I couldn't have wiped the enormous smile off my face if I tried. "I got accepted at Fairfield, too."

"You might want to keep your options open, then," Mr. Steve said as he walked into the kitchen. "Take the weekend to think about it."

"You'll have plenty of time during those twenty-six point two miles you'll be running on Sunday, that's for sure," Bebe said, shuffling over in her slippers to hug me.

"Why think about it?" I said, hugging her back. "My mind's made up."

"Because sometimes in life, you think you know what direction you're going in," Bebe said. "And then something comes along to completely change it."

When I arrived at school to meet Brina at the appointed ungodly hour, the gleaming halls greeted me with silence. It was weird being there when almost no one else was.

I shuffled upstairs to Brina's locker. By her side was Rodney, one of Brina's arty-farty friends. I wasn't sure what kind of a plan Brina had cooked up, but from the looks of things, it was going to be a good one.

"Hi guys!" I chirped.

"Whoa, you're awfully chipper this morning," Brina said, surprised.

"I got accepted at not one but two good schools, and I'm here for my best friend's coming-out party," I said. "Who wouldn't be chipper today?"

"You did it!" Brina screamed, picking me up and twirling me around the halls. "I knew you could!"

"Look out, LA—Trace and Brina are on the loose!" I said.

Rodney watched us go crazy. "You chicks are loco," he said, shaking his head.

"That's the beauty of us," Brina told him. "You never know what you're going to get. One day we're pissed off—the next day we're ecstatic. It keeps life interesting."

"It keeps life freaky," he mumbled, and went back to helping Brina put the finishing touches on slp's locker. He stepped back and surveyed their work. "Perfect," he declared, turning to Brina. "I'm outta here. You can add the words anytime now. It should be dry enough."

"Thanks, Rodney, I owe you one," she called after him. "Come on, Trace, we've got a lot of work to do before these halls start filling up."

"OK, what's my job?" I asked her.

"You're just here for moral support."

"That I can handle."

I plunked myself down on the linoleum floor and watched Brina at work. Her body blocked whatever she was doing, so I couldn't get a sneak peek at it. Five minutes later, she stepped back so I could see the finished product.

It knocked me out. Their mural was simply gorgeous, and Brina had taken the time to write her lyrics in a flowery script—the direct opposite of the angry slashes that had marked her slp blow-off letter. The locker now read:

> Let me be your Cinderella
> The whole damn fairy tale turned true
> I want to climb into your palace
> And I will love you through and through
> I want to be
> I will be true
> I'm climbing hand over hand
> Love you through and through

At the bottom, Brina had painted a little heart and signed her initials. "So, what do you think?" she asked me.

"It certainly makes a statement, Brina."

"You think it's too much?" she asked, doubt clouding her face.

"No. I think it's just enough," I said, smiling up at her.

Brina pulled me to my feet and hugged me tight. "Good luck in San Diego," she said. "I'll be there with you in spirit, all twenty-six miles."

"That's twenty-six point two, thank you very much," I told her. "And I know you will. So have fun with your sophomore god. And if you can't be good, be careful."

Brina winked at me. "Will do."

Who would've ever thought we'd have both come so far in twenty-four hours?

I was so on edge by last period thinking about the marathon—could I actually run that far? would I hit the wall everyone talks about?—that I almost missed Brina's getting in trouble.

The speaker crackled with static, interrupting a very boring history lecture on Catherine the Great. "Would Sabrina Maldonati please report to the principal's office immediately?" Brina looked at me, her eyes wide with surprise.

"Bussss-ted," Charlie Wanamaker hissed under his breath. Brina gave him a sharp kick in the shins with her big-ass boots and he let out a high-pitched yelp. I wondered where Charlie was the day Brina had beaten the pants off of Greg Cyzynski in fourth grade. Usually the memory alone was enough to keep guys from messing with her.

I waved to Brina as she walked out the door, and then promptly forgot about the whole situation. Today, it was all about me—and my nerves, which felt like someone had jump-started them with a few million amps of electric current.

I scooted out of school the minute the bell rang, drove home like a maniac, and packed my gear: the newer running shoes I'd broken in over the past month plus the old pair, just in case I had second thoughts; my trusty iPod; layers of clothing I could peel off as it got warmer during the race; and the *You + Bliss = Me 4ever* T-shirt.

I was about to switch off my computer for the weekend when I changed my mind and clicked onto my e-mail box one more time. There, hidden among a bunch of spammy offers, was a message from Caitlin, the girl who had been so good to us at Fairfield.

Subject line: Congrats!

Trace,
My friend who works in admissions gave me the great news—congratulations! I know you were considering other schools over Fairfield, but I would be remiss if I didn't say this: Fairfield is perfect for you. Remember what a great time we had when you visited? If not, I've attached a little something to jog your memory. If you're still not convinced after looking at it, promise me you'll at least give it some serious, serious thought. Call or e-mail with any questions.

Your friend the almost senior,
Caitlin

I opened the attachment and laughed out loud. It was a picture of me after I ran into the ocean instead of the finish line during the bat races. I was soaking wet, looking very Medusa-like with icicles hanging off my head. The rugby team was high-fiving me and I sported a grin the size of Texas.

I couldn't believe Caitlin remembered me, much less cared enough to ask about the status of my application. None of the other schools had a clue who I was. Crap, when I was at UCLA, no one would even talk to me.

Wait. What was I doing, dissing the university I was going to next year for the one I was never even particularly interested in? Must be all the excitement, I thought. A minute later, the phone interrupted my crazy thoughts. It was Brina. "Oh . . . my . . . God," was all she could say.

"Oh, my God, what, girlfriend?"

"Oh, my God, you'll never believe what the principal just got me to agree to."

I ran my fingers through my hair. "I totally forgot you got called down to his office. What happened?"

"First, I got a big, long lecture about defacing school property. Then they tried to get me to rat out Rodney, which of course I wouldn't," Brina said. "When that didn't work, the principal gave me a choice of punishments: Stay after school every day for a month to help the janitor clean the place, or let the *Winnetka Times* interview me for a feature article about the whole slp saga."

"Why the second option?"

"The principal's daughter has an internship at the paper, and he's trying to feed her some scoop so she'll get published."

"You are going to look so funny in those gray janitor overalls," I said, picturing Brina in the preposterous getup. "Do you get an embroidered name patch, too?"

Brina cleared her throat. "I picked the story," she said quietly.

"You what?" I screamed.

"I said, I picked the story."

I couldn't speak—I was so blown away. Was this the same girl who wouldn't even skate with Sully just a few months ago because he was an underclassman?

"Trace, are you still there?" Brina asked.

"Yeah."

"Listen, I know Sully won't mind. And I'm not the least bit embarrassed," she said. "In fact, I think every girl at Northshore Regional will be green with envy. Who else spent their senior year getting anonymous love notes from the hottest guy in school? No one."

The drama queen had gone and topped us all again. With Brina, I thought, there's never even a close second.

# CHAPTER
## 17

On Friday night, Bebe, Mr. Steve, and I caught the red-eye to San Diego. As soon as we got to the hotel on Saturday morning, they flung themselves on the bed and started snoring away.

I had a whole different agenda. I threw on my *You + Bliss = Me 4ever* shirt and wrote Bebe a *very* specific note about where I'd be, just in case Shamus turned out to be a psycho killer who didn't even know the Boss-alike. The only detail missing was exactly whom I was going to meet. That I left as pretty vague "old friends."

I grabbed the keys to our economy-sized rental car and soon I was jamming to the sound of the tiny, tinny-sounding engine pinging its way up the coast to Del Mar. I thought about forgetting the whole thing more than once. But then I realized I had fought too hard to get this far and would kick myself later if I turned around now.

I was shaking so much by the time I parked the car, I wondered if my legs were going to give out. They didn't. Slamming the door shut, I looked around until I finally found a sign pointing to the second floor for the Pacifica Café.

I glanced up to see a breezy open-air restaurant with a great view of the ocean. Leaning over the wrought-iron railing was a man who was obviously waiting for someone. I could tell by the way he searched the face of every person that walked in. So far, he didn't look like a murderer. I punched 911 into my cell phone anyhow—that way I'd only have to hit SEND if I got into trouble.

I ran up the stairs, ready for the biggest moment of my life. "Mr. . . . .

uhhh . . . Mac?" I wondered why only one guy was there waiting to meet me, not two like I'd expected.

The man turned to face me but didn't immediately meet my eyes. I realized he was reading my shirt. "Trace?"

"That's me," I said, waiting for him to put two and two together. "Before you say anything else, tell me the answer to my trivia question."

"Bliss," he said, now blatantly staring at all of me, not just my T-shirt.

"You got it," I said. I couldn't believe I was actually face-to-face with my very own father. He didn't look much like Bruce Springsteen anymore—or maybe it was just the fancy suit throwing me off—but if I squinted, I could see some subtle resemblances between us.

"I have something to tell you. . . . It's huge. . . . That's if you haven't figured it out already. . . ." I was having a hard time finding the right words to properly introduce myself as his daughter.

"I have something to tell you, too," he said, looking completely uncomfortable now. "Mac had to go out of town unexpectedly. I'm Shamus."

"Shamus?" Tears sprang to my eyes. "Where did Mac go? When will he be back?"

"He had to head to Europe to visit a sick family member and won't be back until late next week, the earliest," Shamus said, wiping beads of sweat from his forehead with an expensive-looking handkerchief. "But I can see now what you meant about your news being a big surprise. I knew that Mac and Bliss had a big thing going that summer, but I never realized they'd had a child together."

"Yup," I said miserably. Then I had a thought. "Do you think we could call him together now?"

"I'm afraid not," Shamus said. "He's in flight as we speak, and I have no idea where he's staying once he gets there."

"Let's e-mail him, then."

"He was in such a hurry to leave, I don't think he brought his laptop."

"Oh, well," I said, hitting probably the lowest point of my life. "I've already waited seventeen years to meet him. What's a few more days?" The laugh I tried to force came out sounding more like a sob.

Shamus put his arm around my shoulder. "I'm sure Mac will do his best to make up for lost time once he gets back."

I laid my head back against his chest. I felt completely drained, like there was nothing left inside of me. "How well do you know him?" I asked Shamus, hoping some crumbs of information would feed my need until my dad got back from his trip.

"Very," Shamus said. "I'd say I'm closer to him than anyone else in the world."

"Then can you tell me all about him? About his life?"

"That wouldn't be fair to Mac," Shamus said. "I'm sure he'll want to tell you everything himself."

"Fine," I said miserably, getting up to leave. I stuck my hand out. "Thanks for all your help, Shamus. I really appreciate it."

Shamus stared at my hand and then wrapped me up in a big bear hug instead. "Mac's one hell of a lucky guy," he said. "He just doesn't know it yet."

I felt all safe and warm, like Shamus was my new guardian angel. "Maybe since you're the one bringing us together, you could be his stand-in at the end of the race. I'm meeting my mom at the Bitter End after the marathon. It's right near the finish line."

"I'll see what I can do to clear my schedule, Trace," Shamus said. "But I'm pretty booked up tomorrow with business."

When I got back to the hotel, I made some lame excuse to Bebe and Mr. Steve about being tired and locked myself in my room for the rest of the day. They didn't seem to mind in the least bit and took off in search of fun.

"Where are you going?" I asked them, just to be polite.

"Buffalo Joe's," Mr. Steve said, pointing to a big ad in the *Reader* of five guys in humongous Afro wigs. "Some retro band called Dubble Bubble is playing there for happy hour."

"Looks like a blast," I said, picking up the phone to order room service. "Have fun."

My weird combination of dishes—pasta, oatmeal, and beer—was delivered shortly after those two lovebirds left. I had totally lost my appetite after meeting with Shamus, but I hoped I could choke down at least one of my carbo-loaded selections. I needed energy for the big race tomorrow.

I twirled spaghetti around my fork, trying to get out of my current funky state. I had been so close—this close—to meeting my dad. I even had his phone number in my hand. I could conceivably be talking to him in a week. So why did I feel so shitty?

After a lot of thought, I realized what had happened wasn't the end of the world. It's not like I had met my dad and he had run away from me the same way he had run from my mom all those years ago. He was just on a trip, and I'd just have to dig down deep and muster one more week's worth of patience.

The next morning, Bebe and Mr. Steve were trying to sneak in the hotel room as I was getting ready to leave. Both had their pants legs rolled up to the knees, and they were wearing these wild Afros.

"Good night?" I asked them.

Bebe let out a little scream and put her hand to her heart. "You scared the crap out of me, Trace."

"Nice hair," I said, patting her wig.

"We paid the guys in the band for them," Mr. Steve said. He and Bebe collapsed into a fit of giggles.

"I just need an hour power nap and I'll be as good as new," Bebe said, crawling into bed.

Mr. Steve wasn't far behind her. "Me, too," he said, snuggling up against her. "We'll meet you at the finish line."

I gave Bebe a quick kiss and hopped a cab to Balboa Park. The place was already packed to the gills with people who looked like serious runners. I pushed my way through the crowd until I found my posse of nine-minute-milers.

A gut-wrenching hour later, the starting horn sounded. It took a full five minutes before I could even move across the start line. "I hope they subtract that off our final time," I told a guy standing next to me. He was dressed in a white satin jumpsuit, an Elvis wig, and blue suede sneakers.

"Oh, please. I just hope I finish in one piece," he said, pointing to his crazy outfit. "This seemed like such a good idea at the time."

"C'mon, you hunka hunka burnin' love," I said, grabbing his hand and pulling him along. "Let's get moving."

I was so caught up in the excitement, I could practically feel the adrenaline coursing through my veins. I tried to contain myself because I knew I'd need to tap into that energy later, but I was totally out of control. "This rocks!" I screamed as I caught an earful of the first band. Elvis gave me a pained smile and a thumbs-up.

I was feeling lighter than air and trying to etch everything about the experience onto my mind so I could remember it forever. The gorgeous scenery. The enthusiastic cheerleaders, encouraging us to keep going. The rockin' bands that made me forget I would be running for the next four hours. My shoes flap-flap-flapped to the music and it all felt effortless. My training was certainly paying off.

At mile thirteen, I caught sight of Bebe waving a sign that said *Rock on, Trace*. I was impressed. My mom could apparently still party like a high school kid and be fresh as a daisy the next day.

"Where's Mr. Steve?" I panted as I ran over for a hug.

"Back at the hotel, trying to recover from last night," she said, laughing. "He's with you in spirit, though."

As I raced away, Bebe yelled after me, "You're halfway there!"

As soon as the words were out of her mouth, the band launched into Bon Jovi's "Livin' on a Prayer." " 'Ohhh, we're halfway there,' " I sang at the top of my lungs, not even caring that it was one of Bebe's songs that I loved to hate. " 'Take my hand and we'll make it, I swear . . .' "

Elvis was holding his side and looking pained. "I don't know if I'm gonna make it," he told me. "I swear."

"Oh, you will. I'll help you every step of the way," I said, feeling magnanimous. A fleeting thought went through my mind—that it was Zander I should be in step with this entire race and not the King—but I pushed it out before it even had a chance to get settled in. I'd done enough crying, moping, and freaking out about Zander over the past few weeks. It was time to move ahead into my future.

I didn't see Bebe again until mile twenty. "You look amazing, honey. Like you're not even hurting," Bebe said, beaming with pride. "Only six miles left to go. I'll see you at the finish line."

Only six more miles? I got totally revved. I had run twenty miles twice during training. What was six more? Less than an hour's worth of running. No big deal.

Elvis seemed to brighten, too. "I think I'm actually gonna make it," he told me, smiling for the first time in hours.

We slowed for a water stop, and that's when I came toe-to-toe with the dreaded wall. "I'm just gonna walk while I drink this," I told Elvis.

"Oh, no, you're not. That's the kiss of death."

"Smooch, smooch," I said, pissed that this guy I didn't know from a hole in the wall was telling me what to do. "My hips are about to fall out of their sockets. I need to stop for a second."

"No walking, girlfriend. Run! Run!" screamed a cheerleader in blue and gold, waving her pom-poms in my face.

I grabbed one pom and then another, throwing the damn things across the road.

"Bitch," she muttered, picking her way through the runners to retrieve her precious pom-poms.

"You got something against UCLA?" Elvis asked me. "It's a pretty good school."

A crazy thought hit me just then—one that felt so good, I knew it must be the right decision. "Nope. I wouldn't go there. I just realized it's not for me."

"Where *is* for you, then?"

"The land of the Beheaded Deer," I said happily.

"What?"

"I'll be a freshman at Fairfield University in the fall," I said.

"Never heard of it."

"That's what they all say," I told him, not caring at all that it lacked the same name recognition as UCLA.

The exhilaration of making that momentous decision got me through the next mile or so. And then I got completely fed up. "Whose freakin' brilliant idea was it to run this marathon anyway?"

"Uhhhhh . . . I'm guessing now . . . yours?" Elvis said.

"Well, I'm an idiot," I said. "If I could find a wheelchair, I'd be so outta here it's not funny."

"You don't mean that," Elvis said. "Just hang in there."

"I do, too. Can someone get me a wheelchair?" I yelled into the crowd.

The paramedics started running my way, but Elvis waved them off. "You are not quitting on me now," he told me. "You helped me. Now it's my turn to help you."

"The finish line might as well be a million miles away," I groaned to my table-turning friend.

Now it was Elvis who grabbed my hand and forced me to run. I felt like a loping, lopsided, wounded animal. "Can't you just shoot me and put me out of my misery?"

He smiled and kept dragging me along. "Sorry, no."

Not nearly soon enough, the finish line came into sight. "Oh, my God, it's finally here," I said. Tears of relief streamed down my cheeks.

"We did it, didn't we?" Elvis said, sounding like he couldn't believe it himself.

The band launched into "Born to Run" and we started sprinting. Knowing someone was sitting in for Mac while he was away, I didn't even bother to glance up at the stage.

" 'Tramps like us, baby, we were born to run'!" Elvis and I sang as we crossed the finish line pumping our fists. The King singing the Boss with a Beheaded Deer—now, that was one for the photo album.

I said my good-byes to my new best friend Elvis and grabbed one of those metallic race blankets, trying to get my body to stop shaking. Once I was pretty sure I wasn't going to have an aneurysm, or embolism, or whatever it's called, I started limping my way toward the Bitter End. Fitting name, I thought.

Even though the restaurant was only three blocks away, I had totally underestimated how beat-up and exhausted I would feel after the race. With me gimping, it took a good fifteen minutes to get there.

I walked in and pushed my way through the crowd, trying to spot Bebe. But the place was so packed, all I could actually see were other people's heads and shoulders. I finally grabbed a chair and stood on top of it, scanning the crowd. Still no sight of her.

I felt a tap on my leg. "I'll be down in a sec," I said, not even glancing at whoever it was. "I've just got to find someone first."

"You already found me." I looked down. It was Shamus. And he was all sweaty and dressed in a short-sleeved white shirt with the sleeves rolled up, Levi's, and boots. The working-class hero look was such a contrast to his business attire the day before, but I didn't have the wherewithal to give it a lot of thought.

Hopping down from my perch, I gave him a huge hug. "Thanks so much for coming," I said. "It means a lot to me to know a good friend of my dad's was here to share this with me."

"I wanted to talk to you about that, Trace," he said as Bebe finally spotted me and started winding her way through the throngs of people to get to us. As she got closer, I saw that her mouth was hanging open and she looked like she'd just seen a ghost.

"Mac?" she said, her lips still formed into a perfect SpaghettiO. "Is that really you?"

"Close but no cigar, Bebe," I said, putting my arm around her. "This is his friend Shamus."

"Actually, you're both kind of right," Shamus said, staring at the ground and shifting his weight from one foot to the other.

"What?" I screamed, furious. "You're Mac?"

"Well, technically . . . ," he said, trailing off.

I just lost it then. "You mean to tell me you lied to my face? That you ran away from me, just like you ran away from my mother?" I lunged at Shamus and started beating his chest with my fists. "You asshole! How could you do that to me?"

Bebe pulled me off of him the best she could. When I finally stopped flailing my arms around, I buried my head in her shoulder and sobbed uncontrollably. This wasn't the way it was supposed to happen. Not by a long shot.

"You were so right, Bebe," I said. "We've made it this far without any testosterone interfering with our relationship. There's no need to start now."

"Trace, you should be proud. You accomplished your goal. You found your dad," she said, stroking my hair. "Don't you at least want to hear his side of the story?"

"No," I said, still sniffling into her shoulder. "Because his side of the story is that he made up some stupid name and pretended he was someone else to get out of a mess he made a billion years ago at the Jersey Shore."

Shamus looked pleadingly at Bebe. "I did make a huge mess out of things, didn't I, Bliss?"

"That's an understatement," she said.

"I could have kicked myself for breaking up with you that way," Shamus told her. "I eventually swallowed my pride and called your dorm at Fairfield, but they said you never showed up at school. Then I tried you at your parents' house, but they said you didn't live there anymore and wouldn't tell me where you'd gone."

"Bullshit, Mac," Bebe said, as angry as I was now. "My mother definitely would have relayed the message that the father of her unborn grandchild called. In fact, she would've flown all the way to Europe to pick you up herself."

"But she wouldn't have told you Shamus called, right?" he said. "And if she did, you wouldn't have known who it was."

"That's because it's an alias," I hissed. "The one you use to run away from your problems."

"It's not an alias," Shamus said gently. "It's my real name. Shamus McDonohue."

"I was in love with a guy named Shamus?" Bebe said, and started to laugh. It really was a ridiculous name, especially for a twenty-one-year-old guy. I guess he had finally grown into it at forty-whatever.

"Bebe, how could you be so . . . ?" I was going to say "stupid," but then I remembered both Brina and I had been convinced until a week ago that Sully's name was Peter Liam Sullivan and not Sullivan Liam Peterson. So if Bebe had thought her love was really named Mac Donohue instead of Shamus McDonohue, I couldn't really blame her. I turned my attention to my dad instead. "How could you be so cruel, pretending you were someone else yesterday?"

Shamus hung his head. "I . . . I guess I panicked," he said. "I had no idea what you had to tell me, Trace. I was actually hoping all those e-mails were from you, Bliss. I thought maybe you were using a fake name to find me."

"Keep dreaming, lover boy," Bebe said, looking pleased that she could deliver some hurt back to him after all this time. "Just like I dreamed for years that you'd pick up one of my books, realize it was me, and come begging my forgiveness."

"Books?"

"Yeah," I said, feeling incredibly protective of my mom now. "Didn't you ever realize your Bliss was really Belinda Tillingham, the famous romance novelist?"

"Bliss, that's great," Shamus said, looking truly happy for her. "I would have tried to contact you if I knew. But I'm afraid I don't make it into that section of Borders very often."

"That's OK," she said, patting his hand. "The truth is, we both screwed up."

"I still want to know why you lied to me," I said, interrupting their peacemaking.

"When I figured out the surprise was you, Trace, and that you're my daughter . . . ," he said, "well, needless to say, I completely freaked out. So I misled you to buy some time until I could make sense of everything in my head."

"Did you think I wouldn't recognize you the next time we got together?"

He shrugged. "I wasn't thinking that far ahead."

"You were going to disappear again, just like you always do. Right?"

"I promise I'll never disappear again," Shamus said fiercely. "I want to be a part of your life, Trace. I really do."

I stared at him, stone-faced.

"Here, let's try this," he said, extending his hand toward me. "I'm Shamus, and I'm proud to be your dad. May I please be part of your life?"

I felt so lost, I buried my face in Bebe's shirt again and starting crying even harder than last time. "I don't know what to do, Bebe. Help me," I whispered.

"She says she'd love to get to know you, Mac . . . I mean Shamus," Bebe said. "She'd absolutely love to."

# CHAPTER
## 18

When my nervous breakdown was over, Bebe and I caught a cab back to the hotel, with Shamus promising to call me so we could plan an extended father-daughter visit when school was over. My muscles were screaming and my head was reeling from everything that had happened.

"I can't believe it," I kept repeating over and over.

"Me, neither," said Bebe. "He's still pretty smokin', huh?"

"For a dad," I said. "Is he married?"

She examined her fingers like they were the most interesting things in the world. "He wasn't wearing a ring."

"So maybe there's still hope for the two of you," I said.

"Don't go all *Parent Trap*-y on me," Bebe said, still staring at her hands. "Because I am."

"You are what?" I asked her.

"Wearing a ring."

I looked down and saw the diamond glinting up from Bebe's left hand. "Oh, my God!" I screamed, throwing my arms around her. "When did this happen?"

"Last night on the beach," she said. "Steve and I wanted to tell you together, but I just couldn't hold it in any longer."

"Congratulations, Bebe," I said, kissing her on the cheek.

"Can you do me a favor?" Bebe asked. "Can you pretend I didn't say anything about it?"

"Sure thing," I said.

\*  \*  \*

Mr. Steve was waiting for us back at the room, champagne bottle in hand. "This calls for a celebration," he said, popping the cork and passing us glasses.

"To running the race of your life, Trace," he said, toasting me. "And to a beautiful beginning of our life together, Belinda."

"To a great race and beautiful beginnings," I said, and we clinked glasses all around.

"You told Trace already, didn't you?" Mr. Steve said to Belinda, looking disappointed. "She isn't freaked-out at all."

Bebe nodded. "Sorry. I never was any good at keeping secrets."

I cleared my throat. It was such an absurd statement. "Well, except for that one small issue about my dad," I said.

"Oh, yeah," she said. "Well, at least that's over."

"Over?" Mr. Steve said.

"It's not over," I said, correcting Bebe. "It's just beginning."

"What are you girls talking about?"

"It's a long story," I said.

"We'll fill you in later," Bebe told him.

"Did you already tell Trace we picked our wedding song, too?" Mr. Steve asked Bebe.

"No. You do it."

" 'Never Gonna Give You Up,' " he said, smiling now. "Rick Astley."

"Well, it's better than 'Fourth of July, Asbury Park,' " I said. "That was your song with my dad, right?"

"Right," Bebe said. "But I'm all grown-up now. I have much better judgment. About a lot of things."

The phone rang and I hobbled over to answer it. "Hi, Trace." It was Zander. Not that I wanted him to know I knew that.

"Who is this?"

"It's Zander. Who did you think it was?"

"Zander," I said, grinning. I'd kind of thought he might call today.

"So, how'd you do?"

"I did OK, thanks to Elvis."

"I'm not even gonna ask what that means."

"Good idea."

"Trace, there's something I've been wanting to tell you," Zander said. "Something I should've said before you went to visit UCLA."

Oh, Jesus, I thought. Here we go again. He's about to tell me he and Buffy are back together or something equally as vomitous. "Yeah?"

"I love you, too."

"You what?" My legs didn't just threaten this time—they really gave in. I fell to the floor with a splat and shook my head to clear it.

"I was so stupid. I thought that if I broke up with you, my feelings would just go away," he said. "You know, running away never solves anything."

I thought of Shamus. "Ain't that the truth."

"I know I don't deserve it, but would you consider giving us another shot, Trace?" he said. "I'll even book us flights so we can see each other every other weekend once we get to school."

"Twice-a-month cross-country trips are more than my bank account can handle, Zander."

"There are specials from New York to LA. I'll make sure to stock up on tickets every time there's a fare war."

"What's New York got to do with it?" I asked him.

"I finally told my dad I'd rather be a filmmaker than follow in his footsteps," Zander said. "I'm going to NYU."

"And what does LA have to do with it?" I said, toying with him now.

"The last time I checked, that's where UCLA was."

"Who said anything about me going to UCLA?"

"You did?"

"Naaaah," I said. "You've been gone longer than I thought, dude. I'm gonna be a Beheaded Deer next year."

"What?" Zander said.

"You heard me. I'm going to Fairfield," I said.

"Really?" Zander asked.

"Yup," I said, grinning from ear to ear.

Zander let out a whoop. "So we'll only be an hour away from each other!"

"So true," I said.

"When I need a break from the big city, I'll come see you," he said, already planning our future together. "And when you need a little more excitement, you hop a train down to me."

"Hold on just a sec," I said. "I didn't say I forgave you just yet. You still have an awful lot of sucking up to do."

A great feeling came over me after I hung up the phone, and I realized it was pride for everything I had accomplished. Like figuring out Fairfield was the right place for me, even if it wasn't anywhere near as sexy as UCLA. Like running a marathon, especially those last few grueling miles when I wanted to quit more than anything in the world. Like being able to forgive my mom for not working harder to find my dad, and my dad for almost running away again. Like letting Zander off the hook for being human, just like the rest of us.

As I was patting myself on the back, I realized the hunch was finally gone—probably for good. I could stand tall, knowing I had the courage to face whatever life threw my way.

"Sing it with me." Mr. Steve leaned forward and cranked the volume on the stereo as soon as "Sing for the Moment" came on.

"Who's this, bastardizing Aerosmith?" Bebe wanted to know. She really had been living under a musical rock for the past few years, I thought.

"Ever heard of Eminem?" I asked her.

"Christ, what will those marketing guys think up next?" Bebe said. "Imagine, having cartoon candy singing a great old song."

Mr. Steve rolled his eyes at me, and we both started laughing hysterically. "No, Eminem. *E-m-i-n-e-m,*" I said, spelling it out for her.

"Who?" Bebe said. Now I knew how Bebe must feel when she talks to my friends about her bands.

"If you don't know now," I told her, smiling, "you never will."

"Give it up, old lady," Mr. Steve said, giving Bebe a kiss on the cheek. "You're so out of it."

OK. So even though lots of things in my life were never going to be the same, it was looking more and more like some things would never change.

Trish Cook is a freelance writer who, like Trace, survived high school, a marathon (actually two), and being best friends with a hottie/drama queen. She lives outside Chicago with her husband and two daughters. When Trish isn't busy dreaming up new stories, you can usually find her playing electric guitar, running down Sheridan Road, or catching her favorite bands in Chicago.

**books**

COMING THIS SUMMER
# A TOTALLY FRESH LINE OF BOOKS

<u>June 2005</u>
### SO LYRICAL
by Trish Cook
0-451-21508-7

<u>July 2005</u>
### THE PRINCIPLES OF LOVE
by Emily Franklin
0-451-21517-6

### CONFESSIONS OF AN ALMOST-MOVIE STAR
by Mary Kennedy
0-425-20467-7

<u>August 2005</u>
### ROCK MY WORLD
by Lisa Conrad
0-451-21523-0

### JENNIFER SCALES AND THE ANCIENT FURNACE
by MaryJanice Davidson
and Anthony Alongi
0-425-20598-3

**Available in paperback from Berkley and New American Library**

www.penguin.com

# ROCK MY WORLD: A Novel of Thongs, Spandex, and Love in G Minor

## by Liza Conrad

"*A nd on the sixth day, God created Nick Hoffman's voice, Liz Phair's lyrics, Kurt Cobain's angst, and Lenny Kravitz's guitar licks. And He saw that it was good. So He just said, Screw it . . . tomorrow I'm resting.*"

I looked across the table at Carl Erikson, *Rock On* magazine's editor-in-chief, as he put down my essay, "Creation of Rock and Roll," that had run in my high school newspaper. I held my breath.

"This is really quite clever, Livy," he said.

I relaxed a little. "Clever" is a lot better than "What were you thinking, clacker?" or "Cheesy"—and I so wanted this summer gig. I tried to picture Carl forty pounds lighter. With hair. And an earring. In tight jeans. With eyeliner. Back when he was cool, or at least not bald and "pleasantly plump," back when he and my father used to hang out after Babydolls' concerts and smoke an ungodly amount of pot. And Lord knows what else. Trying not to laugh, I simply said, "Thanks."

One time, my father said, when I was four years old, Carl stripped naked and played air guitar in our living room during a party. I don't remember that, which is just as well. If I'd been able to recall Carl's flaccid—my father remembers that detail perfectly—penis, I was quite positive I would have fallen on the floor in hysterics and wouldn't have been able to do this interview.

"You know what we're asking you to do, right?" Carl raised an eyebrow, his reading glasses perched on the end of his nose.

I nodded.

"Good," he said. "I like the way you write. At seventeen, you're better than half of my staff, and I mean that—though don't tell them. *Rock On* is for the MTV set. We're not like *Rolling Stone*. They cover the whole spectrum, and they're oh-so-self-important." He took his glasses off and laid them on his desk. "We want readers mostly your age . . . and into their twenties. We've got gossip and lots of photos. Backstage candids. Interviews with actors. Do you read _Rock On_?"

I nodded, even though I didn't. I thought most of it was crap.

"Of course you do. All teens in your age bracket do."

"Sure," I said convincingly.

"Well." Carl leaned back in his enormous leather chair, a view of the New York skyline behind him. "I don't have to tell you what the Baby-dolls mean to rock and roll history. I'm sure you meet people all the time who tell you what an amazing musician and singer your father was—and is. And the reunion tour is going to be the hottest summer stadium ticket both here and in Europe."

"And Japan," I said. "That's where the tour starts."

"Yeah. The Japanese love them. And now he's got that American Express commercial. Hysterical. Comes across as uber-hip. And with the Wolves opening for the Babydolls on the tour . . . Jesus, I wish I was twenty again." He smiled, and for a split second, I could see the twenty-year-old Carl. His eyes were less tired, and his dimples showed.

"Well, Livy . . . I'm sold. What I want is a series of articles—you could make them like journal entries—from the road. Places like Madison Square Garden, L.A., London . . . Wherever they are—wherever you are. And then mingled with that, I'd love to read the story of the Babydolls . . . and your life with your parents and the band and so on. I'd love to connect this tour with readers your age—they'll be able to relate to you."

"Like Kelly Osbourne without the pink hair. And the foul mouth—most of the time."

"Yeah. Minus the pink hair and the f-word." He smiled at me. "I like how you think. You're quick—like your old man. I'll give you my e-mail, and Rob's—he's a very sharp editor. He's good, and he's excited about this."

"Great."

"I'd also like you to take digital pictures—candids—of the tour bus, the jet, the crowds, the band, the Wolves."

The Wolves were opening for my father's band. Nick Hoffman was so good-looking that grown women got wolf paw tattoos on their breasts. I remember being five or six and seeing women throwing baby-doll pajamas on the stage at my father. Though tossing pajamas and permanently inking your body seem like two entirely different brands of fan obsession.

"Sure." Photograph Nick Hoffman? I could just imagine my best friend Cammie's response when she heard that: *Can we take his picture with his shirt off?*

"One story a week for the summer tour . . . We'll put you on the pay-roll for two hundred dollars a week; fifty bucks for every photo we use."

"Deal." I said it calmly, but I would have done the stories for free—just to start building up press clippings. My dream was to someday start my own rock magazine. Getting *paid* to write? That meant I could actually *say* I was a writer. For real.

Carl stood and shook my hand, then came out from behind the desk. Suddenly, and without warning, he enveloped me in a bear hug. "God, I remember when you used to toddle around the house in your diapers. Can't believe it. You look like a model, and you're taller than I am."

"That's not hard, Carl," I said, looking down at the top of his bald head. I'm five foot eleven. He had to be five foot five.

He laughed and put his arm around me.

"So you think if I was as tall as your dad, *I* would have gotten all the groupies?"

"Not unless you put on some spandex back then."

"Oh, I had spandex."

"Well, you know how chicks dig musicians. And you can't play any-thing," I teased.

"I once played the tambourine on stage with the Babydolls. At Wembley."

We left his office in search of my father.

"Tambourines don't count."

"Yeah, well, I had hair then, too." He looked over at me and winked.

Down the hall, I heard female giggling. Lots of it. Along with a coo-ing sort of fawning. It could only be for my dad—women still fall all over him. He says it's because he kicked hard drugs, so he didn't age like Keith Richards, the walking cadaver—though that's giving cadavers a bad name. They don't make the corpses on _CSI_ look that bad. My father still looks young. He wears his hair to his shoulders, and it's as thick and dirty blond as when he was twenty-one. He has blue eyes and a lanky build, and he speaks with a raspy voice like some late-night DJ who's chain-smoking through the night shift. He wears boot-cut jeans, custom-made lizard-skin cowboy boots, and tight black T-shirts that show off his body. He looks, all the time, like what he is: a rock star. All my life, girls tried to be friends with me because of him. It's beyond creepy to go to a friend's house and see a poster of your father in her bedroom—when you know in her fifth-grade mind she's kissing him. _Gross!_

Carl opened the door to _Rock On_'s conference room. And there was my dad, Paul James, black Sharpie pen in hand, signing the left breast of some woman, her top unbuttoned to her belly button. She blushed and covered up. The other women were laughing. Not just women my dad's age either. There were interns there who looked just a couple of years older than I am—college girls. I rolled my eyes, and Dad came over and kissed me.

"Well, baby?"

Carl smiled. "She's hired. We worked it all out. Have some paperwork to fill out, but it's all set."

"Cool. That's my girl."

We hung around the office, took care of the paperwork, and then Dad and I went downstairs where our limousine waited. My father got his fifth DUI before I was even in junior high. After that, he never bothered to get his license back again. It's kind of pathetic when you have to drive your own parents around. My mother's from England, and she never did learn to drive on our side of the road. What a pair they are. At least, however, I have a convertible. I mean, if you have to drive your father around, might as well drive something you're not embarrassed by. And when I don't drive, then it's the limo. Toby is our driver/bodyguard. He used to drive me to school every day until I got my license. He also keeps all the liquor in the house under lock and key.

In the back of the limousine, Dad grinned. He has this lopsided smile women have been swooning over forever.

"You're all grown up, Livy."

I rolled my eyes. "*Please* don't get all mushy on me."

"Well, it seems like yesterday. I mean, holy shit, I can barely remember you when you were small. And now you've got your first job as a real writer. Next thing it'll be college. One year. Christ, just one more year. Then next thing you know you'll be hosting *Total Request Live*."

"Dad, I'm a writer, not a TV host. They read cue cards."

"Well . . . where did the time go?"

"The time went down the sucking vortex of drugs, Dad. You can't remember me because you pretty much went through the 1990s in a blackout."

"Ahh, yes. And now, unfortunately, I'm constantly reminded you're way too clever with words, courtesy of that very expensive private school you go to . . . so you can mouth off to me—and I get to remember it all because I have no blackouts to help me forget," he sighed. "Anyway, I'm sober now."

"Yes. Now."

"What's that supposed to mean?"

"Dad, sometimes I don't think you really . . . think things through. Have you thought about this tour, Dad? I mean really thought about it?"

"Yeah. . . . At least I think so. Why?"

"Sex, drugs, and rock and roll, Dad. . . . You're going back on tour with Greg Essex and Steve Zane. Neither of whom has ever met a drug he didn't like. And you and Charlie have been trying to go to AA. Have you thought about what the tour bus is going to be like? What backstage is going to be like? Not to mention the whole Paris incident. The stuff of legend, Dad. Are you sure you can handle this?"

"Since when did you get so fucking smart?"

"Since I raised myself. Toby went to more of my school events than you did."

He leaned his head back, shut his eyes, and pretended to sleep. I could see Toby in the rearview mirror and knew he was hoping I'd let it drop. I watched my dad fake-sleeping, trying to remember a time when he was responsible, and pretty much recalling none. We rode back to Nyack in silence, and Toby pulled into the gate and up our long driveway. Dad pretended to wake up. As we got out of the car, he grabbed my hand.

"I love you, Livy. You're my girl. I hate fighting."

"I know."

Dad let go of my hand and went into the house. I got my purse, feeling aggravated. I was one of those big "surprises" in life. Mom was a backup singer who had fallen in love—like the whole world—with Greg Essex, lead guitarist of the Babydolls with the biceps and forearms of a sex god. They were together first, then he broke her heart when he suggested a threesome with another woman. She ran into the arms of his best friend, my father and lead singer, and five months later—just starting to show—my mother married my dad. There was some question about my paternity . . . but I happen to have my father's blue eyes. They are this weird icy blue. And I'm his. Much as I sometimes wish I wasn't.

Our house—for a couple who never had any other children—is way too big. Eight bedrooms. Which is okay, I guess, since there always seems to be *someone* crashing—usually a musician. I once spent three months sharing a bathroom with David Drake, the bassist from the Kung-fu Cowboys. He had a nervous breakdown and spent the entire summer building model airplanes. Whatever.

Our house is on the Hudson River in Nyack, New York. Kind of trendy. A perky talk show host who never ceases gabbing about her children on the air lives next door. Guess what? The kids are raised entirely by nannies. I'm surprised Ms. Perky Talk Show Host even knows their names. But we can barely see their house for the big pines that surround our property. Our house is pretty, with a big back lawn that touches the water. My room is on the third floor, in what used to be the attic. My parents finished it off so it's my own living room and bedroom. And no more sharing the bathroom with musician houseguests.

I shut the car door and started to head up to the front porch. Toby cleared his throat. "Liv?"

I turned around. Toby weighs a good 280—all muscle—and he shaves his head, but he has this enormous handlebar moustache that curls around his mouth and makes him look like some kind of weird kewpie doll.

"Yeah?"

"He's trying."

"I know."

"Cut him some slack. He's going to need a lot of support on this tour."

I nodded. Toby was in AA, too, but unlike Dad, Toby had been sober for twenty years or something like that. My father pretty much fell off the wagon about every six months. Now he had nearly a year under his belt. I hoped he could stay out of trouble on the tour—no women, no drugs, no alcohol. The last tour ended with him in rehab. The tour before that with two nights in jail.

"I know, Toby. We're all just worried." I turned and climbed up the steps and into the house and then kept on going—all the way up to my room. When I was little, in my mind I used to pretend Toby was my father.

When I got upstairs, I turned on my stereo and popped a CD in—one I burned myself. I make a CD every week of all my favorites. That changes from week to week, song to song. Sometimes I can get into a "phase"—like only Nine Inch Nails for two or three weeks. Sometimes I hear an old song—like from my parents' generation, like the Rolling Stones' "Sympathy for the Devil," or from the Seattle grunge era—and I can literally listen to the same song two hundred times. It's in me, part of me, whatever. I put on my current set of favorites and started jumping up and down on my bed. *Holy shit! I got it! I got it!* Rock On!

I called Cammie, my best friend, who had talked her parents into letting her go on tour with us for two months. They thought it would be a great opportunity to see the world. I wasn't sure what they thought of my father's reputation, but I also knew they were so close to a divorce that maybe it didn't matter—just having Cammie away while they tried to work things out would be good. They were letting her older brother live in Boston that summer. He's going to college there. Anyway, her father could never say no to her. She had him twisted around her little pinkie.

"I got it, Cam!" I screamed into my cell phone. I had stopped jumping and flopped straight backward down on my bed. For some weird reason, I love doing that—except for the one time I hit my head on the wall and had to get stitches.

"Oh my God! That's _so_ great!"

"They're even _paying_ me."

"Wow! Next thing you know, you'll have your own reality show. Paul James's daughter as rock star critic. You could call it _Livy's Real World_."

"No, I think my life has enough reality in it already."

"I'm so happy for you."

"I can't believe it. My name in print . . . in a real magazine."

"You'll get into NYU's journalism program for sure."

For as long as I can remember, Cammie and I have been planning to go to New York University together. She wanted to study filmmaking. We had visions of sharing an apartment in Greenwich Village.

"You excited?" I asked her. We'd been planning this summer tour together as soon as the Babydolls announced their concert dates.

"Two days and counting!" She sounded like she was hyperventilating.

"One suitcase, Cammie. You can't get nuts." I was picturing clothes from one end of her room to the other.

"I know. One _big_ suitcase."

"Yes, one big suitcase. One carry-on. But it's not like the suitcase can be the size of your closet, so I don't know how you're whittling down all your crap into one bag."

"I'll manage."

Cammie was a major clothes horse. Juicy Couture and Abercrombie & Fitch—her two favorites. What she didn't have, she borrowed—from me. She was also a makeup nut, and I think she had no less than fifty-two kinds of shampoo in her bathroom. I kind of liked sleeping over her house because I felt like I was at a spa—getting to pick shampoos, conditioners, soaps, cleansers. You can't see her bathroom counter it's so full of stuff.

"Anything new on Operation V?" she asked me.

"I refuse to help you anymore."

"Oh, come on."

Cammie was determined to lose her virginity—in a scheme that made our history teacher's description of the landing at Normandy in World War II sound like a casual battle plan.

"All right. I just found out this morning that Steve Zane is not bringing anyone on the tour."

"No one?"

"Nope. His latest girlfriend left him."

"Operation V is going according to plan."

Cammie intended to lose her virginity to the drummer of the Babydolls. He's younger than my dad by maybe ten years, and he's a total slut. But Cammie had a theory about losing her virginity.

"Are you *sure* you want to go through with this, Cam?"

"Absolutely. As I have said a thousand times before, I have yet to meet a single person who ranked their virginity-losing partner as anyone great. I mean, sure, you think you're in love with some hot guy and you lose your virginity to him. Twenty years from now, he's just some dumb guy you lost your virginity to. Most people are lucky if they remember the guy's name. But if I lose *my* virginity to Steve Zane, even when you and I are ninety and have false teeth and side-by-side rocking chairs in the nursing home, I'll remember exactly who it was—and to top it off, he's probably quite good at it."

"Whatever, Cam. Just don't say I didn't warn you. Every nanny I ever had in my life quit because he'd sleep with her and then dump her a week later in a different city. They'd all go home crushed."

"But *I* know exactly what I'm doing. I'm losing my virginity for historical reasons. I can tell my *grandchildren* that I did it with Steve Zane."

"Yeah. I often discuss sex with my grandmother."

"Well, you get the idea. This isn't about a relationship. It's a quest. You can't tell me you don't think Steve Zane is totally fucking hot."

I admit it. He was. Brown hair, blue eyes, really full lips, high cheekbones. He was the Babydoll the magazines said was "the pretty one."

"Cammie, you know my rule."

"Yes," she sighed. "Livy James's first rule of the opposite sex: No musicians need apply."

"Trust me, Cam. After a few weeks on the road, you'll never look at a band the same way again."

Sex, drugs, and rock and roll.

It's not always all it's cracked up to be.

But then again, it's the only life I've ever known.

# The Principles of Love

## by Emily Franklin

Just to get this out of the way: yes, it's my real name. And no, I wasn't born on a commune (not unless you consider Boston, Massachusetts, circa 1989, to be a commune). In the movie version of my life, there'd be some great story to go with how I got my name—a rock star absentee father who named me in his hit song, or a promise my real father made to his grandmother in the old country. At least a weepy love story of two people so happy about their daughter they had to give her my name. But there's not—there's just me.

Love. My name is Love. Maybe this makes you think of your first kiss (mine = Jared Rosen, who managed to knock out my top left tooth at the beginning of the summer and provide my first kiss—a peck—by August's end). Or maybe you cringe when I introduce myself, wondering if I come complete with a tacky poster of cuddly kittens tangled in wool. (I had one in third grade that showed a tabby clawing the wall, saying HANG IN THERE! Thank God for paper recycling.)

Trust me: Despite what my name conjures up, I am not the sort to have a bed piled with fluffy kitties or well-loved stuffed animals. I actually don't even like cats all that much, not since I hugged little Snowball, my old neighbor's cat, right before the freshman formal last year and wound up sucking down antihistamines and nursing facial hives in my gown. Not pretty.

Then again, pretty's not all it's cracked up to be—or so I hear. I'm not what you'd call pretty, not the even more tantalizing *beautiful*, though maybe I've got potential. Right now I suppose I could fall into the category of appealing. My Aunt Mable's always saying the girls who peak in high school show up looking downright average at their tenth reunion, so I'm hoping (hoping = counting on) that my best years are still ahead of me. I don't want to look back on my life and have sophomore year of high school stand out as a blue ribbon winner, though the chances of that happening are slim at best. Part of me wouldn't mind trading places with the shiny, perfectly blond and still summer-tanned girls who probably emerged from the womb with a smile as wide as a Cadillac and legs from a music video. But since my life isn't one of those Disney movies where the heroine gets to swap places for a day and learn the secret to life, I have to be content to know only what it's like in my own life—and all I can say is it's too soon to tell.

We've been here (here = the Hadley Hall campus) for four days. Four days and six hours. And still not one decent conversation, not one promising smile-nod combination over mushy tuna sandwiches and lemonade outside, courtesy of FLIK, the school food supplier. When my dad told me about orientation for Hadley, I guess I imagined days spent lounging on the quad, soaking up the last of the summer rays while meeting cute boys, bonding with my two amazingly cool new best friends, and somehow forgetting that I have a forehead label— New Girl. Love, the New Girl. And not only that (here I'm imagining some lowly freshman pointing me out as someone who's even more lost than he is); I have the privilege of being the principal's daughter.

When my dad and I arrived on campus, typical trunk loaded with boxes, laundry hamper filled with my still-dirty duds, some overly en-thusiastic tour leader showed us to the faculty housing. I followed my dad up the slate pathway toward the front door of a yellow Victorian house. Huge and with a wraparound porch, the house overlooks the playing fields and the rest of main campus. I stared at it, thinking of the card my dad gave me for my seventh-grade birthday—one of those 3D cards that you unfold into a whole building—a large house with a tur-ret and a carousel. I used to stare into that card as if I could get sucked into its landscape and experience some magical life for a while. This is what I thought of when I saw our new digs, minus the merry-go-round.

"This is Dean's Way," the tour guide boy explained, his hands flail-ing as he pointed out the features of our new abode—porch, view of central campus, door knocker in the shape of a heart. I stared at the metal heart and wondered for a minute if this could be an omen (heart = love = me) but then I rolled my eyes at myself. I hate when I give myself Lifetime programming moments.

"This is for you," Tour Guide said and handed my dad a large manila envelope and reached out to shake my hand. It still feels weird to shake hands as an almost-sixteen-year-old (almost = just under eight weeks until I'm highway-legal). Plus, Tour Guide never even asked my name. Around here, I guess I'm just a faculty brat.

My dad took the keys from the envelope (an envelope labeled, by the way, PRINCIPAL BUKOWSKI AND DAUGHTER, as if I have no other identity), and began to fumble with the front door lock.

"Ready?" he asked, and smiled at me.

I nodded, excited. Dad and I have lived in some pretty grim places before—the apartment on Yucca Street that lived up to its name, the rent-reduced properties on the campus of Seashore Community College—so I never planned on living large. We've moved around a fair bit, actually, and one of the reasons Dad signed the contract with Hadley Hall was to make sure we could stay in one place. The thought of living here, of calling this home, or not peeling up anyone's old apartment buzzer labels and slicking ours on top, feels both comforting (stability = good) and trapping (sameness = confining)—or maybe I just mean revealing.

Dad rushed in, ever eager to explore new places and see what problems (kitchen bulb out, bed in the wrong place for optimum light) he might fix. That's what he does, problem-solve and rearrange. Me, I'm more cautious. I lurked for a minute in the doorway, holding onto the heart knocker and wondering what I'd find.

And I don't just mean that I stood there wondering what my new bedroom would look like. It was like right then, at the front door, I knew everything had changed—or would change, or was changing. The morphing process of leaving freshman year and the already hazy memories that went with it. Soon, sophomore year at Hadley Hall—*the* Hadley Hall, with its ivy-coated brick and lush green lawns, its brood of young achievers, lacrosse-playing boys, and willowy girls—would begin. And I'd be in it.

\* \* \*

In the made-for-television movie of this day, I'd wake up in my new house and while sipping my milky coffee, I'd meet my new best friend. We'd bond over loving the same sappy lyrics to 1970s songs (example = "Brandi (You're a Fine Girl)"—lame but awesome song from sometime in the late seventies). Then, later, I'd be getting ready to go for a jog (and by jog I mean slow, but hey—it's something), and the Kutcher-esque hot guy I saw yesterday by the track would happen to be running by and take time out of his exercise regimen to give me a guided tour of campus . . . and of himself. Heh. Unlikely—but then, it's a movie.

The reality of my life is this:

Outside, I can hear the buzz of bugs and the grunts from soccer and field hockey players from the fields near the house. I am decidedly un-motivated to get out of my bed—even though it's eleven o'clock. Last night, I caught my second, third, and fourth winds and wound up flip-ping stations between a *90210* rerun on cable and some infomercial that nearly convinced me to order that bizarre brush/hair-dye combo thing that supposedly makes it easy to home-color. Not that it'd be useful for me, since my hair is different enough already: penny-hued, with some bright bits at the front (not so suitable for highlights or lowlights—more like dimlights). I think about adding some wild streak of blue or something, but mainly this is when I'm PMSy. As my Aunt Mable al-ways says, Let No Woman Attempt Hair Change When Hormonally Challenged. This was, of course, after the Miss Clairol mishap that took her three trips to the salon to correct.

Actually, I kind of pride myself on never having ordered from TV before—not that there's a fundamental flaw with it, but there's a prin-ciple there. Maybe I feel like if I started, there'd be no turning back, and pretty soon I'd wind up with that weird mop and the orange goop that strips paint and the hair-braiding contraption that I know would create such tangles I'd need to cut off great lops of hair. So I avoid potential psychological damage (and smelly fumes) by refraining from any and all made-for-TV offers.

Plus, Aunt Mable already signed me up for the Time-Life Singers & Songwriters discs. They arrive each month. She wants to edu-ma-cate me on the finer decades of rock and folk, long before OutKast and Britney. Most of the songs sound like an advertisement for deodorant, but I love the cheesiness of the lyrics, the mellow strumming of the guitars. Instead of John Mayer introspection, there's just old-fashioned lust or odes to seventies fashion. Half the time the guy's singing about making it with his lady or the woman's crooning about how her disco man done her wrong—what's not to appreciate there? Plus, sometimes Aunt Mable will listen with me and tell me how a particular song makes her think of being a cheerleader, eating grilled cheese, and making out with Bobby Stanhope in the back of his Camaro.

With so much late-summer sunshine streaming in my window, I can't stay in bed any longer. It's harder to be a lazy slob in warm weather— hiding under the covers is much more gratifying in winter or heavy rains. I slide out of bed and onto the floor, pressing PLAY so I can hear the latest disc—it arrived yesterday, my first piece of mail to this new address. The typed label proved that I don't even need a street number anymore—just my name, Hadley Hall, Fairfield, Massachusetts, and the ZIP. Fairfield is "just outside Boston"—that's how the school catalog describes it, although my dad and I clocked it in the car and it's nearly twenty-four miles, so it's not as if you can walk it. Probably because of my own moniker, I am name-focused and tend to overanalyze place-names, so when my dad announced ("Love, pack your bags— we're going to prep school!" as if he'd have to endure the mandatory school blazer with me) we were moving to Fairfield, I couldn't help but picture green expanses and fair maidens traipsing around in long dresses, books carried by the same guy who'd throw his blazer over a mud puddle for easy-stepping.

Anyway, I was partially right. Fairfield is easy on the eyes, as are most of the Hadley students I've seen so far. Doing my usual shower routine, lathering all parts and hair while lip-synching, I wonder for a minute what life would be like here if the town were called "Hellville" or "Zitstown"—but when I emerge, clean and wet, and wipe the steam from the window, I can still see the soccer players and beautiful full elm trees. No ugliness here.

"She's going to be here any minute," my dad yells up from his post in the kitchen. I know his routine so well that I can tell he's already come back from the gym and eaten the first half of his multigrain bagel. He doesn't use jam, he squashes fresh fruit onto the bread and munches away. He will have already set aside the last cup of coffee for me in the microwave, which he will nuke for forty-six seconds prior to my arrival in the kitchen. We have a system. It's what happens when you live with just one parent—either you don't know each other at all or you're way too familiar.

"Hey," I say, right as the microwave beeps to signal my caffeine is ready.

"Big shopping day?" Dad asks. He flips through a book. I shrug. I'm not Prada-obsessed or anything, but I enjoy looking around at what's out there. Mainly, it's an excuse to get off campus and be with Aunt Mable, who gives me regular reality checks.

"What's that?" I lean over his shoulder. Dad smells like strawberries and the original Polo from the green bottle. Dad smell. "Or, better yet, *who* is that?" The book in front of him contains black and white photos.

Dad puts on his game-show announcer voice, "The Faces of Hadley Hall!" I reach for the book. He holds it back and says in a regular voice, "I'm just trying to familiarize myself with the rest of the faculty. You'll get your own copy later in the year."

"And the IPSs?" (IPSs=Issue Prone Students—teacher code for screwups.)

"Maybe," Dad says and bites the rest of his bagel. "Eat something."

A car horn beeps. I can see Aunt Mable's car out the front window. She emerges from the driver's side and sits on the hood of the rusting black Saab 900. With jean cutoffs, black tank top, and Ugg boots the same camel color as her ringlets, Aunt Mable always looks like a rock star herself—Sheryl Crow's lost sister or something.

"I gotta go," I say. "You know I'll eat more than my fair share with Mable. She's taking me on a culinary tour as well as showing me her personal fashion finds."

"Here," Dad hands me a key. "Your name here."

"My name here," I say back. This is our "I love you."

I take the house key and head outside. He could ask when I'll be home and I could answer that I don't know or make up some time frame, but the truth is, Dad doesn't set rules like that for me. He knows I'll call and tell him where I am and what I'm doing, and it's not a big enough deal to bother setting up some structure that I have to follow. Besides, I'm a lousy liar, and I never want to lie to him. It's his Jedi mind trick: He figures if he gives me enough freedom, I won't actually want it all. Here's the thing: Up till now, it's been true.

Before I even reach the Saab, my senses are overwhelmed. Mable's new carfume wafts from the rolled-down windows, and my aunt sits cross-legged on the hood of the car, singing along to Guns N' Roses ("Sweet Child o' Mine") at the top of her voice.

"Skipping decades?" I ask, and join in on the chorus.

"After you are thoroughly informed of the 1970s, you will pass Go and move on to obscure eighties tunes," she says.

"Axl Rose is not obscure," I say.

"True." She nods and slides off the hood to hug me. "But this is a classic."

Mable drives the twenty-four miles into Boston using back roads, and explains the various towns and subway stops along the way. We pass suburbs and slumburbs, a country club or two, industrial buildings, and a huge water tower splashed with brightly colored paints.

"Supposedly you can see faces and words in the mural," Mable says, pointing to the tower. "Personally, I think you can see Clapton's profile in the red part."

We make our way over Mass Ave., where hipsters and homeless people mingle. Passing by Berklee College of Music, I watch as students heft guitars, keyboards, and massive drums in the late summer heat. Aunt Mable watches me absorb the scene.

"Here we are, the mecca of vintage apparel," she says, sweeping her arm towards a storefront like it's a new car on display.

"Baggy Bertha's?" I'm skeptical. Let me state that my own personal style is not fully developed. Not that I don't know what I like—I do, and I'm well aware of what makes me gag—but I'm sort of all over the place when it comes to picking out clothes. I have no trouble finding items that appeal (a pair of black flip-flops with plastic red flowers on them, faded Levi's 501s, two close-fitting tops—one electric blue, one layered white and gray), yet I have no idea how to put them together. It's like I'm a crow drawn to shiny things. After shopping I usually get home and sift through my purchases only to find there's not one presentable outfit in the lot. It's why I tend to stick to music instead.

"Perfect," Mable says of the suede jacket in front of her. "This, too. And let's try this."

She collects clothes, and I wander around the vintage shoe section, agog at the array of coolness and crap up for grabs. Next to thigh-high pleather boots (think Julia Roberts in the hooker phase of *Pretty Woman*) are Mary Janes and saddle shoes, Elton John disastrous sparkly clunkers circa 1976, and then—the black ankle boots I've longed for, like a riding boot only not in a dominatrix way. Plus, the heel would give me an extra couple of inches (I'm what the pediatrician called "on the smaller end of the growth chart"—better known as five-foot-two). I hold up my footwear find to Mable, who's clad in a bonnet and purple boa yet still manages to be sexy.

Mable makes me try on the Aerosmith-inspired Lycra outfit she's picked out, and I make her don a dress out of a fairy tale—not a Drew Barrymore kind of fairy tale; the Little Bo Peep kind. We stand in front of the three-way mirror, looking at the flipside images of ourselves.

"I'll never be this kind of rock star," I say, toying with the fringe on the sleeves. Mable smoothes her frilly petticoat. "If I placed an online personals ad with this picture of myself, would I find the love of my life?"

As I wait for Mable to get changed, I look at the old posters for Woodstock (the real one, not the Pepsi-mudfest) and *The Rocky Horror Picture Show,* the framed black-and-whites of Mod girls in thick eyeliner and go-go boots standing by their Vespa scooters. Was life better then? More fun? Simpler? Sometimes I think of life-as-told-by-a-Robert-Doisneau-poster (you know, the master of romantic photography, who took those pictures of people kissing in Paris or the woman walking down the street in Italy), and how the days must have felt—I don't know—bigger somehow, more important. But then, I know I'm fantasizing because in these imaginings, I'm never in high school or doing dishes or tying shoes. But even the posters of hippies hanging out in front of the Metropolitan sign in Paris seem cooler than the midriff-baring teens we passed near Harvard Square. Maybe the past is bound to seem better, because it's done with.

Reading my mind, Mable pays for my boots with cash, glances at the hippy posters, and says, "It wasn't any different than today." Then she tilts her head, reconsidering. "Okay—a little bit. No e-mail, lots of polyester, and too much patchouli and smoke."

Boots in hand, I suddenly wish I were someone who felt that back-to-school shopping were the start of the rest of her life. But I'm not. I can't help but think it'd be easier if I gained redemption or enlightenment with a new purchase, or that getting a cool outfit meant my year would work out. I think of my dad, fortysomething and still picking out his ties as if he were presidential, as if superficial coatings mattered.

"Hey, lighten up, Brick," Aunt Mable says. She calls me Brick when, in her opinion, I'm thinking too hard or weighing down an otherwise pleasant moment.

"Sorry," I say, shaking my head to shrug off my thoughts. I roll down my window, rest my arm on the door frame, and let the wind wash over me.

"Look at us. We're like that Springsteen song." Mable smiles. I don't have to ask which one. She means "Thunder Road." She mentions it all the time. She loves the line about not being a beauty but being okay just the same. I always wait for the one about how highways or roads can lead you in whatever direction you choose—forward or back, able to take you anywhere.

Just like that, I'm out of my small funk and say, "I can't wait to get my license."

"That's right! You should be practicing. Drive. Hop in."

We swap sides, and I attempt to drive standard in the highway hell better known as Downtown Boston (hell = one way meets merge meets six lanes and a blinking red = huh?). Once she's fairly certain I'm not going to kill or maim us, Mable starts a round of RLG.

RLG is the game we devised—basically a musical Magic 8-ball. The rules for playing Radio Love God are elementary (though open for discussion and warping depending on how desperate the situation). The idea stems from the fact that we all do those stupid little tests with ourselves like "If I get this wrapper-ball into the trash on the first shot, so and so will like me," or "If the song ends by the time the light turns green, I'll get the job." Sometimes the tests work, but of course the odds go down if you start doing the "It's 11:11, make a wish and touch something red" and then you wish to become Paris and Nicky's other sister (but, hey, if that's what you're wishing, you have other, worse, problems).

Anyway, to play RLG, you have the volume down and say something along the lines of "Whatever song comes on next is from—to me," or "The next one is how my summer will go." We make sure the volume-down rule is strict, because otherwise you can sort of cheat and, in the middle of "Your Body Is a Wonderland" say, "Oh, by the way, this is from the campus hottie to me." And that's just plain wrong.

The best part of this slightly loser game is that you can twist the lyrics to suit your particular situation. For example, even if it's an ad for Jolly Jingle Cleaners and you've stated that it's from your long-lost summer love, you could interpret "We'll clean you, steam you, get the wrinkles out" as "See, he's wiped the slate clean from when I kissed that other guy. He's steaming—meaning he's still hot for me, and the wrinkles of our relationship are gone." And then you can go home and e-mail said boy, only to humiliate yourself when he doesn't write back. It's brilliant fun.

Mable takes her turn playing RLG and is saddened when she asks how business will go tonight and the reply is "Alone Again, Naturally." Mable runs her own coffeehouse, Slave to the Grind, with comfy couches, a laptop lounge, and amazing lattes, so she's constantly surrounded by people. I couldn't take that much face time. I like my alone time—balanced, of course, with a good friend or conversation.

Mable lets me parallel park (parking = getting it on the second try!), and we go for greasy cheeseburgers and sweet potato fries, splitting a vanilla frappe (frappe = East Coast milkshake).

"Are you thinking about the scene in *Grease* when Olivia Newton-John and Travolta hide behind their menus in the diner?" Mable asks.

"No," I say, sliding two fries in my mouth, whole, and then using dentist office-speak for a minute. "Ibuzthinknboutthishotguy."

"What hot guy?" Mable asks. She has an uncanny ability to understand dentist office-speak.

"Someone at Hadley. He's probably an idiot."

"A really gorgeous idiot?"

"Yeah, that. Plus, I was thinking how much I miss singing."

At my old school, I was in a band. Maybe not the best band, but Baby Romaine ("Baby," as in the girl from _Dirty Dancing_ who won't be put in a corner, and "Romaine," as in lettuce, as in _let us_ play—hey, it was freshman year) gave me an outlet aside from Mable's car and my shower for singing.

"Well, you've got an incredible voice. What about Hadley? There's got to be—what—an octet group or something . . . like in _American Pie_." Yet again, Mable references movies and songs to prove a point, but this one's lost on me.

"Yeah, I know. But I don't want that—"

She cuts me off. "Then write your own songs."

I want to protest or crack a joke, but I don't. I just eat my burger and nod. I'm so afraid of sounding cheesy in songs, or derivative, that even though words sometimes swirl in my head, I don't write them down.

Bartley's Burgers turns out to be this famous place. Harvard undergrads, former presidents, movie scouts on location, all come here for the grub. The walls are blanketed with peeling bumper stickers (ENVISION WHIRLED PEAS, ELVIS HAS LEFT THE BUILDING) and NO NUKES signs.

Mable sees me checking out all the paraphernalia and wipes her mouth on the little paper napkin. "Your mom and dad used to come here."

My hand freezes before my mouth, a quivering sweet potato fry stuck in midair. No one ever mentions my mother. Ever. Not even in passing.

"Sorry," Mable says and quickly slurps some frappe. "It was a million years ago."

By my quick calculations, Mable's overestimating by about 999,987. "No—wait—go back."

Mable shakes her head. "Never mind, it's late. I should drive you home."

"It's not home, it's Hadley," I say, annoyed at how teenagery I sound. "Seriously, Mable, I'm not being Brick, I just have to know something. Tell me anything."

"Fine." Mable takes a breath and looks around. "Once, I saw your parents sitting in that corner over there, sharing some sproutburger or whatever alfalfa mojo your mother liked then. Your dad drummed the table, as per usual. He's done that since we were kids. And your mom put her hand on his like this." Mable flattens her own fingers and leaves her hands resting on each other. "And . . ."

She looks at my face. Probably I look too eager, too desperate. She cuts herself off. "And that's all."

I open my mouth to demand further details, but Mable's gone up to pay the bill.

The car ride back to Hadley Hall starts off stilted, with no conversation, just the radio's declaration, over and over again, that summer is over. WAJS plays tributes to this effect, with songs talking about empty beaches and seasons changing. This, plus the sight of the Hadley campus, makes me cloud up again.

Chin on my hand, I stick my face partway out the window like a dog. In front of the house—our house—my house—Mable stops the car.

"Listen—forget what I said back at Bartley's. Say hi to your dad for me, and just enjoy the here and now." I know she's not just talking about movies and songs and decades-old hippy posters. She means forget the maternal mystery, don't dwell on what could be—just live in the present.

After dinner, I sit on the porch while my dad commits to memory student names from the face book. People here have names that seem more suitable to towns or buildings: Spence, Channing, Delphina, Sandford. I mean weren't Pacey and Dawson enough of a stretch?

Outside, I can't get comfortable—first too hot in my sweatshirt, then too cold in just my T-shirt. Then the porch slats cut into my thighs, so I stand up.

"It's less windy on the other side," says a voice from around the turret-edge of the house.

I go to discover the person to whom the voice is attached. Sitting on one of the white Adirondack chairs in the front of the house with her knees tucked up to her chest is:

"Cordelia, as in one of King Lear's daughters, and a fac brat just like you."

She rattles off other information—about me, my dad, the house (turns out the heart-shaped door knocker was put on by some old headmistress who died a spinster, so not a lot of romantic omen there).

"I'm Love," I say, even though Cordelia knows this already. And before she can make some joke about it, I add, "Bukowski. Love Bukowski."